Eskimo Money

Design by Heather M. McElwain

Published by WILLOW CREEK PRESS
P.O. Box 147, Minocqua, Wisconsin 54548

For more information on other WILLOW CREEK titles,
write or call I-800-850-9453

This book is a work of fiction. Names, characters, places and incidents are either products of the author's imagination or are used fictitiously. Any resemblance to actual events or locales or persons, living or dead, is entirely coincidental.

Library of Congress Cataloging-in-Publication Data
Landers, Gunnard.
    Eskimo money / by Gunnard Landers.
        p.   cm. -- (Wilderness badge series)
    ISBN I-57223-149-I
    I. Walruses--Alaska--Fiction.   I. Title.   II. Series: Landers, Gunnard.
Wilderness badge series.
PS3562.A4755E84   1999
813'.54--dc2I   99-I3800
                                    CIP

Printed in Canada

Eskimo Money

by Gunnard Landers

WILLOW CREEK PRESS

ACKNOWLEDGMENTS

The story line and characters in *Eskimo Money* are entirely fictional. However, the violations upon which the book is based are real.

Federal wildlife agents are involved in assisting state conservation officers as well as enforcing national laws such as the Endangered Species Act, the Marine Mammal Protection Act of 1972, and the Lacey Act, which in part involves violations regarding the selling and interstate shipping of wildlife for profit. There are only 200 federal field agents and nine in the Special Operations branch. The Special Operations branch targets undercover operations against commercial game violators.

A 1989 headline in the *Anchorage Times* read, "Man Admits Trading Drugs for Raw Ivory — Walrus tusks swapped for marijuana, rifles." Operation Taxidermy originated in 1987. Among items confiscated were 5.3 pounds of cocaine, $28,000 in cash, skins or parts of mounts of 18 wolves, 18 polar bears, numerous other animals, and 769 pounds of walrus ivory. 36 people were charged for illegal trafficking in wildlife parts and other infractions of federal and state laws.

A 1981 headline in the *Anchorage Times* read, "Key Figures Tied to Ivory Probe." The lead paragraph read: "The president and chief executive officers of a native village corporation, a medical doctor, a legislative lobbyist, an Anchorage millionaire and members of the local Brothers motorcycle gang have been implicated in illegal sales of marine mammal products to undercover federal agents."

Operation Whiteout in 1992 included charges against an Anchorage ivory dealer, the seizure of 67 untagged walrus tusks, but also polar bear hides, seal skins, and sea otter furs that were illegally marketed for cash and drugs. Alaskan fish and wildlife agents report they spend close to 50 percent of their time working illegal ivory trading cases.

There are an estimated 250,000 walrus in the world. Every five years the U.S. and Russia conduct joint surveys of walrus. However, the results of these surveys can be profoundly affected by weather and ice conditions.

Weather and ice conditions also impact the harvest. Alaskan Eskimos take 3,000 to 5,000 walrus per year. Estimates run that as many more walrus may be struck-and-lost.

There are an estimated 20,000 to 25,000 polar bears in the world. It does not appear that there are sufficient resources committed to gather reliable harvest figures of polar bears.

Special thanks is given to Dave Hall who was the agent-in-charge of the 1981 case. Other assistance was provided by federal agents Wally Soroka and Kim Speckman. State Biologist Bob Nelson provided information as did State Trooper Joe Cambell. Ike Larsen talked of his hunting experiences. Other background information was provided by taxidermist Bob McConnell, registered ivory dealer Angie Larson, and federal wildlife biologists in charge of walrus monitoring. Other assistance was provided by Pat Harings for his original research and Bob Neidhold for editorial help.

CHAPTER ONE

The Cessna 205 flew west and south, following the brown waters of Cook Inlet away from Anchorage, skirting the green expanse of Lake Clark National Park, crossing the sparkling cold waters of Iliamna Lake. Rich Swanson, senior agent-in-charge of the ten U.S. fish and wildlife agents assigned to cover the entire state of Alaska, dropped the airplane to five hundred feet, low enough to give them a good look at occasional moose, a grizzly bear, and several black bears.

"Beautiful country, you lucky bastard," Special Agent Reed Erickson said above the engine drone. He was a medium-built man with brown hair, a light beard and brown eyes that never ceased their restless movement. He sat with a navigational map, tracing their progress, as usual familiarizing himself with every piece of terrain he crossed. It was part of being raised in the outdoors — always know where you were at, otherwise you could never figure out where you were going.

"Must be Iglugig down there." Reed indicated a tiny, remote village on the west end of the lake. "When I get out of the undercover business, I just might put in for Alaska." His voice dropped. "Of course there's not much for family that would come along. Trish maybe, once she got out of high school. A man needs family, something stable when you get away from all the bullshit."

Rich glanced at Reed, wondering on the tightness in his voice. "That's the truth," he agreed. "We'd be pleased to have you." Rich was tall, lean, a serious family man not given much to ribald humor. Reed's reputation was familiar to every one of the two hundred field agents the department's Law Enforcement Division had assigned to cover the entire United States. Reed was part of Special Operations, a nine-member unit assigned to conduct covert operations against commercial game violators. From deer poaching to taking bighorn sheep out of national parks, Reed had been known to directly take himself into whatever the situation demanded. The stories got pretty profound. And of course when Special Agent Abe Kramer started his walrus ivory investigation and then just flat out disappeared, no trace, nothing, who volunteered to follow in his footsteps but Reed.

"I'm surprised you're up here like this," Rich said seriously. "After Abe. You know how deep these connections go. The smart ones have seen every trick we can pull. The gift-store front has been used before."

"A play is only as good as the actors," Reed said.

Rich continued his lecture, getting in his say while he could. "Every step will take you a little deeper, a little further away from support. You get out here and there's no prospect of backup. I mean, Jesus Christ, Abe hadn't even started and he just disappeared. Not a trace. And you're following after him?"

Like he was stupid, Reed thought; although Rich was not being unkind. What could he say? That he was a dumb 18-year-old kid ripe for being cannon fodder in Nam? That he'd once had everything a man could ask for and that somewhere along the line it had all gotten away? Pam, Stacy, maybe even Trish. A family was the basis of life. Forty years old, on the road and this job was all he had. Who'd confess to that? He wasn't a man to feel sorry for himself. Just get out and move, don't think, bore in, never step back. Abe disappeared. Reed had approached Peter. Hell, he'd take care of that.

"I'm just going to do some probing, Rich. One step and then another. There'll be contact. There's no worry about that."

"Well, I sure do feel for Abe's family. I'll give you that. I did one long-term undercover case against those guides. That was eight years ago. It still eats me up."

Reed turned away and stared at the boggy, lake-filled bottoms below. Both men were silent. The motor droned, numbing their senses. The wilderness and isolation stretched as far as he could see. In time the gray waters of Kvichak Bay slowly drew into view. Tendrils of late-morning fog still covered the water, soft mounds of mist reaching out over the green, dripping-wet foliage of a low, brushy shoreline.

"Any sign of a trawler?" Rich asked. They'd received the call the afternoon before. Two government-contract social workers, out studying native village life, had observed a fishing trawler named *Winch God II* stopping at their village. Word passed that the skipper was looking to purchase fresh walrus tusks, something forbidden to a non-native by the Marine Mammals Protection Act.

Rich crabbed the Cessna through a persistent crosswind and brought it in on the end of a short, bumpy, dirt and gravel runway at Levelock.

* * *

ESKIMO MONEY

The two researchers, a man and a woman, seemed happy just to have the company. The man was lean, athletic. The woman was thin, a nervous and sensitive soul with an abundance of compassion. The isolation and the realities of life in the far north had hardened her face and erased some of her youthful idealism. They hadn't witnessed the purchases directly, but they'd spoken with some villagers who had.

Reed and Rich asked around. Most of the villagers were noncommittal, but one, the village mayor, a man named Bernard, stated he'd personally witnessed the captain, a man named Dale Woodruff, carry two thirty-inch-long walrus ivory tusks onto his boat.

"But you don't know from whom he purchased the tusks?" Reed asked. He and Bernard stared, two men of similar nature and understanding. Bernard shook his head in the negative. "I knew you didn't. I just had to ask." Bernard reflected Reed's hint of a smile. They both knew he could not give up one of his own people.

Rich took Bernard's signed statement. "Enough for a warrant. Of course we have to find the boat, then we have to fly back to Anchorage to get the warrant, then fly back, find the boat again and find a way to serve the warrant."

"So what's your problem?" Reed asked.

Rich looked quizzical and then smiled, blue eyes sparkling, lines crinkling up in his weathered face. "I don't know. Us northern boys just like to complain."

After little more than an hour on the ground, they reboarded the airplane and flew down Kvichak Bay and soon discovered the *Winch God II* had stopped at the villages of Kogguing and Naknek and then headed west in the early morning hours. Rich turned the Cessna out over the waters and bucking-air turbulence of Bristol Bay.

"There's a hell of a lot of water out here. We can check up as far as Dillingham and then refuel. After that I don't know."

"Has the commercial fishing been down this year?" Reed asked.

"That's the word. The salmon just aren't there. They're staying out because of the late spring. Water temperatures are down and baitfishes are staying out. The Japanese are taking too many. Sport fishers are taking too many. Every year it's something. Boats sink, fishermen get swept overboard. It's a tough way to make a living."

The bottom line, Reed thought, especially for the villagers, subsistence living in a world with a cash economy. It didn't seem to mix. The problem, as was always the problem with the ever-increasing influx of human beings, was that nature paid the price.

"There's a boat up ahead," Rich said. He pointed out a small white wake in the water. "I'll keep her up a thousand feet, belay any suspicions. There's a pair of ten-power binoculars behind your seat. When we get overhead, see what you can tell."

As they passed to one side, Reed peered down with the binoculars. "It's the right color and shape, black hull, low stern, white housing with red trim around the bridge. Slow but steady, just like a tugboat." He hesitated, adjusting the binoculars for the best visibility. "Can't make out the letters, but there're two names and numerals behind. That has to be our man."

"If he maintains this course he'll put in at Ekuk or Clark's Point. The question is, should we give him a look at Ekuk and try to make a case, or turn back for a warrant? Two white men in a village with a hundred and fifty Eskimos has a tendency to stand out. If he hears we're there he might spook."

"We can't board the boat without seeing him take something on or unless we have a warrant. You don't have a parachute in here do you?"

Rich stared. Although such was the man's reputation he was momentarily uncertain if Reed was serious or not.

"Just joking. You drop me off in Clark's Point and I'll round up a boat while you go back for the warrant. If he stops in the village, I'll lie low and try to witness something. At the least I can maintain contact."

Reed disembarked at Clark's Point. He waited until Rich took off then hiked down a gravel pathway toward the beach and past a line of worn and battered houses, little more than cabins. The yards were littered with used snowmobiles, all-terrain-vehicles and various pieces of boats and wooden flotsam. Scattered pole racks had lines of salmon hanging to dry in the open air. Uninsulated plywood shelters provided minimal protection to the dogs chained out front. Animal bones littered the dung-covered ground within the reach of the chain. A series of pens closed in with chicken wire held a dozen sled dogs who stirred and whined at his passing. On the side of some houses, sealskins were stretched and drying. The odors were strong: curing meat, dog dung, oil smoke, the seaweed-and-salt smell of the sea. This wasn't nature and it wasn't the city, that was for sure.

Two young girls wearing blue jeans, earrings and nylon jackets watched as he passed. The old and the new, the clash of cultures, the destruction of a people. Some real contrasts, Reed thought, centuries-old traditions side by side with modern behavioral roots that barely touched the ground. Cultural diversity, like him and Stacy, his oldest daughter with her elaborate makeup, bracelets, and defiance of society norms. It was a good thing the Eskimo had the ability to adapt.

The arguments were familiar. What the situation demanded was concentrating on the task at hand. Forget about the personal and figure a way to get at this guy and see where it led. Reed shrugged at the tightness across his shoulders. He just had to think on that.

There were a number of boats, mostly aluminum, but also including a couple of skin-covered umiaks, that were beached on the rocky ground above the high-tide mark. Because of crushing ice and high and powerful tides, building docks was impossible. Boats were rolled into the sea on a series of logs set one behind the other. Besides the umiaks, there were two modern boats, open-hulled aluminum, including a twenty-foot Boston Whaler with a hundred-and-fifty-horsepower motor. This was the boat he needed, Reed thought. Ironically, the owner, Lester Tobias he learned from one of the young girls, was probably the biggest walrus hunter in the village. Whether Lester engaged in wasteful hunting or sold ivory illegally was another matter. There was little room to maneuver. He had to take a chance.

Lester's house, such as it was with brown, peeling paint and faded yellow trim around the windows, was located on a patch of gravel in front of a thicket of scrub willows. Lester was a rich man; three ATVs and parts of others littered his gravel yard. Two young boys, playing with sticks and a can, stopped their game as Reed approached. A black husky with pale-yellow eyes growled low in its throat but did not move off the roof of the dog house. This was absurd, Reed thought. Everyone in the village knew he was here; they just did not know who he was.

A thin man with a scrabble of a goatee answered Reed's knock. It was Lester Tobias, an Inupiaq and owner of the Boston Whaler. Reed took him aside and showed his identification.

Lester glanced at the identification and then away. Like a man embarrassed, Reed thought. He suppressed a smile. Lester expected to be arrested. But for what? If Captain Dale Woodruff of the *Winch God II* came to Clark's Point, Lester Tobias might be a man Woodruff wanted to see.

Reed spoke easily, trying to put Lester at ease. "What I'm here for is to ask if you and your boat are available for hire for a day or two?"

Lester's dark eyes looked at Reed as if judging his sincerity. The stiffness across his shoulders seemed to ease. He spoke in clear English, a man who'd spent eight years in schools in Anchorage, a man well-acquainted with the capitalistic way. "Five hundred dollars a day, plus gas."

"I need all the gas you can carry."

"I have three twenty-five-gallon drums lashed inside the boat. The tide will be in in three hours. But I can lower the boat with logs and a come-along."

"I'll hire the boat as of now," Reed said. "But we may not use it. Two things, don't mention to anyone who I am. And is it possible for me to stay inside your house until I'm ready to depart?"

"Sure," Lester said. He'd adopted the tone of a man who had nothing to hide.

As to keeping a secret from the other villagers, highly unlikely, Reed thought. If Captain Woodruff made regular runs like this, someone would talk. But if the captain was cruising on speculation from village to village, no one would have reason to talk, except for those who hated fish and wildlife, and there were always some of those.

Reed trailed Lester into his house. It was close, dark and smoky. The two young boys trailed after, eyes wide and silently watching this Caucasian in their midst. Lester's wife, Sally, was portly and friendly. She invited Reed to sit at the Formica-topped kitchen table. She immediately served homemade bread, smoked moose meat, and bitter black tea. A young girl, about fourteen, Trish's age, peeked in from the back bedroom and came and sat on the living-room sofa next to the darkened television. Lester sat at the table and his two sons stood behind him, watching as Reed ate.

"This bread and meat are excellent," Reed said. "The smoked flavor of that moose is quite unique."

Sally seemed to nod. They were friendly enough, Reed thought, but he was an intrusion, an interruption on their family life and they had no idea how to react.

"I could be here a while," Reed said. "I'm waiting for a boat."

"A big boat?" Lester asked.

"A fishing trawler."

"You can sleep. The boys will go and watch."

And tell others, Reed thought. But he nodded and Lester sent the boys outside. Sure, why not, he had little choice.

He finished his tea, bread and meat. Sally offered more. Reed said no, he was full. They sat in silence.

"How was the walrus hunting this spring?" Reed asked.

"Very good," Lester said. "Last summer hunting was very poor. The ice fled north very fast. The walrus stayed out to sea."

"And the kings?"

"It was a good run," Lester said. "Soon the silvers will be in. Then we will go to fish camp."

"That'll be some work," Reed agreed. "I've always loved salmon, especially smoked." He stifled a yawn.

"You could lie down," Sally suggested.

Sleep while five- and six-year-old boys stood his watch, Reed thought. The boat could come and go. Rich would not be amused, the great Reed Erickson asleep on the job. Reed looked at Sally, a friendly face he could trust. Even Lester seemed all right, a friendly man who did not believe in laws — at least the white man's laws. "Sure, a nap sounds good," Reed said. At least he'd be out of their way.

Two hours later he awoke. He stared at the gloom of the bedroom ceiling and sensed quiet movement in the outer room. Quiet for his sake, the intruder in their midst, a few minutes disruption and then he'd be gone, a figure out of the air, a fish and wildlife agent, not a human at all.

Reed slowly rolled to a sitting position. He hadn't done anything really physical and still he was stiff. Getting old, a tiny voice said. But he could still outrun any poacher he ever saw. He laced up his leather boots and went into the outer room.

Sally, Lester and the girl sat side by side on the sofa watching television without any sound. Lester smiled. Sally rose to get him a cup of tea.

"That was a good nap. Thanks," Reed said.

The girl rose and turned up the sound on the television. The door opened and the two young boys entered. The older one whispered in his father's ear. The other boy crowded against his knees. Lester looked at Reed. "The boat is dropping anchor in the bay."

"Thank you," Reed said. He handed each of the boys a dollar. They shrank away and looked at their father for instructions.

"Go ahead," Lester said. "It's wages for your work. You never turn down wages for your work."

Reed sat at the table sipping tea. He hadn't even started the case and could see it would be hard. The isolation was a blessing, but the prospect of going at people who were doing little more than trying to make a living out of nature was the crux. It was a way of life. But parts of life in a modern world were destructive. Parts were illegal. He'd be tearing families apart, just like his own. Tearing out his own guts.

Gloomily he stared out the window and across the desolate landscape. He loved being out here. He could see the fishing trawler in the bay. A small outboard-powered Zodiac rubber raft was headed toward shore. He sipped black tea and waited.

A half-hour later a man came to the door and asked for Lester Tobias. Lester went outside. Reed peeked through the window. The man, Captain Dale Woodruff, Reed presumed, was short with a protruding stomach and the thick hands and powerful arms of a fisherman. He was mid to late forties with a pugnacious face as hammered as an old tramp steamer that had faced storms and sun and salt-spray and was further reddened from decades of booze. He wore tan pants and the top of a filthy, yellow rain slicker. Either he knew Lester from before, or someone had given him Lester's name. In either case the two were engaged in close conversation. Whether they were talking about the presence of a fish and wildlife agent inside Lester's house or the prospect of buying fresh raw ivory, Reed couldn't say.

Five minutes later Lester returned inside. Reed sat quietly, waiting until Lester spoke. "The man wanted to purchase raw ivory. I told him it was against the law for a native to sell to a non-native, but he said he didn't care about that. I told him the season is late. The ice is far to the north in the Chukchi Sea. All my ivory is gone."

"Thanks," Reed said. Lester was probably telling the truth. If he'd told Woodruff more it'd do no good to ask.

A half-hour later the Zodiac returned to the *Winch God II*. Woodruff carried a canvas duffel bag, Reed observed through the binoculars. The bag was empty. Either no ivory was available or those with ivory were not willing to sell. Or, more likely, word had circulated that Reed was in the village. But had the villagers passed the word to Woodruff — that would be the key.

The *Winch God II* weighed anchor. Decision time: "Follow or wait for Rich and the warrant?" Reed thought. He had no direct probable cause.

"Lester, do you have a set of oil slicks I can borrow? Then I think we better get your boat ready for sea."

"The tide is almost up. It will not be hard."

An hour later they were ready to depart. Reed, clad in a hooded sealskin parka and pants, felt like an Inupiaq ready for the hunt. He stood on a beach of stones pounded round by ice and thundering waves. The *Winch God II* was a small speck five miles out, heading down the coast toward Nushugak or Dillingham. Twenty minutes more, he thought, and then Lester pointed at the sky and the red and white Cessna 205.

An hour later, after picking up Rich with an ATV, Lester had the Boston Whaler pounding through the gray waters of Bristol Bay. Lester stood at the center console, feet widespread as he balanced easily with the roll of the boat, working the motor back and forth as he expertly quartered the three-foot-high waves.

Reed grinned across at Rich who was clad in a green Gortex parka. A cased rifle lay at Rich's feet and a bullhorn leaned at his side. Reed's hair and face were plastered from icy salt-spray. "This is the life, out pounding the surf," Reed shouted. "Yesterday morning I was in Washington DC."

Gradually, over the course of three hours, they closed in on the *Winch God II*. What Captain Woodruff would think of their approach, Reed could only guess. If he'd been informed that a fish and wildlife officer was in Clark's Point, the drugs and ivory would already be dumped in the ocean. But then maybe not. Besides, people stayed greedy. Marijuana that cost two thousand dollars in Anchorage could purchase ten thousand dollars worth of ivory in remote villages.

"He doesn't like us following him. He's turning," Lester pointed out.

Heading back out to sea. They'd both agreed they'd take him when he anchored off Nushugak, Reed thought. He stared at Rich who nodded agreement at his unspoken thought. "Lester," Reed pointed that Lester should cut the corner. Lester nodded and, without instructions, pushed the throttle wide open.

Reed and Rich, half-sitting and half-crouched for balance on their toes, held on to keep from being slammed onto the deck. Reed's fingers were numb from the biting cold water. The pounding was taking its toll on his legs and back. Only the angry whine of the outboard motor, the wind and spray in his face, and the higher white froth from the speeding trawler, provided an adrenaline kick. Reed could see Rich, as sopping wet as he, fingering the bullets and glancing at the cased rifle held firm beneath his feet. The two men grinned.

They closed in, running beside the trawler with its huge, throbbing diesels. Lester throttled back, running at about fifteen knots. The only man visible appeared to be Captain Woodruff inside the small enclosed bridge. The captain stared straight ahead, not even looking in their direction. Reed understood the game.

Rich raised the bullhorn and mashed the talk button. "Winch God Two, Winch God Two, this is the U.S. Fish and Wildlife Service. You are instructed to heave-to." The trawler plowed straight ahead, as Captain Woodruff looked straight ahead.

Reed motioned and Lester moved the deep-veed Boston Whaler to within ten yards off the port side, just outside the high bow wave. Rich repeated his call. Captain Woodruff looked straight ahead.

"Run up across his damn bow," Reed shouted.

"What the hell, do you think we're Greenpeace or something?" Rich shouted.

Lester throttled up, cutting twenty yards in front of the raised bow, one way and then the other. The thin Inupiaq villager grinned at the excitement of his maneuvers.

"Slow her down," Reed said.

The *Winch God II* bore straight ahead, looming at their stern like a whale over a tiny kayak.

"He isn't stopping. Get out of here," Rich bellowed.

Lester looked at Reed. Reed nodded and Lester gave throttle.

"Jesus, Reed, we were so damn close he couldn't even see us."

"Just checking out Lester's seamanship," Reed shouted.

"Uncase that rifle and get it loaded."

"He's pretending not to see us. It won't do any good even if I shoot across his bow. He knows we won't shoot him."

"Get it ready," Reed said. He turned to Lester. "Can you swing off and come in from behind, inside that bow wave?"

Lester grinned, gunned the motor and swung around in a tight circle. Reed quickly began to slip out of his sealskin parka and pants even as Rich began to jam wet shells into the wet magazine. They flew over the bow wave and Reed, with his pants downs to his knees, was slammed to the deck and against the center console. Lester just grinned.

"You're a bastard, Lester," Reed yelled with an excited grin. He turned to Rich, "Give me that warrant."

Rich reached inside his coat. "This is crazy. It isn't worth it. We'll get him another day, follow him in the airplane, something." He handed Reed the typed warrant that was already sodden with spray.

Reed slipped the warrant inside his shirt. Lester maneuvered the Boston Whaler in beside the trawler, fighting the secondary bow waves that alternately threatened to push them away and then suck them in to where the tiny Whaler would be pinched between the trawler hull and a wave. The bow could be pinched down, flood with water and instantly tip them underneath the trawler and back through the huge twin props. Lester, a smile fixed on his brown, goateed face, worked the motor, direction and prop, giving full throttle at times to fight the pinching effect of a wave.

Reed stood on the seat, one foot poised on the gunnel, hands gripping the rail, judging the yawing back and forth, bracing against the sudden lurching as they were sucked in by a wave. Water streamed down his face. His hands were numb. The back part of the fishing trawler was low, without a rail. He stared at a cross brace. Four feet seemed as close as Lester could get.

"He's looking now," Rich yelled. "There's a crewman with him in cockpit. Maybe you should wait." Lester swung out, and Rich called over the bullhorn. The *Winch God II* continued out to sea.

"Get her in there, Lester, I don't have much time left," Reed yelled.

Lester swung the boat back in. He caught a wave and the boat bore in hard, he gave throttle and turned. Jump, Reed thought, but then the prop caught and the Whaler lurched up. Reed jerked to one side and felt a hand as Rich hauled him back into the boat.

"I'm getting too old for this," Reed said.

"Then don't jump. It's too dangerous," Rich said.

Reed pulled away. Rich didn't understand, he had to jump, he had no choice.

The boat swung sideways, following in the trough of two waves. The pattern was established, as the front wave took their bow it drew them down and in, Lester gave throttle and they would lurch free and buck up and out. But just before that, just before the lurch, they were closest to the trawler.

Reed poised on the gunnel. He stared at the dark water, the sliding hull of the trawler. The Boston Whaler bore in, bow sinking, sucked down and in by the force of the wave trailing out from the trawler. The throttle whined and the weight of water sucking them under forced Reed down as well. He struggled up against the pull. And then he leapt, eyes fixed on his target, hands reaching. He went too far, hitting the cross brace with some force, slamming his head and chest as he twisted and curled in on the trawler's gray deck. Reed gasped for air. A small line of blood dripped down his forehead. He looked up. Captain Woodruff stood ten feet away, rifle in hand.

"You sonofabitching pirate," Woodruff yelled. He started to level the rifle.

"Federal agent," Reed bellowed. He had to establish command through force of presence. "You level that thing and it's a major felony. There're two witnesses right there. What the hell do you think you're doing?"

He saw Woodruff's eyes swing toward Rich and Lester, a hint of the rational there. It was the irrational ones that would shoot you dead. Rich had his rifle poised, if Woodruff shot, Rich would shoot. Which left him with a hole, Reed thought, but that was the way the game sometimes worked.

"You have no right to board my boat," Captain Woodruff said.

"I'm reaching inside my shirt. I have identification and a warrant to search this boat."

"Where the hell did you get a warrant?" Captain Woodruff asked. The wild bitterness had left his tone. He lowered the rifle to point at the deck.

"Anchorage. A judge signed it this morning."

"Sonofabitch," Woodruff said. His blue eyes looked around, a man facing defeat. He waved at the bridge and the trawler throttled back.

Reed glanced at the bridge. The helmsman was little more than a boy, twelve or thirteen years old.

"My son," Captain Woodruff explained. "I've been teaching him the ropes."

"Buying fresh ivory? Trading drugs for ivory? What the hell kind of ropes are those?" Reed jerked the rifle from the captain's thick hands.

Woodruff glared in defiance. Even on the windy ocean Reed detected a whiff of alcohol. "It's been a tough year. Equipment failures, a crewman chopped off part of an arm, insurance cancelled me. One engine needed a complete overhaul. A new net. And the fish just haven't been there like always. A guy has to survive."

"This isn't the way," Reed said. "You could probably lose your boat, your commercial license."

"I found that ivory, it's fossil."

"We have witnesses that will say otherwise, and a serologist in our laboratory in Oregon can check. Don't fight us, Captain. Cooperate. It'll be the best, for you and your boy."

The strength seemed to fade from Woodruff's face. The jowls sagged. His eyes were twisted, staring, misted over with tears. He did not look Reed in the face. "I put my life into this boat. Fishing's all I know."

"You help us, we'll help you."

Woodruff looked at Reed, understanding what was being asked. "You want some real ivory traders?"

"That's right."

"I can get you inside. All I ask is four things; keep my name out of the paper; I keep my boat; I keep my commercial fishing license. And you don't question my boy about what I've done."

"How big of operators are you talking about?"

"Tons."

Here, facing defeat, the man was ready to talk, Reed thought. But later, once time passed and he got onto home footing, could he be trusted?

Yet, it was an avenue into the big-time ivory traders, those men who knew the business and knew how to protect their backs. And it might just lead him to Abe, following down the same path, toward oblivion, like the man had never been.

CHAPTER TWO

Reed had never met a more suspicious man than Kurth Breismeister. Over the telephone, after an introduction from Captain Dale Woodruff, Kurth had been rather pleasant. But that had been six months previous. Now, at their first face-to-face meeting, the pleasant attitude had disappeared.

Kurth was a slight man, red-faced and with thick, wavy blond hair and blue eyes. A real rake with the women. He seemed quick to smile, but was just as quick to squint and glare. He'd take them for a ride, he said. But as they climbed into his brown Bronco, he whirled. "If you guys are agents, the best thing, the safest thing, would be to get out right now. No harm done."

"What is this?" Reed demanded. He understood the testing game. If Kurth wanted to play tough, he'd play tough. "Over the telephone you say you want to deal. Now you're backing out?"

"Oh, no. I didn't say I'd deal. I said we could talk. Well, I'm telling you, if you're not level with me, you can leave right now. It will be the smartest move you've ever made. Don't think I won't check you out, up one side and down the other."

"I'm working in my uncle's gift shop here in Anchorage," Special Agent Pewter Torbino said from the backseat. "I also am a partner for a shop in Hawaii that needs carvings. I know carvers out at Lahaina. I carve myself. Since the ban on elephant ivory, raw material is scarce. You said you could help. That's why Mr. Woodruff called."

"Dale Woodruff and I were a long time ago." Kurth muttered like a young boy going to church against his will. He turned and his eyes held Pewter's. He pointedly checked her body then smiled as if to invite her inside his confidence. "First time in Alaska?"

"I've been here a few months. My uncle had a stroke. I wanted to come see the last great frontier."

Kurth laughed and smiled back. He started the vehicle. "I'll show you around. Although, like everyone says, Anchorage is Anchorage, everything else is Alaska."

Reed gave Pewter a brief look of reassurance. Second time undercover and she hadn't held back, spoke right up. Few people could handle undercover. Her initial response was a pleasant surprise.

Pewter had deep, sloe-brown eyes almost like his. Her shampooed hair was short cut and dark. Her skin was smooth, without flaws, as naturally tan as if she'd come from the South Pacific. He'd seen her first at a conference for field agents, then briefly partnered up with her as an operative on a Texas game-farm case. As quickly as Reed looked into her eyes, he looked away. Pewter thought he'd asked for her on this case because she had some knowledge of ivory, some history as a carver, because he assured her she wouldn't have to do deep cover, just work in Anchorage, handle the shop.

What the hell had he been thinking. Already he'd been forced to take her into the field. Not where she belonged. Too middle class. On the game-farm case she didn't want to be a shooter, had never hunted, never killed an animal much less a man. Reed turned away, trying to conceal his sense of unease, his awareness of weakness at a time he needed strength.

Kurth drove them down toward Turnagain Arm, Seward, Homer, the towns south. They passed shopping malls, scattered commercial areas gone to seed, smaller residential areas.

"The town's going to hell," Kurth continued with his running commentary, most of which was directed into the backseat at Pewter. "What we need is another shot of oil. If we could plug a few of those damn conservationists and open up the Arctic National Wildlife Refuge, this economy would take right off."

"Maybe you should open a season, like you do for bear or moose," Pewter suggested in an easy tone.

Kurth looked into the backseat and laughed. "That'd be a good idea. I'd get me all the tags I could. Maybe even mount a conservationist on the wall."

"So where are we headed?" Reed asked. They'd turned into the Chugach Mountains and were steadily climbing, passing more upscale houses, those with modern design, surrounding forest and a magnificent view of Turnagain Arm and Cook Inlet.

"Up the mountain," Kurth said.

"I can see that, asshole," Reed snarled.

"Oh, touchy, aren't you? If you're a legitimate buyer you don't have anything to fear."

Kurth made a turn onto a gravel road with ten-acre lots and scattered residences. "Take it easy. C'mon. We'll stop by my place. Have a drink, a bite to eat, maybe a hot tub."

"Sounds great," Pewter said. Kurth turned around and gave her a grin and a wink but Pewter did not respond.

Kurth lived in a large, cedar-sided house high in the foothills of the Chugach Mountains. He introduced his wife, Wynona, a dark-haired, green-eyed woman with milk-white skin that had looseness under her arms and chin as if stretched and shrunk too many times. Wynona nodded in greeting, a pretty woman filled with suspicions and without a hint of warmth. Her judgment on him was instantaneous Reed observed, a note of disdain like he was a working type she cared nothing about. But with Pewter, wearing fashionable clothes, a flowered blouse and green slacks, she showed some interest. Clearly Pewter had taste and class.

Reed glanced around. Given Kurth's background, the son of a hard-drinking father who crewed on Valdez fishing boats, Kurth had done rather well. Background checks indicated Kurth owned a semi-tractor truck that hauled goods back and forth to the North Slope. With income from a one-man trucking business he'd built this house, bought a nice ocean-going yacht, and had two twenty-thousand-dollar vehicles sitting in the yard. Kurth and Wynona Breismeister were definitely people to watch.

"What a view," Pewter said. She glanced briefly at Reed as if seeking direction, or perhaps assurance. She had a soft, almost vulnerable demeanor, part of her upper-middle class background, Reed had presumed. But she was a fitness freak, ran marathons, flew small airplanes, had spent two summers as a whitewater raft guide near Glacier National Park. She'd mentioned mountain trips hiking and camping alone in grizzly country. He'd discussed her with Doug. She was strong, but he just didn't think she was tough.

"And she might have to back you, partner. Pull down on some guy. Then where the hell will you be at?"

"Nah, I won't let it come to that," Reed had insisted.

"You like it?" Pewter asked.

"Yeah, honey, I could retire to a place like this," Reed said. He avoided her eyes and pressed his chest against Pewter's back and took her elbows. For a second Pewter stiffened, but then she folded into him, a warm loving girlfriend with lithe athletic lines and a distant touch of perfume. What she desired in life he had not a clue. They gazed through huge bay windows down a greening mountain slope to the distant gleam of the bay. A large cedar deck held a covered tongue-and-groove wooden hot tub. Inside, the house was bright and clean with pinewood siding and a tasteful scattering of Alaskan and Native artifacts. Reed closed his eyes and smelled the shampoo of Pewter's black hair.

"Later, if you like, we can take a hot tub, drink a little wine, enjoy the evening," Kurth said. "If we're lucky, maybe a moose will wander past. There are quite a few in this area."

"Do you take hot tubs outside in the winter?" Pewter asked. She gently extracted herself from Reed. She shot him a glance as if questioning if he understood that it was just pretend.

Reed felt the red creeping into his face. What would she say if he told her he did not?

"Hot tubbing in the winter is the best time," Kurth said. He was standing beside Wynona, but he held Pewter with his eyes. "That's when you can see the stars, and the Northern Lights. Sit back in the steaming hot tub, drink some wine and watch the show." He winked and grinned even as Wynona looked from him to Pewter.

"I hate men who stare," Pewter said firmly. She spoke and looked and carried herself with the confidence of a career criminal. But Reed saw her drink, clutched in both hands, the liquid vibrating from a trembling inside. Given her exterior confidence, he was surprised. She was scared to death.

Kurth grinned. "Yeah, but you'd hate it worse if they didn't."

"Why? Do you think you're indispensable?" Pewter shot back.

"Irresistible, Wynona claims."

"No, impossible," Wynona snapped. She gave Pewter a slight nod of thanks.

They settled down in the spacious living room with the cathedral ceiling. Reed savored the adrenaline kick, once again involved with the consuming intensity being undercover. Everything they said was a lie. Everything they said was measured, a general design to lead these people to sell them illegal ivory.

"I'd really like to shoot a walrus," Reed said to Kurth. "That and a polar bear. We've got a guy looking for a skin."

"Polar bear fall under the Marine Mammals Protection Act. You have to be a damn Eskimo to kill one legally. But then you still can't take the hide back into the U.S., so what's the point?"

"But people do," Reed insisted.

"Sometimes," Kurth allowed. He studied Reed and then Pewter. His eyes narrowed like a man trying to see inside a crystal ball. Abruptly he jumped to his feet. "Why in the hell are you guys coming after me? I warned you."

"Kurth, please," Wynona said.

"What the hell are you talking about?" Reed demanded in a belligerent tone. One thing about these guys, you could never back away, never appear weak, never reveal your doubts.

"I'm talking about making up stories. I'm talking about looking me up. Making me a target. You don't think I don't know the way you feds work," Kurth yelled. "You bastards would sell your own mother down the river. I've seen it before. You can tell an agent, all you have to do is look him in the eye."

"Well, that's good," Reed said. "I'm sure glad you know something, because I don't know where you get off bringing us up here with the pretense of doing business and then you pull this crap. Honey, let's get the hell out of here."

"Why not," Pewter said. Her voice cracked and she forced a harder tone. "I've heard men talk all my life. Most of the time that's all it is, talk. We haven't seen anything to buy."

Reed rose as did Pewter. He gazed at Kurth, seeing the man's uncertainty, a war within his mind, caution tempered by greed. A clear picture, Reed thought and had to force himself not to smile. No matter what people said, he could still play this game. He started toward the door.

"No, don't go. I'm sorry," Kurth said. "I just . . . I do that sometimes. I was arrested once, years ago. It stays with you."

"Then don't take it out on others," Reed said. "It's not appreciated." He glared darkly. "Understand?"

Kurth grinned. "Oh, I understand. Let me get you a beer. Then what do you say we have that hot tub?"

The four of them spent a half-hour in the hot tub and watched silently as evening cloaked the mountains.

"Hell of a nice place," Reed said.

"I'm not bragging, but we worked for this," Kurth said.

"Wynona and I both started with nothing. And I mean nothing. Wynona waitressed. I've worked winters on the pipeline, summers on factory fishing trawlers out on the Bering Sea.

"Did you know that at the height of the fishing season in Alaska one fishing boat a week sinks? My old man had two boats sink under him. No, when you work for stuff, you appreciate what you've got."

"And if it's given to you, you just don't give a damn," Pewter said. But then, as Reed nudged her, she quickly amended herself. "But if you're like most people, you just want more."

"And which one are you?"

Pewter spoke in a husky voice, like she was stating an obvious truth. "I want more. Why do you think we're here?"

Kurth laughed.

"I think you've had enough," Wynona snapped. "Why don't you call Eddie."

"Sure. Be right back," Kurth said. He grinned and winked and kissed his wife on the mouth and then jumped from the tub.

Reed watched. It was going as he figured. Kurth would go through their things, check out their identification, maybe even make some telephone calls, verify their covers. He'd seen it coming. The Nagra reel-to-reel recorder he'd wrapped against his ribs had been stuffed behind the toilet tank when he changed. Of course Kurth would check, he'd warned Pewter. All the security was a plus. It demonstrated Kurth was a big player. It established his intentions.

But Kurth did not deal, at least not that evening and not in his home. Two days later Reed received the call, they'd go with Kurth and take a drive.

As he hung up the telephone he turned to Pewter. "He wants to meet again, with both of us. I think Kurth's taken a shine to you. It might be a plus, but it could be a problem as well."

"I should be able to deal with Kurth," Pewter said. "The way you described it, I didn't think we'd get this close and personal this fast."

"Are you all right about this?"

"Hell yes," Pewter said defiantly. "Just thinking out loud. If I have doubts, next time I'll keep them to myself."

"Sorry." One thing he had to keep straight, Pewter would not be pushed, just like Stacy. He spoke carefully, suddenly unsure of himself. "You look like you're dressed for a business meeting in Washington."

Pewter shrugged. She wore black-checked slacks and a black suitcoat with padded shoulders, an outfit that went well with her black hair. "I'm new at this game. If you want to prescribe my wardrobe, come take a look. I'll even wear wrinkled pants and scuffed leather boots if you like."

Reed laughed. "No. I was just speculating aloud. I don't know how this guy perceives us yet, what he expects."

"Maybe he expects someone serious about business."

"Possible."

"Are you going to get ready?"

Reed smiled. His clothing was constant, seldom varied. "Now you're pushing it."

"No, I was being serious," Pewter said without the hint of a smile.

Kidding, Reed thought, but again he could not be sure.

Thirty minutes later Kurth picked them up at their apartment. They weren't going to Kurth's house for they soon passed beyond paved roads. Deal time, Reed thought, the last house had been two miles back.

Tires over gravel roared beneath the Bronco. Occasionally a rock thumped the bottom. Reed sat easily, fully alert. At least he was armed, a legitimate excuse to protect the ivory-buying money he carried inside his belt.

Still Kurth carried on, asking them again if they wanted to get out before it was too late. Paranoid, Reed thought. He'd covered the situation with Pewter, the games, the posturing, it didn't mean that much. It was just hard to tell what was real. Kurth was that kind of man, nervous, edgy, like a high-strung colt. He did not have an ounce of fat, a man who used calories driving his Bronco down the road.

The grade steepened, forcing Kurth to downshift. They rose above the treeline. Scattered patches of snow still lay where thick drifts had piled in low spots. In the wide valley of a high mountain meadow, rising out of black rock and scrub brush, an A-frame sat as gaudy as a cluster of relay towers on top of a hill. It was a quarter-mile from the nearest cover to the huge tri-level house. A garage-storage area was built to one side. A dozen or so motorcycles, mostly chopper-type with gleaming chrome, sat in front. Reed pulled his pistol. "Hold it right there. What the hell's going on here?"

"What do you think you're doing?" Kurth angrily demanded.

"I'm protecting my assets, not to mention my ass," Reed snarled. "I won't tolerate funny business, understand?"

"Did you want to deal or not?"

Intimidation, posturing, playing games. It was part of the business, Reed understood. But so was living, dying, and he didn't know Kurth enough to understand his goals.

The big problem was the tape recorder burning underneath an elastic bandage against his ribs. It was a Swedish Nagra, reel-to-reel, supersensitive but large enough to be easily detected if someone ran a hand over his ribs.

"Sure, let's deal," Reed said. "But no funny business. And no one touches my gun. Let's understand that right from the start."

"That's cool," Kurth said. He grinned at Pewter. "Your boyfriend's a little touchy, isn't he."

"I don't know why," Pewter said. "It's my money, not his."

They pulled in among the motorcycles. "In my younger days I used to run with these guys," Kurth said. "Just the trips, down to California once. Spent a week cruising with the Hell's Angels. These guys came from there."

They walked into the devil's arsenal. Uzis's, AK-47s, M-16s, sawed-off shotguns, 9 MM Glocks. The Chinese 9 MM pistol he'd lifted from a dead Viet Cong lieutenant in Vietnam felt like a joke. They were in an open living area with a cathedral ceiling. A small fire burned in an open fireplace under a black chimney that stretched up through the ceiling. The sofas and chairs were squashed, well used. The wood floor was covered with throw rugs and a light covering of sand. A large moose head hung from one wall and the bleached skull and tusks of a walrus hung from the other. There were half a dozen men, mostly bikers wearing dirty bluejeans and an assortment of T-shirts and denim. For the most part they had long, stringy hair and beards, and an abundance of tattoos. They watched Reed, but especially Pewter. Reed felt her vulnerability. What she faced, he did not.

"This is Eddie," Kurth introduced one of the men. Eddie was clean-shaven, with shorter hair and a single tattoo of a black panther crawling up his arm. A human skull sat on the walnut table to his front.

Reed scarcely nodded. Eddie was not a man with whom one shook hands. Reed looked at the skull.

"It's an old girlfriend," Eddie said. "She had a big mouth."

Reed picked up the skull. "Judging by her teeth, she must have been sixty or seventy. Or maybe you just like them old."

Several men laughed.

Eddie's eyes narrowed, just a flicker, enough to show a man who could hate, and a man who could get even.

What the hell was he thinking, Reed wondered. He knew better than to be provocative when odds were stacked like this. He could feel Pewter's stare, her wondering on just what he was trying to pull putting up a macho front.

"Maybe I could get a pliers, pull your teeth and see if they compare," Eddie said.

"Are you the guy that deals?" Reed asked easily.

"The guy that deals what?" Eddie demanded sharply.

"Are you the guy who deals ivory, or are we getting jerked around here?" Reed kept his voice in neutral.

"I'd say you're getting jerked around," Eddie replied.

Two men stood and moved in behind Reed. Reed glanced back and then circled slightly away. They were cold-eyed buggers, men who saw nothing wrong with causing other people pain. One man stood six feet six inches and weighed a hundred and seventy pounds. But his knuckles were well scarred and there was a wiry, long-armed reach about him that said watch this guy during a fight. The other guy was a built like a fifty-gallon oil drum with a belly that protruded from a black T-shirt. He was so muscled his arms barely reached in front of his chest.

Yeah, Reed thought, he had a mouth. If he backed they'd ridicule. If he pushed too hard they'd show him soon enough who was boss. He tried not to swallow against the dryness in his throat.

ESKIMO MONEY

"I ain't taking any bullshit here. You better tell them, Kurth."

"Where do you do business? Who do you know?" Eddie asked.

Always checking, Reed thought. He glanced at Pewter who took the cue and handed Eddie a business card showing her as manager of the Rare Species Shop, Morgan Zanke owner. "He's my uncle. He had a stroke. I've been helping out. I used to be in Hawaii." Her voice was quiet, almost inaudible as if diminished by the presence of so many bikers and guns. She did not look at Reed, like a spouse showing her displeasure by ignoring his existence. She talked of the carver's society in Lahaina, people she knew, world-famous carvers. Eddie knew the questions to ask. Pewter knew the answers.

Maybe, Reed thought, bringing her had been the proper move.

They stayed ten minutes. They had a drink. They bought no ivory. Eventually they took their leave. They drove across the clearing. There'd be no easy raid here, Reed thought, not for guns, drugs or ivory; not without substantial advance warning to those inside. He turned on Kurth, "What the hell was the point of all this?"

Kurth laughed. "If you don't know that, you're in the wrong business. Ain't that right, Pewter."

"I don't appreciate being frightened," Pewter said.

"You didn't look frightened to me. You had those boys in there moved. They couldn't take their eyes off you. Of course your boyfriend there almost bought the farm. Not many men pimp Eddie like that and live to tell about it. You're lucky you were with me and it was your first visit."

"No, that wasn't very smart," Pewter said to Reed.

"He was just pulling our leg," Reed argued more vehemently than he intended. He turned to Kurth. "Where'd he get the skull?"

Kurth shrugged. "His girlfriend."

"Sure, and gold prospectors find gold bars lying in a stream. So are you going to deal or not?" Reed demanded.

"We're going up north. I can get other sources."

"You're crazy. Those Eskimos don't take much to whites out in the villages. Oh, you can get a couple of tusks from the drunks in the bars. But that's not steady, it's not reliable. You could use lose everything you've got."

"Maybe that's just the way I have to go," Reed said.

"Maybe," Kurth said.

Reed slouched in his seat. What ever made him think it would be easy? He had to get past Kurth, and then Eddie, get out into the field, find the original source of ivory, find out what happened to Abe. Who could predict how long this would take or even where it would lead. He thought of Pewter.

He'd told her a few months, through spring and summer and maybe the fall, him and her playing girlfriend and boyfriend. Living together in a small apartment, building a life where he had no life. The case could take more than a year. They'd get to know each other, one way or the other; it was all he'd wanted from the start.

CHAPTER THREE

After an afternoon and night climbing and camping beside Exit Glacier, Reed and Pewter entered their Anchorage apartment. They were located in the top story of a duplex located near the international airport and across from an open gravel pit. Reed set his rucksack on the robin-egg-blue carpet. He glanced around. "Something's not right. Weren't those magazines stacked nice and straight? That's the way you usually keep them."

Pewter stood poised, like a suspicious deer about to step into a clearing. She looked all around. "Yes. The shelves look disturbed."

"Check your room," Reed said. He walked back to the front door. He returned to the living room, as did Pewter. "There are a couple of scratches. I installed that lock myself."

"Someone was here. It's not messed up, but they were here."

"Is there anything at all that could give us away? Your name in a book, magazine, mail, anything?"

"No. I have that last letter from my mother in my purse."

"Get rid of it. From this moment on assume we're always being watched. No outside contact except through the avenues we discussed."

"I didn't think it was going to come to this, at least not so soon," Pewter said with deep anguish. "You feel so violated, like you have no privacy, no life. They could come in here any time of day or night."

"I know it's going to be hard. I hope you can stick it out. No problem if you can't."

Pewter snapped, "I'll do my damn job. I didn't say I wouldn't." Her dark eyes glittered in defiance.

"No offense, no offense," Reed said. He held up his hands as if to ward off a mock attack.

Suddenly the apartment seemed smaller, a dark little dungeon like his one-bedroom basement apartment in Washington DC. Reed hadn't done anything and already they were at odds. He wasn't questioning competency; it was a matter of safety. He'd asked for her, she assumed, because he thought she could do the job. And already, thoughtlessly, he'd brought that into doubt. Well, what the hell, he thought, might as well make a hard case difficult.

Reed cleared his throat. "Maybe we better check for bugs. I doubt it, but then I didn't anticipate something like this so soon either."

"Sure," Pewter said. Her hard tone hadn't ebbed. "Then I have to get down to the shop. Morgan expected me in by three."

The Rare Species Shop seemed to hold an example of every species of wild animal known to man. Reed stood just inside the door. Fascinating, exotic, decadent, it was a top-line example of the world demand and continuing trade in wild animal parts. Bengal tiger and snow leopard skins decorated the walls along with horns from water buffalo and the head of a gazelle. Tibetan jewelry, New Guinean penis gourds, Indonesian spirit sculptures were mixed in with an upturned bear paw that was made into an ash tray. A shined and twisted narwhal horn served as a reminder of the days narwhal were slaughtered and their horns sold for a fortune as the alleged horns of unicorns. Sperm whale teeth with faint scrimshaw etchings sat on a shelf next to a wicker basket filled with the hard, six-foot-long whips of whale baleen. In the Alaskan section, which dominated the front of the store, three-foot-long fossil walrus tusks with black scrimshaw etchings were stacked in various glass cases. One entire case consisted of the dried cartilage of *oosiks*, walrus penis. It was their front, their cover, a store that Morgan Zanke had owned for more than a dozen years.

Morgan was a tall, bent man with thinning salt-and-pepper hair and parched and weathered skin. Red railroad tracks up the side of his neck revealed where they'd cleaned out a vein. An old boozer, Reed thought, of course on an international scale. He'd heard the stories, Hong Kong, Tokyo, Taiwan, Africa, Malaysia. The man had been around. Now the vestiges remained. The stroke had left signs of immobility on the left side of his face and in his left arm, a misfortune they took advantage of for part of their cover, having Pewter as Morgan's alleged niece coming over from Hawaii to help manage the store.

That Morgan knew of their operation naturally was a danger. In spite of the goods carried in his shop, Morgan was strictly legal. His paperwork was scrupulous. Ten years previous he'd approached Fish and Wildlife with information on individuals attempting to sell him raw ivory. He'd worked as an unpaid informer for Fish and Wildlife ever since, providing targets, never once having to testify in court or have his name publicly listed as the basis for a warrant. "You can trust Morgan," Rich said. "I wouldn't look for any danger from that area. But I'd just as soon use his shop strictly for a front. Don't get him involved and don't compromise his position as an informer."

Reed watched as Pewter hugged her alleged uncle. Morgan smiled and patted her shoulders in appreciation. Pewter was dressed for business and wore a gray skirt, white blouse with padded shoulders and a tangerine scarf. Dressed for impact, Reed thought with a note of disdain. If he was attracted to her, there was also something about her that set him off. But she'd made an impact on Morgan, she'd made a friend.

Reed picked up a tiny ivory figurine with a peaked head and ferocious expression. He rolled it over in his palm.

"It's a billiken," Pewter explained. "Some people think it's native. But actually it was introduced into Alaska around 1909, after it was the mascot for an Alaskan-Yukon-Pacific exhibition in Seattle. Walrus-hunting sailors aboard whaling vessels have used billikens for centuries as good-luck figurines."

Morgan grinned. "Pewter knows her ivory. She's been teaching me. Take it. It's Native carved, part of Alaska's Silver Hand program to promote Native crafts. When you go out to the villages, you can do some legal buying on my behalf. It's too bad Pewter can't go along. But that'll help get you in. It'll be a sign of good luck."

Reed considered. A tiny hole at the base of clenched teeth provided access for a neck chain. He'd never been one for decorations, absolutely refused to wear a wedding ring. But that was the old Reed. Times were changing. He had to adapt. "Sure. Maybe I'll need some good luck."

A Japanese family entered the store and began to browse. "My main clients on the exotic and more expensive stuff," Morgan said to Pewter. "Don't push, but be available if they ask. I'll be in the apartment." He motioned upstairs.

"So now what?" Pewter asked after Morgan departed.

"I guess we wait," Reed said.

Reed glanced in a display mirror. He was six years older than Pewter, divorced, two daughters. There was a touch of sag around his eyes and even under his chin, although that was mostly concealed by the light beard. He felt as he looked, a little worn, weathered. He'd never thought that much about aging before. But it was sitting there now, sore muscles and sagging flesh making mockery of his lies.

The bell tinkled from the shop door. A woman with long, straight blond hair and a conscious attitude about herself sauntered into the shop. She wore blue jeans and a black tank-top T-shirt with no bra. Two nickel-size tattoos decorated either side of the base of her throat, one of a scorpion, one of a vampiress with blood dripping from her fangs. She smoked a cigarette and strode around the shop, poking and prodding at merchandise that held no fascination. A walking advertisement for filth and disease, Reed thought. Pewter hadn't met many like this. He backed off to watch the show.

"Excuse me, ma'am, there's no smoking allowed in here," Pewter said.

The woman turned, her blue eyes blazing like someone ready to kill. Her pupils were tiny pinpricks of black in a sea of blue and yellow-red. "Oh, really? How the hell do I get rid of it? There're no ashtrays. How about the carpet? Would that suit you fine?"

Reed thought to step forward. The Japanese family was watching, more taken with the woman than the merchandise.

Pewter paused and then reached behind the counter and held out a Styrofoam cup. "I'll take it."

The woman took a long drag and pointedly exhaled into Pewter's face as she dropped the butt into the cup. Pewter's lips were a compressed line. Her voice came out cold. "Feel free to look around. I'd appreciate it if you didn't handle the merchandise. If you have questions, I can answer them."

"You know what all this shit is? Where it came from?"

"Yes. This is a horn from a narwhal. It swims in the ocean. Once people sold these and said they were from unicorns. This mask is an Indonesian spirit sculpture."

"Jesus, what do people do with this crap?"

Pewter smiled sweetly. Her condescending tone came with little effort. "They decorate their mansions. They talk about them. It justifies adventures they make up in their minds. It's exotic. People like exotic."

"I like erotic," the blond snarled. "It's the same damn thing." Her eyes locked with Pewter's, a challenge from which Pewter refused to turn. The blond stood with her hands on her hips and surveyed the store. She briefly glared at Reed. "What the hell are you looking at?"

"Not much, I presume," Reed said.

"Yeah, right. Next time you sleep it better be on your belly and keep a tight asshole."

Reed shrugged. He could not get into this.

"What's your name?" the blond snapped at Pewter.

"Who asks?"

"Who asks?" the blond mocked the superior tone. "My, my. I asked, you dumb bitch."

"You can leave, and now," Pewter said.

"Or what, you'll call the cops? Message. Your name's Pewter?" Pewter barely nodded. "You and your boyfriend are suppose to get your money together and drive south on Highway One toward Portage. Start out at six PM. When you see the one, follow the one. It'll lead you to some real goodies." The woman started away.

"Wait a minute," Pewter called. The blond gave her the finger.

The Japanese man stood at the counter. He indicated a carved walrus tusk with a series of arctic scenes, an Inuit hunter with a spear, a seal, a polar bear. The carving was without fine detail, impressionistic and with the seal of the state's Silver Hand Program to indicate it was Native carved. The price tag read thirty-two hundred dollars. Pewter rang the sale through a charge card and carefully wrapped the carving in tissue paper and packed it into a box. Reed stood nearby, patiently waiting. Pewter's hands shook, from rage or fear he could not tell.

Reed used a backroom telephone to call Doug LaRue, a sometime partner and fellow agent up from Washington. They'd established a fund for making purchases of illegal ivory. However, each buy had to be recorded. Doug would get the money into their post office box. As to being a backup, trying to tail them down the highway and into a who-knows-what situation would be something they could only cover in part. "Or not at all," Reed vetoed the idea. "They'll be watching us too close. I don't know if these bastards are going to make a legitimate sale or just rip us off."

"And you're taking Pewter? We discussed that. She shouldn't be out exposed or acting as backup." Doug was a beefy agent, a hard-drinking man who would never shy from physical confrontation. That he'd been relegated to a liaison and bureaucratic role had not gone down well, Reed understood. His old partner felt betrayed.

"She's been handling it pretty well. It's a bit more than I bargained for, but I don't see how I can back out now. If I'm carrying money, I'm carrying my pistol, and I'll have it out and handy. They'll understand that. A guy's going to protect his investment."

"Yeah, but one man alone with a nine millimeter against automatic weapons doesn't count for squat, partner. This is getting hot and heavy pretty fast. The original design was for Pewter to be a nice, safe little shop girl. But, what the hell, she volunteered. It isn't like anyone went out and gave her an ultimatum."

Reed stood silently, eyes closed.

"Partner?"

"Yeah. I'm here. Just thinking about ultimatums. They're not always as clear-cut as you think. Get that money, Doug. Stand by the telephone. As the masseuse said to her client, I'll be in touch."

"As my fist is going to say to your nose, don't keep me waiting," Doug growled. He hung up.

Reed and Pewter drove south out of Anchorage down Highway One. The brown waters of Turnagain Arm lay off to their right. The tide was out, revealing the bay mud that lay hundreds of feet deep, an anthropologic treasure trove containing everything from gigantic mastodons to human beings, including those from recent days who'd been sucked into the mud and, even while their rescuers tugged in vain, had been covered by the turbulent tide. Minor mounds of the Chugach Mountains lay to their left, dotted here and there with mountain goats in plain sight for gawking tourists. No time for scenery now, Reed thought, but he still liked to look.

"What the heck are you smiling about?" Pewter asked. Her jaw was clenched. The lines at the corners of her mouth were pulled tight. Her small, soft-looking lips were barely visible. She wore slacks, a sweatshirt, hiking boots and carried a pistol at her waist. Reed wore a Nagra reel-to-reel tape recorder and carried five thousand dollars. There would be no body searches, he'd declared.

"Just thinking how beautiful it is out here and what kind of crap we're going into."

"And that's funny?"

"Ironic. There's a motorcycle up there about a half-mile and there are two choppers behind us. One of them is closing fast."

Pewter glanced in the side mirror. Good girl, Reed thought. The biker pulled up beside them; it was stringbean, the long, lean one with scarred, bony fists and the reach of an ape. His hair was long, black and stringy and he wore a gold earring in his left ear. He wore small, round sunglasses. He pulled up three feet away and stared. Reed crooked his little finger in a wave. The man just stared, driving down the centerline between passing cars.

"These bastards like to intimidate people," Reed said. "These guys are more vicious and mean than anything you ever imagined. I didn't know they'd be involved. I should have anticipated something."

"You can't cover everything," Pewter said. Her knuckles showed white as she gripped her purse.

Reed exhaled sharply. He'd never panicked for himself. It was a trademark, but now, with Pewter. He knew he was close. "Listen, I'm sorry about this. I . . . I really don't know your background. I know down there in Texas you didn't want to do any killing."

"What are you talking about?"

"Could you kill one of these guys? No hesitation. None."

"This is nuts."

"No. You have to have your mind set ahead of time. If you have to kill, you have to kill. It's nature, real life. It's for your own safety."

"I'm qualified. Don't cut me out. I can do my job."

"It's too quick. We're not prepared. Next corner, when I make the turn, I want you to get out."

Pewter whirled. Her naturally tan face turned dark with rage. "Are you mad? Now? Why the panic? You don't think I can cut it?"

"No." Just outside Reed's window the motorcycle roared. The man stared. A truck approached and it seemed as if the handlebar would come in through the side window. A little jerk of the wheel and he could splatter the guy under the truck, Reed thought. "I know you'd do fine. I didn't . . . I wasn't suppose to get you this deeply involved like this."

"Then why the hell did you ask me on the case?"

Reed glanced at the black glass of the staring sunglasses. It could be a setup. They could get shot and these bastards would just take their money. A motorcycle gang. He'd never figured on that many bodies. He ground his teeth, every time he tried for his own life . . . every time. He swallowed. "Look, I know your competence from down in Texas, from reports. But this is deep undercover, no backup, something different than I described. I needed your expertise on carving and ivory for the shop. But not this. You see I was attracted, I thought if we got to know each other . . ."

"You sonofabitch. That's it? That's why I'm here, for your benefit. Dammit!" She whirled away, her face as purple as deep dusk on the side of a mountain.

The motorcycle burst ahead. The driver had a big white 1 drawn on the back of his leather jacket. "He's the one," Reed said dryly. "The second coming right here in Anchorage. An old man's dream."

Pewter laughed madly. "You bastard. You beat me down and then you make jokes?"

"He's signaling a turn. When we make the corner I'll pull over. I don't want you killed." Reed slowed.

Pewter's hand strayed toward the door handle. "No. Can you imagine what the guys would say? Don't bother. I'm not getting out." She shook with rage. "We'll take it through. Jesus. I'm paid just like you."

Reed saw her anger. Had it been just this morning they'd stood at the top of the mountain, next to Exit Glacier, at one with the world? He slumped, like a man who'd publicly lost control of his bowels. What timing. It reminded him of his last days with Pam. Logic had no place in marital strife.

He made the corner and drove on. Somehow he found the strength to say the hollow words, "I'm sorry."

If Pewter nodded he did not see it. She was crowded against the opposite door, as far away as possible, her body tensed, closed up, without an ounce of warmth. And Pewter was as warm as anyone he'd ever met.

Reed drove on. His hands were numb. His mind revolved like a tidal whirlpool churning in the bay. He thought of a thousand pieces of advice and kept every piece to himself. There could not possibly have been a worse way to handle this, he thought, and congratulated himself on that.

He concentrated on driving the Bronco after the motorcycle. They had Alaskan plates on the Bronco, the whole works, registration and insurance in Pewter's undercover name, everything they could think of to insure a tight cover. People would check, which meant nothing here. Stay in a position where he could always use his gun, he thought, at least get in a couple of shots. It was all he had.

Stringbean wheeled into a somewhat secluded turnout, a gravel parking area at the base of hiking trails leading into the mountains. He motioned for Reed to park and then pulled out of the lot.

Reed and Pewter sat in tense silence and looked around the empty lot. "They have it covered pretty good," Reed said. "Backup never would have worked. They'd have spotted it. We'd be in the cold."

"I think we already are," Pewter said dryly.

Time passed. The strain did not ease. Reed spoke lightly, "I knew you'd be bored. I thought I'd double the strain."

"Congratulations, you did a good job."

Reed smiled, Pewter never missed a tick.

"Ohh!" Pewter moaned. A man wearing a fake, flaming-red beard emerged out of the brush just to her front. Reed jumped out of the vehicle, pistol in hand.

"What the hell are you doing with that?" the man said in a rough gravel voice. He revealed little sign of concern, a signal he was well covered, Reed thought. He looked down and saw a tiny pink laser light on his chest. The laser moved slightly, making a sign of the cross. Reed casually imitated the gesture, just to let the sniper know he knew.

"For a moment, I had the illusion I could protect my assets," Reed said. He thrust the pistol into his belt. "Guess it shows who's a fool. You have the ivory in your pocket there? It doesn't look like much."

"Real smart ass aren't you," Redbeard snarled. "There's a wooden trunk down near that outcropping in the brush. Girly there's the expert. She can give it a look. You stay here with me. If it's all okay, you give me the bread. And then you all just sit until we're all gone. As simple as pie if no one messes up."

"You're calling the shots," Reed said. "No pun there, I hope." He jumped up on the hood of the Bronco. "See the outcropping of those rocks," he said to Pewter. She stood in the open, five feet away from the man with the red beard. Five-feet-ten, two hundred pounds, Reed estimated for his report — bit of a paunch, worn jeans, black biker boots, the round bulge of a snuff can in one rear pocket and a black belt with a nickel-plated buckle of a man on a cycle with a bare-breasted woman riding on his back — undoubtedly one of Redbeard's fantasies most unlikely to come true.

"Down by those willows?" Pewter asked. Her voice cracked and Reed could see her anger at herself.

"That's right. Watch for snakes. They have those red lasers in these parts. But they don't move very fast or climb very well."

Pewter's eyes locked with Reed's. If they were enemies five minutes before, they were bosom partners right now.

Pewter reached into the back of the Bronco and took out a small scale and a canvas duffel bag. The red-bearded man with sunglasses and brown hair watched closely. Reed, the laser sight still playing on his chest, watched as she walked down toward the spit of rocks and brush. She did not look back before she stepped into the foliage. But he could see she stopped and bent over.

Time passed. Reed lounged against the Bronco. "So how do you think the Seahawks will do this year?"

"You better ask how you're going to do. It'd be more to the point."

"You can tell your jerkoff friend up there that if he keeps sticking that sight on people someone's going to come along and stick it up his ass."

"It might be a little tough with a hundred and eighty grain bullet in your lungs."

A hundred feet away Pewter emerged from the brush. She started back.

"Just stay right there, honey," Redbeard said.

Pewter stopped. "There's a hundred pounds. Eighty pounds is pretty good."

"How much?" Reed asked.

"Fifty dollars a pound."

"Oh hell no. That's too much. I can get it in the villages for a lot cheaper than that."

"Then fly the hell out there and get it. Fifty dollars. We've got other outlets that pay almost that. We'll just keep with them."

"Forty-five."

"I ain't here to dick around. Take it or not."

"Forty-eight, but just for the eighty pounds," Reed said.

"No. Fifty for all of it, or nothing."

Reed straightened. "Well, thank's for showing us. Tell Kurth when he wants to go for a fair price, we're interested. That's too far out of line. Pewter."

"Wait a minute." Redbeard seized Reed's arm in a powerful grip. "We ain't setting up and running all the way out here and you don't buy. That's not the way it works."

Reed gazed at the dark eyes behind the sunglasses. This guy was on the edge of anger and had an arsenal waiting in the hills. How far could he push? He tightened his stomach against the fluttering inside. "Kurth says he wants to do volume, he has to deal."

Redbeard looked away, clearly uncertain. "I don't like this dicking around." He looked toward the brush. "Ah, take the eighty pounds. Forty-eight dollars." He whirled on Reed. "What do we care. We know you're government agents. You're giving us government money. We don't care if you have it painted with ultraviolet paint. We don't care if it's marked. We can get rid of it all. Government money's as good as that of anyone else."

"Nice line of bull," Reed said. He circled the Bronco, hoping to put the vehicle between him and the laser sight. "Pewter, pick out the eighty pounds and put it in the duffel bag." Reed turned and opened the back door of the vehicle.

"What are you doing?" Redbeard demanded.

"Did you want money or is our credit good?"

"You've got a mouth, don't you. I was told that if there's a good enough excuse it was all right if you lost some teeth. It was also all right if the girl over there had a chance with a real man or two."

Reed lifted the seat and took a small bag from a slit near the base of one seam. Bent over inside, Redbeard peering over his shoulder, he counted the money. He turned. "There, thirty-eight hundred and fifty dollars, an extra ten so you can buy the boys a beer. They must be tired sitting up there in the brush, using up the batteries in their laser sights. Some guys do that, and about the time they get into a fight their battery's dead."

Redbeard stuffed the money into his pants. "When you drive out of here, you drive south. Don't stop until you get to Girdwood. Understand?"

"You've got the guns," Reed said. He started down toward where Pewter was dragging a heavy canvas duffel bag stuffed with full-length walrus tusks. By the time he reached her and picked up the bag, Redbeard was disappearing into the brush. Reed looked at his chest.

"What are you looking at?" Pewter asked. Her dark eyes were bright and her hands shook.

"Some joker in the hills has had a red laser sight fixed on my chest half the time. Either the battery's giving out or he has it turned off. Are you all right?"

"I've been better," Pewter said. "Let's just load this and get out of here."

Reed threw the tusks into the back. He had to steel himself not to run as he circled the Bronco. And he had to fight to keep from ducking behind the dash as he started the engine and backed away. He kicked up dirt and gravel as he sped away and turned south toward Girdwood.

"I just glimpsed a motorcycle back in the woods on one of those trails," Pewter said. "I wonder how many there were?"

"More than enough," Reed said. He exhaled and rolled his head to relieve the tension.

"I'm exhausted. But there's no way in hell I'll go to sleep," Pewter said.

"Two or three days to unwind," Reed said softly. "That's what it takes me. Then you'll sleep. It's just like combat. It tears you up."

"So what do you think these guys are up to?"

"I think they were fronting for Kurth. Maybe we've established enough linkage here so we can get a warrant and look at his telephone logs. We don't have a case, but we made a buy. The guy claimed we were government, but he didn't have much conviction. They'll be back. What we have to do is get inside, get a link to their source, a link to where they sell."

"We?" Pewter questioned. "I thought you wanted me out of here. I still haven't killed anything or anyone. Not like the great Reed Erickson." The sarcasm was unbridled.

"I don't know what got into me out there. It's not normal. I can assure you. Lately I haven't really been myself."

"Let me know when you are yourself. Then I'll know the real you. It's like my father; all his life he wanted me to follow him in biology. He said I'd never last on this job. Now you tell me the same. I guess you were trying to build my confidence."

"I don't doubt your competence," Reed protested. "It was the false pretenses that I initiated. And then the danger. That was unfair on my part. It was my mistake, not yours."

Pewter's eyes narrowed. Her face was drawn, the muscles tense, erasing her youth, taking away her joy. "I wish I could believe you."

"It's true."

Pewter motioned him away, the dismissive gesture of an embittered woman. "I don't want to talk about it anymore. We'll just do our jobs. When we have to be girlfriend and boyfriend, I can pretend. I did it with Mike, I guess I can do it with you."

Reed recoiled from her disgust. He'd evolved a long way from home to make a mistake like that. Undercover, judgment was all you had. He managed to nod. She was right, there was no need to talk. If anything it would be a mistake.

They returned to their apartment. They'd have to log the ivory in, somehow get it into storage without being spotted. Reed ducked into the bathroom to shower, to wash away the stink of shame. If he'd ever pulled a bigger gaff on a case, he couldn't remember when. It always happened when you mixed in your personal life, like you were suppose to be insulated, like nothing else mattered except the case.

When he left the bathroom the living room was empty. A neatly written note lay on the coffee table. Pewter had gone for a bicycle ride on the paved trail along the coast. Don't wait on supper, she said, she'd eat downtown.

Reed stood in the silence of the apartment. The stillness echoed. You had to trust your partner and he'd shown no trust at all.

He went to the refrigerator and opened a beer. The skull and thirty-inch tusks of a walrus sat on the kitchen counter, forty-eight dollars a pound, Eskimo money. It must have made a hell of a journey, through the Pacific Ocean, down the Bering Sea, onto some ice floe where some hunter had gunned it down. Did the carcass go to waste? Did the walrus die naturally, a revered participant in the ancient tradition of the hunt? Or was the kill modern-day head hunting, a simple matter of greed?

Reed closed his eyes. Few people handled undercover with aplomb. He'd liked it from the start, a raw excitement he dared not explain. The rest of life paled. He could do this, handle these guys, keep himself in check even facing that gang. But he couldn't maintain the lie with Pewter. There he'd failed, unable to maintain the deceit with someone he liked. There was no logic at all.

The hell with it, he snarled. He'd go out on the town, see what Anchorage offered for night life. He'd been celibate long enough. A man had a right to live.

ESKIMO MONEY

CHAPTER FOUR

There was no way to make amends for his gaffe, Reed thought. A partnership was like a marriage — once a wrong, always a wrong, never forgotten, always there. So he wouldn't even try. Shrug it off, go on. He could play hurt as good as anyone.

From now on he'd treat Pewter strictly as a professional. He'd keep her on the case. But no more out in the field. In the shop, maybe out with Kurth and Wynona. They'd work together. They'd reside in the same apartment. But they'd relate only as regarding work. If Pewter changed to go jogging or biking, he did not ask to go along. If she wanted to ask him, fine. Whatever their relationship outside work would be up to her, Reed thought. He would not give her any pressure. He didn't ask about her family; he didn't ask about her philosophy; he didn't ask about her life. If they talked, it was about the case, options, things they might try in their efforts to penetrate the ivory trade.

Three days after they'd made their ivory purchase from the motorcycle gang, Reed saw Kurth in the Rare Species store. Kurth, lean and tan with his wavy blond hair and quick smile, wore black denim trousers and a black shirt with the sleeves cut off at the shoulders. God's gift to women, Reed thought irritably. Kurth leaned on the counter, face to face with Pewter. The two of them laughed. That Reed felt a reaction was a warning, a signal that he had a long way to go in order to achieve nirvana.

Fortunately the store was empty of customers. Reed strode across the room, circling past the full scrimshawed head of a walrus skull and tusks and past a wicker basket filled with tiny bottles of crude oil, allegedly from the *Exxon Valdez* spill; two dollars each, another Alaskan souvenir, something to replace the two-dollar bottles of crude oil gift stores had sold when the pipeline first opened. "You sonofabitch!" Reed snarled.

Kurth turned, still smiling. He held up a palm to stop Reed's advance. Reed spoke as harsh as he could. "You send us out there to be jerked around by a bunch of goons while some guy's pointing a laser sight at my chest. I should tear your goddamn head off."

Pewter stared in wonderment, uncertain if Reed was acting or not. "It wasn't suppose to go that hard," Kurth said. He touched his palm against Reed's chest to hold him back. His eyes betrayed a sense of uncertainty, as if he read Reed's anger as genuine. "Just take it easy. Checking things out. Next time around there'll be some accommodation."

"You're damn right there'll be accommodation. On the way we do business, and damn sure on the price."

"I can't do much on the price. The market's set by demand. Right now demand is awfully damn high."

"If there's not enough margin, this isn't worth doing." Reed glanced at Pewter as if looking for confirmation. His voice came out several octaves higher than he ever intended. "Isn't that right, honey?" Reed winced at Pewter's glare.

"Whatever you say, honey," Pewter said.

Kurth's eyebrows arched at the frosty reply. He smirked at Reed then turned to Pewter. "I'll call you."

"What the hell do you mean you'll call her?" Reed demanded.

Kurth started away then turned and smiled. He spoke easily, like a man who never worried. "About business. You know. When I have the goods and you have the money." He stared long and hard at Pewter and then took his leave.

"That was all an act, right?" Pewter asked.

"Yes. I wasn't happy with that kind of a setup. We were vulnerable. Kurth has had his chance to look us over. I won't go through that again. But you have to play as hard with these guys as they play with you. What did he want?"

"Just talking," Pewter said. "He's coming on to me. How do you think I should play it?"

"We're suppose to be engaged."

"Even Kurth can see that isn't working."

"Yeah, I'm sorry. I was a little too peeved at Kurth. I just didn't like that sight playing on my chest. Whatever you think. I trust your judgment."

"That's a surprise. Or are those just words you think are right? Sometimes it's hard to tell."

"Yeah, for me also. We want to get a direct buy we can record. And we're going to have to keep Kurth on the line for a long time. You know the rules. We can't get too involved or it blows the case. Kurth's a pusher."

"He's also an adulterer, that's plain to see."

Reed nodded. "I got together with Doug. They've been going over the telephone logs. There were a number of calls to a Vitus Inokenti. He's a half-

Yupik who lives up in Eagle River. We took a look. His house isn't much of a place, pretty junky. But he has several kids and his wife works in a convenience store. As far as we know Vitus doesn't have a regular job. But he does have an old airplane. And he still has relatives living on St. Lawrence. He can legally buy and trade ivory with other Natives. He recently filed a flight plan for St. Lawrence. I'm going up there and see if I can buy some legal carvings for the shop here and also meet with Vitus."

"We'll have to talk with Morgan and see what kind of carvings he wants and what you should pay," Pewter said. "I can write out a list. When are you leaving?"

"This afternoon."

"This afternoon!"

"We've been watching that Terry Grason from Fairbanks. Abe had him on a list, but we don't know that he ever made contact. Woodruff gave Grason a call for me once. He wasn't interested. The field agent in Nome called. She said Grason's in town. I want to make the bars tonight and see if I can bump into him."

"This is all pretty fast."

"I know. Things break this way sometimes. I'm running back to the apartment to throw some clothes together. If you can make out a list of those carvings, I'll swing back."

Pewter nodded. "What about Kurth?"

"Keep him on the line. If he offers a buy, tell him you won't carry that much money around by yourself. If he's stupid enough to bring it into the shop, tell him it has to be when Morgan isn't around. Doug can set up in the back room and record things."

"All right," Pewter said.

"Watch yourself," Reed said. "Keep that chain on the door. No one's been around for a few days. But they might return. At least you get the place to yourself a few days."

"I don't think it'll feel any different than it does right now," Pewter said.

Another shot, Reed thought; or an opening. Lately with Pewter he could not tell. Or perhaps he could never tell. He didn't know her that well. "Does it bother you being there alone?"

"You mean because people break in and are sneaking around with guns in their hands?"

"That's just work, other than that." He forced a smile.

"When you're an only child and you move around a lot you learn to get on alone, even if it's not what you prefer. And I've worked in San Fransico for five years. Hardly any of it really outdoors; all import/export stuff, animals and plants. The job isn't what I anticipated. There are only a few female agents. Most of the guys try to be accommodating. But that's the problem, almost worse than those who don't think we should be here at all. Taking this case was my mistake. The Texas case was exciting. I thought this was an opportunity."

"Look, I don't know how I can make this up."

"First step, don't try. Besides, I joined the health club in town. I met some people."

"Don't forget . . ."

Pewter glared. "Sorry," Reed muttered. Always lecturing. It drove Stacy mad. "I'll stop back for that list," he said and turned around and left.

Reed took a commercial jet up to Nome. Vestiges of snow and ice still coated the higher elevations to the north and east. Brown patches of frozen tundra and leafless willow bushes served as scant break against a bleak, windswept landscape. The arctic town of four thousand was quiet, a black bear still shrouded in hibernation before the brief summer onslaught of gawking, camera-laden tourists. A few bundled residents, the majority of whom were Inupiaq and Yupik, stalked the sidewalks. The sun shone bright in a pale blue sky and the wind blew in cold off the Bering Sea. Back around the turn of the century they'd discovered the beaches of Nome were laden with gold dust. The boom had built a city.

Over the years storms and ice had turned the beach over. Modern-day panners with gasoline engines still set up camp during summers, shoveling sand off the beach and sluicing out as much as an ounce of gold a day. It was a way to make a living, just enough money to sit out a long, dark winter.

Reed checked without reservations into the Nugget Inn on Front Street, next door to the Bering Sea Saloon and Fat Freddy's Restaurant. "Double room," Reed told the young, Inupiaq receptionist. "I don't like being closed in small spaces." The girl smiled. The two months after the rush of the Iditarod sled dog race, modestly known as "The Last Great Race on Earth," there were an abundance of rooms facing the Bering Sea.

As soon as he reached the room, Reed called the local fish and wildlife field agent. She'd checked and, at least as of two hours earlier, Grason's silver de Havilland Beaver was still tied down at the airport.

Within the hour Reed began to make a round of the gift shops that were open. Morgan had named some contacts so he posed as a legitimate buyer of Native-carved ivory. He hit as many shops as he could, the Arctic Trading Post, Board of Trade Ivory Shop, Polar Jewelry and Gift Shop.

Even with Morgan's business card the owners were wary of a new buyer. As the opportunity presented itself, Reed followed the prearranged script and dropped hints. The Native carving was good, but it didn't always exhibit the detail some of their more upscale clientele demanded. He had business interests in Hawaii. And of course there was the matter of a carver's reputation. A Garth Hobart carving commanded thousands of dollars. Reed walked around the shop, examining the artifacts, mukluks, billikens, fur coats.

Melvin, the owner, was a short, dark-haired man with a pale, wrinkled complexion and the air of a man who'd endured too many hard times. He was suspicious but Reed managed to continue in an even tone. "A great many of the island scrimshanders and carvers can't get the quality raw ivory to carve anymore. As I mentioned, we can use fossil ivory, however, it's too dark and striated in order to obtain the best quality pieces. Besides, there's that guy from Oregon who has those Vietnamese carvers; he seems to buy all the fossil ivory in sight."

"If you're looking for raw ivory you came to the wrong place," Melvin said in a high-pitched voice. He stepped back as if to escape. "I don't know who you are or what you're up to, but if you're looking for raw ivory, you're looking for trouble."

Reed stalked over to Melvin and leaned on the counter. The tiny billiken on a chain around his neck hung out from his plaid blue-and-black-wool shirt. "I'm not looking for trouble, Melvin. I'm just a man looking to make a living. Just like yourself." He winked. "You know, consenting adults."

Melvin wasn't amused. Melvin's an honest man, Reed thought. Sometimes, working with the dregs of the world, he had to remind himself that honest people still commanded a healthy majority. Melvin didn't give one signal he wanted to deal.

* * *

That evening Reed made the round of taverns, the Arctic Native Brotherhood Club, the Polar Bar. Ten o'clock at night and the town was still as light as midafternoon. Eventually, at the Board of Trade Saloon, he finally saw his mark.

He was blinking against the gloom and surveying the bar and his target stood out as distinctly as a grizzly bear standing in a path. Terry Grason was six-feet-four, with broad shoulders and thick curly hair. He wore a leopard-sealskin vest over a plaid shirt, and blue jeans held up by a huge silver belt buckle with the carved figure of a grizzly bear. His hands were knobby clubs with knuckles well scarred from numerous bar fights and torn skin from working on his airplane in the freezing cold. A genuine Alaskan frontiersman, Reed huffed.

Reed selected a stool several down the long bar from where Grason sat. Behind the bar three yellowing oosiks, walrus penises, hung one below the other. He ordered a beer from the woman bartender, a saucy Yupik wearing tight jeans and a loose gray sweatshirt.

Reed waited, avoiding eye contact, trying to figure an opening that would not make Grason suspicious. He'd never met the man, but of course he'd seen his picture. And, as a result of Captain Dale Woodruff's introduction, he'd talked to Grason some months back. But that was over the telephone. Grason had no interest in dealing with anyone for anything. The conversation had been short. It was doubtful Grason even remembered his undercover name.

Fifteen minutes passed. He might have but one chance at this guy, Reed thought. He sipped at his beer in an effort to wet the dryness in his mouth. He got off his stool.

"Did the bartender call you Grason? Terry Grason?"

Grason turned and stared. His eyes were clear, steady, a man who'd never felt a sense of physical inferiority. Up close, even in the gloom of the tavern, the lines of age were beginning to show in the sag under his jaw and the slight puffiness in his jowls. And yet there was an undeniable hardness about the man, like a Marine, a construction worker, someone who'd spent his life working with back and hands. He stared, a man who had no reason to speak.

"If you're the Terry Grason from Fairbanks, I called you a few months back. Dale Woodruff gave me your name."

"And what's your name?"

"Reed Goodnow."

Grason gave a slight nod as if recalling the conversation. "Woodruff's a scavenger. He picks up scraps off other people's tables. He ran a guide boat for me some years back. How'd you meet him?"

"We did some business together last summer," Reed said.

"But you're not from Alaska?" Grason said.

Reed slid in against the bar next to Grason. A low buzz of conversation filled the bar, locals whiling away the night as the days slipped on toward another summer without dark. "No, I'm from Wisconsin. Just up here doing a little business. Great country."

"It used to be," Grason growled. A man named Sealskin Charlie tipped off his stool into Grason's side. Grason gently helped the little man back onto his stool.

"Get him out of here," the bartender yelled. "He's had enough. I told you before." Two men came and helped Charlie out the door.

"That's what I mean," Grason said. "It's all going to hell. You should see Fairbanks. Back before they put in the pipeline it used to be a frontier town. Now it's four-lane roads and fast-food joints. The day they put in a McDonald's I knew the town was dead."

Reed nodded in sympathy. He ordered a beer, pointedly not offering to buy one for Grason. "Yeah, the unique diversity in every part of the country is being destroyed. Everything's so bland, the same, just like television. That's why I like Alaska. I still think it's unique."

"You're fifteen years too late," Grason said. He apprised Reed closely, the worn, casual clothes, the scuffed leather boots, the short beard. It was natural, used, not at all a practised look. "What the hell do you think you're doing up here?"

Reed laughed. "Actually I just wanted to see some of this country. Although I am suppose to be doing some business. My fiancée is running her uncle's gift store in Anchorage. I'm buying carvings and native crafts for the shop."

Under Grason's quiet questioning, Reed told about the Rare Species store. How Morgan Zanke had had a stroke. How his niece, Pewter, had carved ivory in Hawaii and had an association with shops in Lahaina. He'd talked Morgan into letting him make this trip up to Nome and out to St. Lawrence. The trick was not to say too much, don't volunteer any part of his story unless Grason asked.

"So you don't have a job?" Grason asked.

"I've only been here a few of months. And then last summer for a visit. There's not much work available. I help out in the shop. Drive a little taxi. Although there's not much business until summer gets going."

"Everyone who ever worked on the pipeline is driving a cab," Grason growled. He motioned at Celise to give him a beer and to give one to Reed as well. "They're all divorced, waiting on the next big oil boom so they can collect their fortune and blow their wad again. Everyone up here loves their oil. They just don't get the picture that it's oil, people, money that's destroying everything that made this country great." Grason sipped his beer. "But you have to have progress. Can't stand in the way of progress. I'm just glad I was born when I was. I got to see the real Alaska, the real frontier."

"It looks like there's still a lot of country to me," Reed said. He spoke with genuine empathy. Grason's attitude came as a surprise. Maybe Captain Woodruff had steered him wrong in an effort to save his boat and commercial fishing license. But then again what was Grason doing in Nome? His guide and outfitting business operated out of Fairbanks. "From the time we took off from Anchorage I never saw a village or a town. Of course there were a lot of clouds."

"You were at thirty thousand feet. Oh, there's a lot of land out there yet. But it's going. If you want to see Alaska, you have to get right down on the deck. When are you going out to St. Lawrence?"

"About noon."

"If you want to see some country, I'll show you some country. Meet me for breakfast at Fat Freddy's at seven. I've got a Beaver. You pay for the gas and meal and I'll show you around."

"That's damn generous."

Grason stood and, without another word or even looking at Reed, turned and walked away. Reed stayed another fifteen minutes. It was past midnight when he took his leave. Traffic in the bar was as heavy as it had been at ten o'clock. He walked down the dusky light of the wide main street toward the motel. He casually glanced around. Down one alley young kids were still playing at twelve-thirty at night. A husky, chained to a bare-wood plywood doghouse, lay in the dust and watched him pass. A cold, hard wind blew in off the Bering Sea. He could not escape the feeling he was being watched.

He entered his motel room. It smelled a little musty from the salt humidity of the sea and from lack of use. He stood naked and stared at the gray, tossing waters of the Bering Sea. Terry Grason didn't seem like a bad sort. There was a hell of a lot of power with that guy. Six-foot-four and built like he lifted weights. Fortunately the power seemed controlled.

Reed turned and looked at the twin beds, the empty room. He looked at the ocean and recalled Lester crabbing the Boston Whaler in on the *Winch God II*, spray flying, the boat lurching like a sick whale. He recalled the cold spray against his face, the sheen of water between him and the trawler, his precarious balance, the throbbing of his heart. Just as there had been the silent beauty of the mountains, the cool wind, the clouds huddled down below, Pewter lying at his side in the little tent, her hair shiny, the light scent of perfume like the smell of fresh pine. There were things worthwhile — they were just so hard to hold.

Reed woke at six-thirty, took a quick shower and then met Grason for breakfast, after which they drove to the airport in Grason's rented pickup truck. Without preamble or even a cursory preflight, they climbed into the silver Beaver. Grason fired the engine, gave a brief call to the tower and taxied to the main runway. The morning sun poked through tendrils of fog and promised a bright sunny day. As casually as if driving an automobile, Grason did not bother to rev his engine or check his instruments. Before he made the turn onto the runway, he pulled the throttle out and with a roar, a shake, and considerable vibration, the Beaver lifted upward into the air.

"How many hours do you have?" Reed asked.

"Thousands. I hardly log them anymore," Grason said. "Too damn many regulations, lawsuits, you name it. Did you know forty percent of the cost of an airplane is just for liability insurance? Even up here lawyers are running us into the ground. I should have stayed simple. When I started my outfitting business it was with pack horses and mules. I didn't have any debt. Now I make more money than ever and I have more debts than ever. It doesn't make any sense."

"Pack horses would be the way to go," Reed agreed. He peered down at the wide-open vistas of tundra. They passed over a scattered herd of reindeer raised for cutting off the blood antlers and selling them to the Orient, although they were also raised for meat.

"They round the reindeer up with helicopters," Grason said. A few minutes later he pointed out a small herd of musk oxen. He banked the airplane and headed out to sea.

Grason continued to talk above the roar of the airplane, like a man talking to a priest or psychiatrist. "We'd go out for two weeks, live in tents, catch fish in streams, eat off the land. Really rough it. When you shot a moose, you packed out the meat, one load after the other. When you shot a bear, you walked up to it on foot. Men challenged themselves. Not anymore."

"That's probably true," Reed agreed.

"You're damn right it's true," Grason roared. "Now days these fat slobs come up from the Lower 48 and they want a ten-foot bear right now. They don't want to work for it. They don't want any danger or any inconvenience. They just want the goddamn skin so they can hang it on the wall and tell everybody how great they are. Hell, I've had them ask me to bring the skin to their motel. Some of them ask me to set them up with women like I'm a pimp for Chrissake."

"It's all an illusion these days," Reed agreed.

"Nothing's real."

"The bastards got money falling out of their pockets," Grason continued. "But they've got demands falling out of their mouth. You don't know how many times I wanted to drop some of them off and just fly off. Let them work their own way back."

Reed laughed. "Problem is if they survived they'd sue. If they didn't their relatives would."

The airplane droned on and soon approached the Arctic Pack Ice.

"I'm surprised that there's this much ice, this late," Reed said.

"Hell, there's ice down here in June some years," Grason said.

The men talked of bears, of leads in the ice where the bears hunted seals.

"There he is," Grason said. He banked sharply, standing the airplane on one wing a few hundred feet above the ice pack and the blue-black leads of the Bering Sea. Blood drained from Reed's head and in the midst of the gut-wrenching turn he wondered if Grason flew this way all the time, or if he was just being macho for his benefit. Grason pointed out the small, yellow-white of a polar bear walking in a slow, pigeon-toed gait near an open line of water.

"Looks damn young, two or three years old," Reed said.

"Probably," Grason said. He dove the airplane and they whipped past less than ten feet above the ice. What from a mile high had appeared to be a relatively smooth carpet had turned into a series of mounds and upheaved pressure ridges of ice twenty feet thick. The pale blue striations of clean cut ice served as an appealing contrast to a world of white.

"Eskimos take polar bear," Grason said. "Hell, Eskimos take walrus, sell the tusks. When they settled the Native claims they gave the Eskimos damn near a billion dollars. Set up all those Native corporations. Damn near every one is bankrupt. They made it so complicated lawyers got most of the money. I feel for these people. They're dying, inch by inch, their culture just being eaten away. Like Sealskin Charlie there last night. He's hand-harpooned ten whales in his life. Going right up to them in a boat and sticking that harpoon into fifty tons of flesh. Now that was a man. What the hell was that we saw there last night?"

"It's sad," Reed agreed. He could only wonder on where Grason was going.

"What are you after?" Grason asked. He pulled the stick slightly and the airplane bounced up over a towering pressure ridge.

Shards of ice whipped past at terrifying speed. Grason was serious, Reed understood. This flight hadn't been just an exercise in building friendship.

"Like I said, I'm buying Native-carved ivory for Morgan's store. But Pewter knows all these carvers in Hawaii. Since the ban on elephant ivory, carving material is hard to come by. I guess the Native-carved figures are a little rough. Some people like fine detail. There's a market. If I can make a buck, I try to make a buck."

"The feds have run a half-dozen sting operations in the past decade. They had buyers from New Orleans. They had a store that was a front for agents. They caught some big dealers at first. Now they catch the small-timers, guys dealing dope for ivory. Great conversion price. I don't deal. And if I did it wouldn't be with some stranger walking in out of the blue."

"That's all right. I do appreciate the flight. This is just beautiful country."

Grason slowly turned the airplane and began a slow climb back toward land. "Friendly piece of advice. Game wardens aren't much liked up here by anyone, Native or white. Game wardens killed my son."

"No! They shot him?" Reed tried to sound incredulous.

"Might just as well have. They ran him down. He crashed. He died."

"That's a shame," Reed said with forced empathy. He knew the story. Jeff Grason and another man were out drinking. They shot a moose standing beside the highway. State Troopers from the conservation division received a tip, drove up and gave chase. Jeff ran and crashed his truck into a tree. His partner was not harmed.

"If a warden came after me, I'd bring him out here. The ice goes for a thousand miles, and hardly a soul around. This is freedom," Grason said with genuine emotion. "How the hell anyone could think about living anywhere else is beyond me. I've talked to many fish and wildlife agents. They'd try to get me when I was a guide. I spotted everyone. They all talk about game management and allocating the resource. Like they're farmers and they own the game," Grason spoke with great contempt.

Reed ignored the threat. "I wouldn't be worried about getting caught out here. They can't patrol all this. It's going back through Nome or Anchorage where I would get concerned." Misdirection, he thought. If you heard a threat you didn't like, ignore it.

He sat quietly, enjoying the flight, feeling just a touch of companionship with Grason, a man as big and tough as all Alaska. Grason saw the past sliding away. Did he care for the land, or did he just use the land? Grason was a hard man to figure, Reed thought. A bitter man.

CHAPTER FIVE

Slate blue leads of the Bering Sea broke through the pack ice in long, rootlike fingers. Tiny white icebergs floated like miniature polar bears in the open water. Vitus Inokenti banked the ancient Cessna so his twelve-year-old son, Samuel, could get a better look at the icy sea. Vitus shouted above the deafening roar, "Ten miles across that big lead. The hunters will be out. Let's go scout for walrus."

"And bear," Samuel yelled. He grinned with excitement. Although he was only one-quarter blood, he had the short, compressed features of a Siberian Yupik, long body trunk, short arms and legs, and thick facial bones. "Grandfather Jake says that one day he would take me out to visit our brother, the bear. If I have respect."

Vitus tousled his son's black hair. In the school outside of Anchorage, Samuel was a very quiet lad. A marginal student, his teacher claimed. But at home, or in the village, or on a hunt . . . Vitus knew his son. Last fall Samuel had shot his first moose.

They leveled off at five hundred feet. The forty-year-old airplane vibrated and throbbed ominously but with a predictable steadiness like a volcano that had been rumbling for ten thousand years. Vitus no longer paid it any heed. Twenty miles away the black line of St. Lawrence Island stood out as a desperate, cold and windy interruption between the annual war between the Bering Sea and polar pack ice. The sun shone brightly, glinting off the pack ice and reflecting millions of sparkling diamonds off the moving water in the leads. But he knew the area of his youth. Rivers of ice fog followed the leads. Full-size fog banks formed quickly, without mercy. They could last for days. As his stepfather Jake often said, "The fog eats the unwary alive."

Especially flyers, Vitus thought and wondered what ever possessed him to bring Samuel. Sissy had said no. Sissy didn't like St. Lawrence. She'd been there only twice, twice in twelve years of marriage to visit her in-laws and the place of his youth. It was, Sissy said, a bleak, forlorn place. Vitus had not said anything; he knew better than to get into an exchange of words with Sissy.

He'd first met Sissy in an Anchorage bar, a loud, buxom woman who'd just been divorced. "I've never been to bed with a nose-rubber, whatdaya say?" she'd said. At the time he thought it was funny.

He hadn't said much, Vitus thought, but within a month they were married, for better or worse. It was the only part of the ceremony he recalled, for better or worse, as if it didn't matter which one.

"A bear! A bear!" Samuel motioned. Vitus tipped the wing to see a female polar bear with a yearling cub making a slow, ponderous walk on the ice beside an open lead. "They stay near the leads looking for seal. You look for seal first and then you look for bear. Next fall she will lose that cub, if it survives. She probably had two. Almost half of them die during the first year. They stay with mama for two years. Then they hunt on their own. It is very hard for young bears. They are not good hunters. It might take ten days to kill one seal. And then a big male comes along and takes it away."

"That's not fair," Samuel said.

"It is the way of the land," Vitus said. He circled over to a small rock island where a dozen walrus had hauled out. A father teaching his son, carrying forward generations of traditions. It was the essence of a man. And Samuel was eager to learn. If only Sissy or Samuel's teacher could see. Vitus pointed. "The hunters will be out. One day soon, you will go."

"Not this time?"

"Your mother wants us back." The words came out sharper than intended, an attitude he did not like to admit. When he thought of Sissy, which he made a point not to do, there was a sadness in him, a wondering on what he was supposed to feel. Certainly she was the mother of his children. Without Sissy he would not have Samuel. Perhaps he should think on that.

Vitus banked sharply so they could look straight down on the walrus. He mellowed, becoming the teacher just as Jake had been a teacher with him. "Did you know walrus hide is so tough they once used it for shields against arrows. And they once cut it into thong for ship mooring hawsers? Even the polar bear is most respectful of the big bulls and cows, just as we are respectful of the bear."

He banked sharply. A thick fog bank was gathering over the western side of the island. He pushed the maroon throttle knob all the way in. The motor roared. The old Cessna vibrated like a tuning fork. "One day I will kill a bear with a lance, like the old days. It hasn't been done in fifty years," Vitus screamed to be heard. "There'll be a great celebration, like in the old days."

He settled low over the tiny village of Gambell, the wooden houses laid out in their rows, snow machines and ATVs sat scattered in the yards along with television satellite dishes. A larger building served as the community hall and Cooperative, another for the high school. Like a bush pilot setting down on a tiny patch of ice, Vitus crabbed the airplane into the persistent twenty-knot wind and touched down within scant feet of the end of the runway. By the time he taxied to the tie-down area they were totally engulfed by fog.

"By the hair on our chinny-chin-chins," Vitus said with a grin for Samuel. He fingered the black, scattered growth of a goatee that covered his brown chin, his gussuk heritage. "You must always watch the weather, always be aware. Weather waits for no man."

The fog was thick, cold and damp. A seaweed and fishy smell carried in from the open leads just offshore. The winter's accumulation of snow and ice was piled up beside the Flight Service Center and hangers.

With Samuel's able assistance, Vitus circled the airplane and tied down the wings and tail. The subarctic tundra and low willows and scrub birch just off the runway were obscured. A huge form, a man six-foot-four suddenly loomed out of the gloom. Samuel started and moved behind his father.

"Grason," Vitus said. "It's early in the season."

"I could say the same for you," Terry Grason said. He wore a wolfskin hat over thick, curled hair, and a leopard-sealskin vest over a plaid shirt. He was clean-shaven with a solid jaw that reminded Vitus of the craggy cliffs along the coast. "You still buying for Breismeister? How much of a cut does he give you?"

"I just come to visit," Vitus said. He followed Grason's stare into the back of his airplane that was crammed with trading goods, rifles, snowmachine suits, canned food and video cassettes. Just the thought of Kurth Breismeister made him sick. Breismeister still owed him fifteen thousand dollars from his ivory buying the last two seasons.

"Been hitting the yard sales again," Grason said. He towered a good ten inches over Vitus's squat, thick form. "How much do you really make out with all your wheeling and dealing and trading and swapping? If it wasn't for the baling wire there this old airplane would just fall apart."

"I bring gifts," Vitus said. "Why do you come? What do you bring?"

"Cold hard cash," Grason said. "You know me, straight up, straight forward."

Vitus nodded as Grason walked away. Grason dealt with the Keelachuck brothers. Everyone knew the Keelachuck brothers gathered more ivory than anyone on the island. Fossil ivory digs at the old villages, fresh ivory, even scuba diving in vicious currents and freezing water at the haul-out areas. The Keelachuck brothers were a law unto themselves, Vitus knew. Not even the elders dared to challenge what the Keelachuck brothers would do.

Vitus sat in the warmth of his mother's house. As usual, despite the three-thousand-dollar per year cost of heating oil, they kept the house excessively warm, a sharp contrast to the freezing weather outside. They were gathered in the smoky dark of the living room, bodies packed side by side and filling every available space; like in the old days, Vitus thought, when families extended four and five generations and all lived together. However, he could not live like that today. Sissy would not stand it, he knew, and wondered if he, after years of living in a world of plenty, could return to such deprivation. There were doubts, his weakness, the gussuk in the blood, the lack of resolve.

But at least he had a visit, he tried to console himself, a visit was the thing. This was a special gathering because he had come from the mainland bearing gifts. His two half-brothers and one half-sister had stopped over with their children. Julie, one half-sister, lived in Anchorage. Vitus had brought a package for everyone, including a package of moose meat for every family. "Samuel shot that," Vitus said casually as if it was not a source of pride.

"It's good the boy can hunt," Jake said. "Perhaps he can spend the summer, hunt bird eggs, go to the fishing camp, maybe even come once for walrus." Jake was short with squat, rotund features. During his lifetime Jake had killed five whales, a man without fear. Once Vitus had watched as Jake circled a wounded bull walrus and finished it off with a lance.

"I've talked about it with Sissy. If Samuel gets his grades up."

"We do not learn our life in a school," Jake growled. "Those are the ways of the gussuk."

Vitus' mother, Lulu, passed around the room a plate with tiny chunks of maktak, whale skin with blubber attached. Vitus plucked two pieces and eagerly began to chew.

They talked of hunting on the island. It had been a long, cold winter, and Vitus was thankful he no longer had to endure such privation. The walrus kill the previous season had been four hundred, a significant drop from the three thousand for the village the season before that. The Whaling Commission permitted the village to strike two bowhead whales. It had been a disastrous year. Both whales struck had managed to escape far out into the Bering Sea where later they would succumb to the tearing of their vitals by the steel shank harpoon.

Samuel told of the polar bear they had spotted. Vitus spoke of the walrus. The leads were opening on schedule. Perhaps it would be a good year.

"When the fog lifts," Jake said, an indication they would take up the hunt. "A few crews have been out. On some nature smiled. Some were closed in by fog. It depends upon how you live."

In time, family members drifted away, taking their packages of mainland meat and clothes from yard sales and returning to their homes. There had been a time when extended families were crowded into houses smaller than this plank house, Vitus knew. Sod and log houses. The Yupik lived underground and buried their dead on top. Now they did the opposite, the white man's way, buried their dead where it was warm and lived exposed to the cold.

Vitus trailed his mother into the tiny kitchen. "That maktak always brings back the memories. If the whaling is successful this year, you must be certain to send more."

"I will try," Lulu said without looking at her son. She was short, round and usually quick to smile.

Vitus touched her shoulder in a sign of affection. But as usual she pulled away. Embarrassed about him, Vitus thought. She had been fifteen when she became pregnant. As they did to many Yupik during the sixties, the Bureau of Indian Affairs sent her down to Seattle to go to school. Lulu would never tell the story, but she became pregnant. They ran her out of school, as if it was all her fault. The village took her back. She had behaved as nature had designed. Eventually Jake married her and accepted Vitus as his own, just like the four children Lulu bore for him.

But he was not the same, Vitus knew. He'd never been the same, not from the moment of his birth.

During the gloom of a cold and foggy late afternoon, Vitus wandered down to the village cooperative. Samuel, full of never-ending talk and laughter, had taken off with his cousins on one of the many four-wheelers. There were five hundred people in the village. A dozen or so were mainland Caucasians, school teachers and government employees. Vitus did not know any of the whites, but he knew the villagers, almost every one.

The late April weather had turned bitter. The rutted, muddy and rock-covered ground had refrozen. People were layered and bundled against the damp chill. The cooperative was noisy, several dozen people sitting around and visiting and drinking tea. Vitus visited, talking of the winter, of the weather, of the hunt and hopes for the coming years. From Native carvers and those in need, Vitus would sometimes trade: rifles, meat, clothes, occasionally money. He gave good deals, spreading the wealth.

In time he learned who had been out on the early season hunts, who had been out at the digs, who had ventured into the stormy sea to the walrus haul-out areas to collect pieces of broken tusks. The next day he made his rounds to individual houses, taking tea, eating smoked salmon, talking of the fall hunting on the mainland, the moose, the caribou, the subsistence harvest from his salmon wheel down at Chitna. And he traded for ivory.

It was not much of a load, four hundred pounds of fossil ivory, much of it small and chipped. The fresh ivory was limited and he obtained less than one hundred pounds, paying an average of twenty-three dollars per pound. He did procure one complete set of two-and-one-half-foot-long tusks, fifteen pounds. He paid three hundred fifty dollars. He knew Breismeister could sell it for six hundred.

It was on the second day of his visit that Vitus was approached by the gussuk, the Cossacks who seldom came, except during summer when bird-watchers or tourists came to gawk and stare and point their cameras in Yupik faces as if the Yupik were animals in a zoo. That the man would specifically approach him at the Cooperative was as troubling as the black, roiling clouds of an approaching storm.

"Are you Vitus?" The man was medium height, slender build, brown hair and a trimmed beard. He met Vitus's eyes direct, a friendly look, without challenge. He shook firmly, but without excess power. He dressed casually in browns and plaids like a working man. There was a sense of casual ease and self-confidence about the man that almost made Vitus relax, but for the fact the man was strange and had no cause to be here.

Reluctantly Vitus inclined his head. He stood silent, trapped against the wall of the Cooperative while the man talked and pressed a business card into his hand. The man was named Reed. He came from a gift shop in Anchorage and was looking for Native ivory carvings for his shop.

"We'd like to set up some direct trade here," Reed said. "That's why we're bypassing the registered dealers. We do a lot of business. Have been for fifteen years. You get the half the profit the dealers get, we save half. And we have a regular and reliable source."

Vitus looked across the Cooperative hall, the neon lights, the tiled floor, the paneled walls. Neighbors meeting neighbors. By more than half they'd adopted Western clothing, canvas and nylon parkas, woolen pants, rubber and leather packs for boots. A few parka helms and hoods, kus-puks, were ringed by wolverine or wolf fur to keep ice away from the face. Some people had sealskin mittens and a few mukluks tied around their calves, and they still gathered at the Co-op as a community rather than an isolated collection of individuals. But it was all fading away, Vitus thought, inch by inch.

ESKIMO MONEY

No one was looking at him talking to the gussuk, but he knew everyone saw. Each time he came home broke, Sissy became more upset. And Breismeister only sometimes paid. But who was this man, coming right out here to the village like this?

"My father does some carving. I could ask," Vitus mumbled.

"It's cold cash, good money," Reed said. "There is one other thing. Is there any chance of tagging along on a walrus hunt?"

Vitus felt the alarm. This guy was an agent, sure enough. But why would he make such a direct approach. It was not smart. "White men can't shoot walrus."

"Oh, I didn't want to shoot. I just wanted to get out on the ice, say I'd been there, see what it's like. I'm willing to pay."

"One thousand dollars."

Reed looked sharply. "One thousand dollars just to ride along? That's damn steep."

"If you go someone else can't." Vitus tried not to smile. The man was shocked by the price. A man from the government would not be shocked, they would just pay.

Reed looked in his wallet. "Look, I have enough money, but that's supposed to be for buying carvings for the gift shop. But who knows if I'll ever have this chance again." He glanced around the Cooperative. "Would you take a check?"

"Cash for one half now. A check for the rest when we get back."

"Great!" Reed said excitedly. "I might have to borrow some clothes. I hope you can set me up. I just asked on a whim. This should be just great, a genuine walrus hunt."

CHAPTER SIX

Reed sat quietly in the motor-driven umiaq as it headed out into the chop of the freezing Bering Sea. He could feel the pulsing of water through the wood frame and seal-skin covering. The excitement began to build.

Besides himself, there were four people in the boat. Vitus Inokenti, Vitus's stepfather Jake, Uncle Talimat, and a cousin named Pukak. By age, experience, and ownership of the skin boat, Jake was the leader, although the venture seemed more cooperative than directed, Reed thought. He'd watched carefully, tried not to get in anyone's way, yet pitched in wherever he could.

Although he was a guest and would eat what was served, in demeanor and attitude he was certain Jake did not want him along, even for the thousand dollars he had paid in cash.

Jake looked every inch like a man born to the harsh life in the Arctic. He was short, compact as if to take the brunt of unchecked wind. His face was deeply tanned from strong sunshine and reflecting snow. Tiny squint lines had formed at the corners of his eyes, and more lines creased the corners of his mouth. Jake would be a man quick to smile, Reed thought, but now he resented the intrusion in their midst, an outsider interrupting the pattern of their lives.

Jake worked the umiaq back and forth, quartering the five-foot chop. The salt spray along with a low, skudding mist soon had them wet and covered with a thin coating of ice. Vitus touched at the ice on Reed's brown parka and grinned. "Now this is hunting, eh?"

Reed grinned and shouted back. "I wouldn't have it any other way. As soon as I can't feel my fingers it'll feel like being back home in Wisconsin."

They crossed ten miles of open ocean in the small skin boat. They had float bladders made of sealskin they could throw out with a line attached to a harpoon. But they had no lifejackets. There was no need, Reed knew. In the Bering Sea in spring, you'd freeze before you had time to drown.

Once distant spray gave away two aluminum boats pounding from wave to wave as they headed out toward the pack ice. At one time the Yupik hunted in close proximity, as teams. Now, too often, they hunted alone or simply in pairs.

The roll and spray and monotonous whine of the outboard began to take its toll. Fortunately Reed was prepared. He'd layered his clothing as thickly as comfortable. He'd surrendered his leather boots for a pair of waterproof snowpacks from Vitus, and readily accepted the offer of waterproof sealskin mittens. He'd even accepted a Gortex hood with a wolfskin ruff that ringed his face. Nevertheless, the chill of the ocean slowly made inroads, stiffening his joints, numbing his fingers and toes, burning as deep as the marrow of his bones.

The long line of the pack ice gradually drew near. Protected by the ice from the wind, the water calmed. They passed individual floebergs and small cakes of ice. A large flock of eider ducks passed overhead. Nearby glaucous gulls rode the wind currents, heads turning as they sought a meal. They passed into the lee of a ridge of ice piled as high as a ship's mast. Vitus nudged Reed's elbow and pointed at the floe. "Big storm."

"Big storm," Reed agreed and Vitus laughed.

Jake, as steersman, idled back and worked the boat in between various floebergs and down long, twisting corridors between floating pans of ice that were often hundreds of yards across. At times the black water shone like glass. Because of the temperature differential between air and water, they moved through a thin fog. They passed one low spot on the ice that was dark and gray. Jake shook his head and passed.

"Rotten ice," Vitus said.

They worked slowly through the ice. Three ringed seals with silver-gray fur surfaced briefly back in a bay surrounded by sheer five-foot walls of ice. Jake turned the boat and they idled into the bay. Pukak, a thick, wiry man in his early thirties, picked up his rifle and rested it at the ready on the thick gunwale.

Jake cut the motor. They sat in silence, waiting. Four minutes passed. The smart seals would swim under the ice to the opposite side of the ice pan, or to a nearby air hole. These three had looked nervous, as if they'd experienced human beings before.

Several hours later they pulled up onto a solid, white, flat pan of ice. They hauled out their gear, food, rifles, hunting bags, and then the umiaq. They dumped water from the boat and then turned it on its side to act as a windbreak.

"It is time to jump," Pukak said with a wide grin and began jumping up and down. Reed and the others quickly joined in, tiny dark figures at the edge of a vast ice pack jumping up and down in order to restore circulation and warmth to their bodies.

After several minutes their circulation was restored, and Jake started a small gasoline stove and brewed strong, black tea and boiled blubber. They ate biscuits, cold caribou meat dipped in fermented seal oil, and chewed on nutlike tasting strips of blubber.

"Yupik food is what keeps us warm," Vitus said. "It's what works in the Arctic."

"I can believe that," Reed said. He sipped at the strong, black tea.

They sat in comfortable silence. The raspy calls of Arctic terns mixed with the creaking of ice, the lapping of small waves, and the whistle of a steady wind. A jaeger swooped overhead. It was a small, rakish bird, half the size of the seagull it pursued. The jaeger had narrow, pointed wings that angled sharply back, and two long, pointed feathers that streamed out beyond it's tail. It easily matched every turn of the seagull it pursued until the gull disgorged a large fish in mid-flight. The jaeger swooped and picked off the fish in midair.

"The jaeger is a thief," Jake said after ten minutes of silence. He looked at Reed as if, for the first time, including him as part of the hunting party. "We will rest, go on lookout. Listen for thunder, like falling water. Aiviq, the walrus. If he pleases, we will hunt."

"Aiviq," Vitus said to give definition to the "he."

Reed nodded. He felt at ease, a part of the team. He had no need to talk. One listened, he observed, he learned. These were hunters of tradition, he understood. They did not kill wantonly for economic gain. Except for Vitus, who bought and sold raw ivory by the ton, they were not the ones he sought.

Reed and Vitus walked across the ice. It was almost midnight and just as light as noon. They passed in the shadow of towering hummocks of ice crushed together by the slow, grinding collision of conflicting ice floes weighing millions of tons.

Turquoise pools of fresh water melted from sea ice formed here and there beneath hummock walls. In one shallow pool tiny shrimp flashed about and Vitus reached in and scooped up a handful and began to crack the shells and eat them raw. Reed ate a few and discovered they were tasty, almost as good as cooked. They climbed the hummock and sat thirty feet in the air, listening closely and peering out with their binoculars at the vast maze of ice. Here and there they could see tiny ebony shapes of seal that had crawled out onto the ice. But there were no walrus and no faint roaring that carried above the wind and sea.

A form of dusk enveloped the ice, a momentary slumbering in a day that never really ended. At three AM the clouded sky began to lighten and they loaded the umiaq and returned to the sea. Hours passed. Vitus missed a four-hundred-pound bearded seal in choppy water. The mist ended. The clouds lifted. Like a beacon of hope from a lighthouse, scattered shafts of sunlight streamed down out of a sky of gray and white.

At one stop Reed pointed. He'd detected a moan, like a foghorn from a distant ship out of sight over the horizon. Jake nodded. They loaded the boat and set out, searching through the maze of ice.

Eventually the roaring grew louder. And then they saw their mark, or to be precise, two marks, what the Yupik referred to as nunavak, walrus on the ice, a brown patch of earth on mounds of white. They paused to discuss the situation. To attack the big herd was to risk massive retaliation. With an aluminum boat and a two-hundred-horse motor they could easily scurry away. Some rumors had it that ivory hunters had attacked larger herds with machine guns.

Jake prayed, a long, monotone recitation of thanks and appreciation for their world and their lives. They loaded into their boat, readied their weapons, and slowly worked through the scattered ice toward the smaller herd of twenty or so walrus that all but covered a small ice pan. Jake steered upwind so the fumes from the outboard did not frighten the beasts.

Even though they crept forward in plain sight, the walrus showed little fear. Only when they closed to within twenty yards did the great herd begin to stir. One massive bull with mounds of blubber hanging in rolls down his neck rose on his great foreflippers and gave forth with a mighty roar that Reed felt all the way down to the base of his spine. The bull lurched back and forth, rolling his eyes until the whites showed. His massive three-foot-long tusks gleamed in the sunshine.

The prolonged, hollow roar startled the rest of the herd. Spasms of loud huffs and groans passed through the herd. Ripples ran through four inches of blubber as some of the walrus began to move. Vitus pointed at a nearby bull as his target. Others picked out a target of their own, picking out those back in the center of the island in order that a wounded walrus would have less time to escape into the water and in order that panicked walrus in the middle would not roll the dead into the water during their rush to the sea. Jake grunted something and suddenly their rifles barked.

The herd plunged into pandemonium. The ice pan rolled with the motion of several tons convulsing across the surface. Blood blossomed in sprays of mist. Tusks clashed. Panicked bulls rolled over cows and calves in their effort to escape.

Amidst the confusion, Reed kept his eye on Vitus's bull. Vitus had aimed just behind the pockmark of the ear. The bull had lurched and convulsed and dropped on the spot. But then it tried to raise its massive head and Vitus put another shot into the thick, blubbery neck.

In a few seconds the ice pan had cleared. Four carcasses lay motionless. Large ribbons of red spread over the ice. One wounded cow fell into the water. A calf sat bawling atop a lifeless carcass. Jake quickly shot the calf lest its cries incite the adult walrus to attack.

Once in the water the walrus moved with ease, dark, agitated torpedoes flashing just beneath the boat. Abruptly a bull walrus surfaced beside the umiaq and lunged up and hooked its tusks over the gunwale just at Reed's elbow. The boat lurched toward the icy sea. The walrus snorted mist into the air. Its stiff whiskers bristled on its flat snout and its red and angry eyes looked directly at Reed.

"No," Vitus cried. He pushed past Reed and smashed at the snout of the walrus with the butt of his rifle. The bull wheezed and blood ran from its nostrils. Vitus smashed again and the bull suddenly eased back, giving up its grip and sinking into the water where it swam away.

Jake quickly gunned the motor and the boat knifed toward the still rocking ice floe. The men vaulted to the ice, rifles ready in case a walrus dared attack. The herd still circled the ice pan, moving here and there to angrily survey their foe. Two walrus moved with the wounded cow. Pukak put a finishing shot into the cow's head. But before Talimat could throw the harpoon, the cow sank into the depths of the sea.

In time the walrus left. The men turned to their kill.

Vitus grinned at Reed. "Now the work begins."

It took several hours of hard labor to process the walrus. Skin and the four-inch thick blubber was cut in long strips that weighed as much as fifty pounds. They hacked off the head, the tusks, and even the foreflippers.

"Rotten walrus flipper is very good," Vitus said.

"I can imagine," Reed replied in such a dry tone Vitus had to laugh.

Pukak cut into the intestines of one walrus and showed Reed the tiny clams and other crustaceans the walrus picked from the sea floor. With his eyes direct on Reed to watch his reaction, Pukak popped a few of the clams into his mouth. He offered a handful to Reed.

"No thanks. Maybe later," Reed said, and again the others laughed.

"Our young men are hardly Eskimo anymore," Jake said. "When I was young we faced starvation. No part of an animal went to waste."

Not like the headhunters, Reed thought, but kept his feelings to himself.

They could not load all the walrus into the boat. So one cow had a small hole cut near one foreflipper and a tire pump was used to force air in underneath the three-quarter inch-thick skin.

"At one time we used our own lungs," Vitus said.

"And lances to make the kill," Reed said.

Eventually, after long, tiring hours, they finished with their tasks. The ice pan was half-covered red with blood. Entrails had been dumped into the water, food for thousands of tiny creatures below. They settled weary bodies in a small circle around the camp stove and ate boiled heart and blubber and drank strong, black tea. Reed ate and drank with relish, replenishing a body that had sorely been used. Once he glanced at Jake and saw a light of friendliness in his dark eyes.

Jake spoke softly, as if, for the only time on the trip, explaining something to Reed. "There is no greater pleasure than to hunt far out on the Bering Sea, to eat from fresh-killed game, and to look forward to a triumphant return home."

Reed nodded. He'd had his hunt, but not with those he sought. He just wished Pewter could see and understand. In too many ways Jake reminded him of his father, Guy. Guy lived exactly as he'd lived for almost fifty years, alone in a tarpaper shack in Northern Wisconsin, cutting pulp with a chainsaw and skidding it out with a horse. Whatever changed in the world, whatever went on outside his tiny circle of life had no discernible impact on Guy. His mother and two sisters had left when Reed was a young boy. He'd remained, living in the forest with his father, a little gnome running through the woods.

But it had been a home, a connection. If the Viking Guy was not warm or demonstrative with affection, he was honest and fair and gave Reed the complete freedom of the forest. There were few rules, few expectations. He had to do his chores, and then he was free. No matter where he went, no matter what transpired in his life, he could return to Guy and know positively everything would be the same. It was a comforting thought.

They loaded into the open boat, situated between huge chunks of meat and strips of blubber. They had but inches of freeboard to spare and yet they set out away from the calming effects of the pack ice and headed out into the ocean in light mist and fog. Reed looked at Vitus as if questioning their direction.

"Jake," Vitus said and pointed at his head. "He knows. Many of the bigger boats have CB radios and Loran satellite navigation systems. Three summers ago, two boats got lost. Their satellite navigation system went out. The old skills were gone and they could not return in the fog. The entire village searched for three weeks before they were located."

The size of the waves increased. On occasion rivulets of ocean slipped over the gunnel as they wallowed back and forth up, and down the gray troughs. Along with the salt spray and the cold and the mist, the relentless motion took its toll. The waves were uneven, and each sickening, lurching, motion hit them differently. The crests would lift them up to where they balanced precariously, dark chasms fore and aft, and an empty, churning sea stretching for miles around. At times the outboard would break free of the sea, whining in the air while Jake quickly cut the throttle. Then they would drop, an abrupt, sliding plunge into the canyon with gray walls moving all around. If they took on one good wave, surely they would sink, Reed thought. If they drowned, they drowned alone, returned to the elements within the sea. They should get rid of some ballast, Reed thought, but knew he could not say anything. Even if it meant he drowned.

Abruptly the boat jerked ahead. Jake had cut away the cow they towed behind. They gained a few inches of freeboard and could maneuver more easily through the waves.

Fatigue and numbing cold and endless motion moved them into a stupor during which there was no sense of time. The agony was endless. They sat wordless and almost motionless, five men bound together in a tiny boat upon a churning sea.

In time a dark line appeared out of the mist, St. Lawrence Island, home once again.

Their spirits revived. A few motionless statues lined the higher banks, children watching for the hunters to return from the sea. Then villagers began to gather, and even Reed felt a joy in his heart. It wasn't the dead walrus, he knew. It was the hunt, the joining with the elements, the life upon the ice and the sea, the struggle to survive. He could not ask for more.

The payoff Reed had hoped for came sooner than he'd ever expected. He'd returned his sealskin parka, he'd eaten a hot meal with Jake, Lulu, Vitus and Samuel, he'd paid his money, given his thanks, purchased some carvings from Jake, and took his leave. Vitus escorted Reed outside. The constant wind blasted in off the Bering Sea, leveling the island of any hint of trees, buffeting the square-built houses, blistering the skin. Reed's hair waved in the wind. Vitus was appraising, trying to make a decision.

Make it easy, Reed thought. "Why don't you show me what you have, Vitus?"

Vitus glanced at the house to see if anyone was watching out the window, then he led Reed to a small metal storage shed set to one side of the house. He removed a padlock and opened a wooden trunk to show an assorted collection of walrus tusks. Accusations confirmed, Reed thought sadly as he knelt to the trunk. He picked up the tusks. Many of them were gray, striated with black lines, mostly fossil ivory, Reed guessed. The fresh ivory would come later, as the hunters got to work.

Reed looked up. Vitus seemed so innocent, so trusting, his brown eyes seemingly as unknowing as the obsidian eyes of a seal. For the moment Reed could not bring himself to speak.

"Forty-five dollars, delivered," Vitus said.

"That seems a little steep."

"That's what the market is. If the hunt is good, maybe the price will drop. Payment in cash."

"If I have to get it to Hawaii, how do I do that?"

"Air freight," Vitus said. "They can't check without a warrant. And they can't get a warrant without probable cause."

"There's a lot of little stuff here that I don't think we can use," Reed said. "My fiancée really buys this stuff. She's a carver. Ran a store in Lahaina."

Vitus closed the trunk. "Don't ever mention this to Jake."

"Jake's a hunter," Reed said. He handed Vitus his business card. "I don't know Pewter's finances, but I think she'll take quite a bit. Her uncle, Morgan Zanke, owns the store. Just like you don't want Jake to know this, we don't want Morgan to know about this. The old folks just don't know how to adjust to changing times. A man has to make a living. It doesn't much matter how."

Vitus nodded. It was a sentiment he could share.

CHAPTER SEVEN

As soon as Reed collected his baggage he flagged a taxi and headed for the apartment. Much like celestial spotlights, the late-afternoon sun filtered in shafts through low, scattered clouds. The late-spring weather was damp and temperatures ran in the low fifties. The first signs of greenery were beginning to emerge after the long, dark winter. His exuberant mood was uncalled for, Reed thought. He had promises of a delivery from Vitus and he felt like he had won the lottery. He could only hope Pewter was home from the shop.

But she was not and within a few minutes his ebullient mood ebbed. He opened a beer and slumped onto the sofa. Ten minutes later when Pewter returned home he did not even climb to his feet.

"Reed, is that you?" Pewter called as soon as she opened the door. Her voice was hesitant, almost frightened.

Reed remained seated. "Yeah, come on in." She looked sparkling, soft black hair, a blue business suit with a white silk blouse and trim skirt. He quickly glanced away. "You sound as if you were expecting visitors."

Pewter stepped forward, almost as if to hug him, but when Reed did not rise she stopped. "A couple nights ago someone was rattling the door at two o'clock in the morning. I've had a couple of motorcyclers following me. That one big skinny guy. He gets up alongside me on the freeway and stays right there."

"He's a bastard," Reed said. Pewter looked drawn, with a tightness around her mouth and eyes. But she'd decided to stay, he thought, there was nothing he could do to help.

"How'd it go up north?" Pewter sat on the edge of an easy chair across from Reed.

"Not real bad. I got out on a legal walrus hunt. I met Terry Grason and he took me flying. I bought a couple of tusks from a local drunk in Nome. And Vitus Inokenti indicated he might want to deal. He should be calling in a week or so."

"You really sound excited," Pewter said in imitation of Reed's dry tone. She stood in a dismissive manner. "Maybe you can fill me in some day, that is if you think I ever need to know any of this stuff."

Reed quickly rose, trying to apologize. "I don't mean to cut you out, Pewter. Here, I have the ivory over here." He got the duffel bag and set it on the living room floor. He took out the two complete heads and lay them for Pewter to view.

But Pewter's anger had blossomed now. "You didn't call like you'd promised. I didn't know what was going on. Doug got after me for not planning and coordinating things better. He reminded me about Abe disappearing, as if I were somehow at fault. I didn't know what to tell him. You've been doing this longer than I have. Why should I have to pay when I don't know what's going on inside your head?"

Reed flushed with embarrassment. "That's my fault. You let me take care of Doug. He has no call to get after you."

Pewter knelt beside the tusks. She picked one up. Her voice was still tight with anger. "Boy these stink. This one must weigh twelve pounds. It sounds like hunting is in full swing."

"Just getting going. They're looking for a pretty good year. The ice is going out on schedule."

Pewter hesitated as if weighing her words. "Do you think the Eskimo should stop killing walrus?"

"Hell no," Reed said. "You should see those people, hunting is their lives. I think the missionaries and government types and city-bred preservationists have done enough to destroy their culture. It's just as much a part of nature for a walrus to die from the hand of an Eskimo as it is to die in the jaws of a killer whale. That's nature, the real world. It's not a talking cartoon out here. There's a quarter of a million walrus."

"But the last Russian-American survey wasn't very conclusive," Pewter pointed out.

"Bad weather conditions. They need another one. But who has the money." Reed regarded Pewter with a critical eye. "You're not anti-hunting, are you?"

"No. It's just not part of my background. I guess I've seen too many skins and hides of endangered species coming into the ports. Sometimes it's unbelievable."

"The more rare a species, the higher the demand," Reed said. "That's the way human beings are."

Pewter nodded. She cleared her throat as if she'd felt choked with emotion. "Well, I'm glad you're back. I was feeling a bit lonely. I guess I hadn't understood quite how much you remove yourself from friends and family and any meaningful relationships once you go undercover."

"The offer to get out still stands," Reed said.

"I didn't mean it that way," Pewter snapped. "I was just talking about how hard it could be, not about quitting. Or haven't you, the great Reed Erickson, noticed? Or maybe it just isn't hard for you."

"I'm sorry. I just wanted to be fair. I didn't want to argue."

"Who the hell is arguing? Jesus Christ, can't a person even say how they feel without you interpreting ulterior motives?"

"Sure," Reed said. "It's just that I started out with other motives, and that screwed everything up from the start."

Pewter's tone eased. "Yeah, I can vouch for that. Just don't close me off. Try to be normal, all right?"

"As soon as I figure out what normal is," Reed said with a smile.

"I'm going to jog in a little while," Pewter said. "I have to burn up some of the bile."

Something was eating at Pewter he knew. Being alone, the visitations on the freeway and in the middle of the night were getting to her. Her words were an invitation, Reed knew, a chance to get back on friendly terms, a normal relationship. But could he keep it at that? "Maybe next time. I'm pretty tired. I'm going to call Doug and set up a meet, get this ivory logged in and see how things are going on his end."

"Are you going to eat with him also?"

"Yeah, we'll probably grab a bite."

Pewter turned away. At the entrance to her bedroom she straightened and turned back. "Kurth's been in the shop a couple of times. One time he saw me eating lunch and sat down. He keeps promising a buy, but he has problems with his supply."

"Vitus," Reed said. "After all was said and done, he approached me. I wonder what Kurth has for outlets when he isn't selling to us. He keeps saying demand is so high. I'd sure like to get after that."

"Why don't we put a transmitter in Kurth's ivory."

"And how would you propose that?" Reed said with more skepticism than intended. Pewter bristled.

"Next time we make a buy. He said I can pick and choose the ivory I need. I can have a piece on me with a transmitter and coated with some of that coded ultraviolet paint they use for tagging ivory in the villages. I'll just slip it in with the rejects. He must get rid of his pieces somewhere."

"Pretty good idea. Of course we don't have much manpower for tracking.

And if they carve into that piece and find the transmitter it could be a real problem."

"I just thought I'd mention it."

"I know. It's something we just might do. I'll have Doug check with Rich, see what they have in stock for transmitters. I'll have Rich talk to Wells about getting some paint."

Pewter nodded. She waited, obviously thinking about saying something more, Reed thought. Feeling the strain, he thought. He knew the feeling well. He had a lot of unwinding to do himself. Nevertheless, he stood and turned away and walked into the kitchen. He should ask her along to the meeting with Doug. But that would put a strain on Doug, take away the camaraderie. He stood leaning on the counter, undecided. He heard the quiet click of Pewter's bedroom door. Next time, he thought, when he was more in control.

A week later Vitus Inokenti telephoned. He had ivory in town, four hundred pounds. "Where did you want to meet?" Reed asked.

"Wherever," Vitus said. "Where do you live?"

The last trusting man, Reed thought. Well, he'd change all that. Reed gave his address. "I don't have enough money for the full four hundred pounds. But we can take a couple of hundred off your hands."

"Sure," Vitus said. He'd be over in two hours.

Reed immediately telephoned Pewter at the Rare Species Store and told her to take some of their purchase money out of the vault. "I'm only going to take a couple hundred of the best pounds here. Hopefully he'll deliver the rest to Kurth and Kurth will deliver some back to us. I'm going to call Doug and see if he can get the biology boys to paint an ultraviolet strip on a piece of ivory. We'll take your idea and slip that into the stuff Vitus has that we're not going to take and see if that shows up with Kurth. That'll prove that connection."

"It'll have to be a piece with good visual markings I can recognize," Pewter said.

After the call Reed went into his bedroom. It was kept bare of decorations, serving primarily as a storage area. They could not afford a lived-in look for this, although this was where he slept. He paused to look around. Not even a picture of Stacy and Trish.

That had been another battle, bringing his two daughters up to Alaska for a visit in the middle of a case. Pewter hadn't said much, but he could tell she did not think it was a good idea no matter how careful Reed indicated he would be. Doug and Rich had been openly opposed, although at least Rich had been empathetic. He knew the cost of this job on family life. There were numerous cases where agents on a long-term undercover operation would move their family forty or fifty miles from the center of their operation and use separate apartments and drop-telephones to conduct their operation. Visiting his daughters would be a good thing. Already he anticipated the time together, something positive beyond this job, something real and whole.

He took a chair into the closet and stood on that and removed a ceiling tile. It was up here where he and Pewter concealed their official Fish and Wildlife identification, their service revolvers, and the tiny Nagra reel-to-reel tape recorder that he took down, loaded with a fresh tape, and fixed with an elastic bandage next to his chest. He took a personal pistol, a Chinese 9-millimeter pistol he'd taken off a dead Viet Cong lieutenant, and tucked it into his belt beneath his shirt. Vitus gave no sign of being a dangerous man, or even a man who carried a gun. But he'd been fooled by impressions in the past.

Pewter returned to the apartment barely five minutes before Vitus pulled into the yard. Doug had a little problem rounding up one of the field biologists and finding some specially coded ultraviolet paint. Pewter showed Reed the six-inch end of a tusk, and then Vitus drove an older, rusting-white pickup truck into the yard.

Pewter tucked the piece of ivory into her skirt. Her eyes were bright with excitement. "This guy's a big-time ivory dealer?"

"He's got a passel of kids. His wife works in a convenience store. His place up in Eagle River is littered with junk. He doesn't work anyplace else. He has an old airplane to keep going, medical bills. He has to pay on the village end and then gets a cut to sell here. It's a tough go."

Pewter glanced suspiciously, as if judging Reed's sympathies.

"Hey," Reed protested the look. "He's got four hundred pounds. I got him to deal. What the hell more do you want?"

"What about price?" Pewter asked. "Forty-five, tops?"

"I'll see how it goes. He's used to me. You talk quality and do the selecting."

"Sure," Pewter said.

There was a light tap on the door and Reed went to answer. He greeted Vitus and then helped carry two heavy trunks into the living room. He introduced Pewter as his fiancée.

"Hello," Pewter said. "You were in the shop earlier."

Vitus nodded. He was stocky, with short arms and legs and dark features. He glanced briefly at Pewter and her bright, fashionable shop-girl's clothes and circled so he stood across the room from her. He had a worried look, and yet a sense of fatalism, like an outdoorsman who's sole response to an unfavorable change in the elements was to hunch his shoulders and endure.

"Beer, soda?" Reed asked.

"Soda," Vitus said.

"Have a seat," Reed said. He went into the kitchen for a couple of sodas and handed one to Vitus, who still stood, as did Pewter. "Let's have a look."

Vitus bent and unlocked the trunks and opened the lids.

Reed whistled at the clutter of white and yellowish tusks.

Pewter gasped at the smell of rotten meat.

"Damnit, Vitus, you could have cleaned these better than that. That smell will stay in this apartment for a week." He quickly closed the lids. "Let's take these outside. I don't think our neighbor is home. We can separate them in the garage."

They manhandled one of the bulky trunks to the cement floor of the garage. Reed and Vitus went back upstairs for the second trunk. When they returned, Pewter was kneeling on a piece of newspaper in front of the open trunk. She began laying larger pieces of ivory off to one side. Somewhere within the jumble in the trunk, lay the piece with ultraviolet paint, Reed knew. Of course if the ivory had been registered in the village, others could be coated as well, but not with this particular code.

Pewter looked at Vitus. "Our carvers in Hawaii like larger pieces, the more fine and white. Female tusks really are ideal. Can you get many of those?"

"If it's a good year, I can get you whatever you want."

"We have a bit of a cash flow thing," Reed said. "So we can only buy so much. When we get paid from the islands, we can buy more. Unless you sell on credit." He chuckled.

"I used to," Vitus said. "Too often I didn't get paid."

"Oh, I understand that. I wasn't asking for credit, just telling you our circumstances."

Pewter picked out two hundred pounds, weighing each tusk on a meat scale on the shelf. Reed negotiated price. Vitus was surprisingly easy, settling for forty dollars a pound, when they'd paid the motorcycle group forty-eight. Reed counted out the money. "Eight thousand dollars, Vitus. That's quite a bundle."

"I have a lot of expenses," Vitus said. He stuffed the wad of fifty- and one-hundred-dollar bills into the pocket of his down vest. He and Reed loaded the trunks into the back of the pickup and Vitus drove away.

Reed and Pewter stood in the open garage, the bare light on overhead, full walrus skulls and sets of tusks stacked all around. "What a trade," Pewter said. "Eight thousand dollars and he's just one guy."

"I'd love to follow him to see where he's going with the rest of that."

"Why not?"

"I don't want to take the chance. He knows our car. There's not enough traffic. We could spook him." Reed stepped outside and looked up. Lead-colored clouds were tinged with pink from the last rays of the sun. A cold breeze touched his cheek, a reminder of his time on the ice, a world removed and yet very connected to Anchorage and cities to the south. The roar of a commercial jet hitting reverse thrusters carried from the airport less than a mile away.

"It's been a long day," Pewter said. "How about going out for a bite to eat?"

"Ah, I just had a snack while I was waiting for you and Vitus," Reed lied. "I want to get this ivory tagged, and get it into Doug and into the evidence locker. Maybe I could meet you later."

"Sure. Later. Let me know if you need any help. I'm always available, in the shop or in my room."

"Hey, I could eat again," Reed protested. "This could wait."

"No, go ahead and take it in," Pewter said. "I think I'll go run."

"It's pretty dark out there. You might run into a moose or a bear."

"Well that would be exciting, wouldn't it," Pewter said with complete lack of concern.

Pewter just didn't understand, Reed thought. He could not afford to get close. He did not have the control.

Three days later Kurth Breismeister met with Pewter in the shop. His supplier came through. He had some goods to sell. "He wanted me to meet him alone," Pewter informed Reed. She sat at their kitchen table eating a full-cooked meal of vegetarian lasagna, salad and garlic bread.

Reed stood in the living room. "So what'd you tell him?"

"I told him I didn't think he was safe. And I said you were still pretty mad about the way things went last time. He said, they had to check us out."

"So no bikers this time." Reed walked past the table and poured himself a glass of water. His eyes strayed to the lasagna.

"Have some."

"Maybe I will," Reed said. "It smells damn good. In return I'll cook a meal tomorrow. Whatever you like."

"Cook what you like and I'll eat part," Pewter said.

"Sounds fair enough." Reed pulled up a chair. And began to fill his plate. "What did you set up for a meet?"

"He's still paranoid. We're supposed to meet him tomorrow night at six in the parking lot of the Safeway store on Diamond Boulevard. We'll follow him."

"To where he has some cronies waiting in the brush?"

He said he'd be alone. No tricks this time. But I don't know if it'll be safe to wear a wire."

"Do you have that transmitter set in that piece of ivory?"

"Ready to go. It's a small, gray piece. Maybe no one will carve on it for a while. And hopefully that piece we put in Vitus's trunk will be there as well. We'll establish that link, a Native selling to a non-native."

"No witnesses to the transaction, but we'll have a hell of a circumstantial link. I'll have it set up with Doug and Rich to be in the area. They can do some tracking."

"It's all working out pretty good."

"So far. As long as I don't get any laser sights pinned on my chest. Just to warn you, I'm going to come onto Kurth pretty hard. He has to understand, I won't go for that bullshit. It's a situation where you have to play them tough."

"All right. But I'm playing the good girl here. Kurth has a few adulterous designs. I don't want to discourage him all the way."

"Oh no. We're going to have to keep him on the string for at least a couple of months. We'll just start squeezing him on price."

It was an easy, enjoyable meal, Reed thought. Home cooking, something he'd missed. The mood, the conversation was easy, planning for the meet, figuring contingencies, on how they might act if Kurth's motorcycle friends showed up. They'd be carrying another five thousand dollars or so. Reed's boss, Peter Ullysses Waldheim, would demand they made a sound investment. He'd want his money back. Pewter laughed, when Reed told her that. It was the first time he'd seen her so warm and open since he'd first met her on the game farm case in Texas. Perhaps they could be partners, he thought. Pewter could travel with him from case to case, a companion, like he used to do with Doug.

The meeting with Kurth went exactly as planned. Just as promised, Kurth was alone. He met them in the parking lot then led them on a five-mile drive into the foothills of the Chugach Mountains. He turned down into a bankrupt housing development where towering weeds slowly devoured a gravel road. He pulled into a lot that was equally filled with weeds. He had what appeared to be one of the same trunks Vitus had concealed under a pile of brush. He appeared, at least as far as Reed could see, to be alone.

As he'd promised, Reed came on hard. Kurth whined, groveled, and then, with Pewter watching, became livid with rage. Pewter stepped in, calming the two down. They got to ivory trading. The one thing Kurth would not give on was the price. He had other outlets, he maintained with sufficient vehemence that Reed was certain he told the truth.

Pewter picked through the ivory, weighing each piece, including one Reed was certain was the plant she'd placed into Vitus's trunk. When she placed the piece with the transmitter into the reject pile, not even he could tell. In the end Reed and Kurth just stood and watched Pewter work.

"You're a lucky guy," Kurth said to Reed. He was trying to make amends. His thick, wavy blond hair, blue eyes and handsome features surely must be an attraction to Pewter, Reed thought. Perhaps to any woman, or at least Kurth thought so.

"What do you mean?"

Kurth motioned at Pewter. "A great-looking chick like this. She has her wits about her, takes care of herself. I haven't looked all over, but I haven't seen any sign of flab. I told her, when she gets tired of you, come on around."

"Wynona would sure like that," Pewter said.

"Hey, I'm Morman when it comes to women," Kurth said. "I can love two; I can love six."

"Shhh," Reed hushed. Pewter looked up. Reed pointed as a cow moose and a calf walked down the gravel road. The cow eyed the vehicles and people, but only slowly ambled on her way.

"Only in Alaska," Kurth said. "Go out to some wasted development and sell walrus tusks while a moose stands watch. That's why I love this land. Someday the four of us have to go out. Do a little hot-tubbing again so I can look at Pewter's body. She was pretty quick in and out of the water last time. Then I have to get you out on my boat. You'll love it out on the ocean."

"Sounds like a treat," Reed said. "I can't wait until the salmon start to run. That and the halibut. You're right, I just might never leave."

* * *

Yes, it all went so well, Reed thought. He sat in the Bronco, side by side with Pewter, watching across a dusty parking lot and through a chain-link fence at a pale yellow, cement-block warehouse. Nearby small airplanes eased in and out of Merrill Field. Warehouse, carving factory, whatever you wanted to call it. Doug and Rich had tracked Kurth directly from their meeting site to this warehouse. When Kurth departed the warehouse, the piece of ivory and the transmitter had stayed inside, one more mark, one more target, although this one had been a surprise.

Local field agents had been aware of the ivory-carving shop for three years. According to the Articles of Incorporation the business was Native owned and Natives were hired to carve Native-delivered ivory. All goods were certified under the Silver Hand program. However, in the last three days two Japanese managers had been seen entering the plant on a daily basis. Plus, not all the workers were Natives, some were Oriental, Vietnamese according to a check of some license plate numbers. Everything had checked out on previous visits. But with only ten fish and wildlife agents for the entire state, how much could they watch, Rich had said? With the transmitter inside there, obviously delivered by Kurth, they had at least one violation of a non-native trading fresh ivory. With close surveillance, undoubtedly they could come up with more.

Reed poured a cup of coffee from the thermos. He motioned at Pewter. "No thanks."

"You can't be a true stakeout artist until you learn to drink bitter coffee and then sit and hold your bladder for hours on end."

"As boring as it is, I think I'd rather work in the shop," Pewter said.

"Yeah, Morgan says you have a nice salesgirl look. At least his sales are up. He gives part of that credit to you."

"Or maybe he's just having a good year. Wait, look there."

A hundred yards away a four-wheel-drive vehicle pulled up to the shop. A heavy-set Native woman walked inside. A few minutes later she emerged with the Japanese, a man named Tanaka. The two looked inside the back of the vehicle. Pewter raised the camera with the three-hundred-millimeter telephoto lens. She began to shoot. Reed looked through binoculars. "Can you see the license plate?"

"Yes. I have a shot."

The two went back inside and two workers emerged and carried several heavy boxes into the building. "Native to Native, perfectly legal," Reed said. "Native to Japanese, then I have my doubts. Damn these laws are archaic. Question is, how the hell are we going to get inside these guys' operation?"

Two days later Reed stopped in to visit Pewter at the gift store. The two went out for lunch while Morgan tended the store. They chose a small tourist's saloon on Fourth Avenue, just down from the shop. The decor was old Alaskan. Chainsaw carvings of grizzly bear, Eskimos and old-time prospectors stood watch over rough-hewn booths and purposely misspelled, hand-lettered menus. As usual Reed was dressed as casually as a prospector while Pewter was dressed for working in the gift store. While Pewter ordered, Reed sipped at his coffee.

"Good, rich coffee," Reed said as the waitress departed. He leaned forward. "I just met with Doug and Rich. That woman who delivered all those heavy boxes is an Inuit. Originally from Barrow, now Fairbanks. Her married name is Altona Mosby. Her husband's Caucasian. Named Brian. And guess who Brian works for?"

"In Fairbanks? Really?"

"You got it, Terry Grason. Brian's one of Terry's fishing guides. If Grason's dealing ivory like Woodruff claimed, he could be using this Altona as a front. She just claims the ivory is hers and there isn't a damn thing we can do."

"And Grason was on that list of people Abe was going to look at."

"But he hadn't made contact."

"So now what?"

"We wait. I made contact with Grason. He wouldn't have taken me for a flight if he wasn't interested. He wasn't simply being sociable. I think he'll come around. For all we know he could be checking us out already. So we have to be ready for that as well." Reed leaned back in the booth as did Pewter, neither looking at the other, neither willing to broach anything to do with either of them. It was the job, and only the job, the one constant in his life, just as it had always been.

CHAPTER EIGHT

Terry Grason walked unannounced into Tanaka's export company head-quarters. It was a small affair with a paneled reception area and two offices, a second story corner of an old office building on Old Seward Highway. Julie, the receptionist, smiled brightly. She was mid-thirties, divorced, and wore a beige blouse and black skirt. She offered coffee and invited Terry to have a seat. Tanaka was with a client.

Grason and Julie talked about Fairbanks, prospects for the summer tourist season, Grason's outfitting business. If he asked her out, the answer would be yes, Grason knew. But Julie was thirty pounds overweight, like his ex-wife, Jeri, the last five or six years. But he didn't notice Jeri's shape, she'd become a real person, a fixture in his life. It was being together that gave him comfort. If he wanted good sex he went someplace else.

Tanaka and another man strode from the office. The second man was Japanese also. Tanaka briefly nodded at Grason and then walked his client to the door. When he turned back, he invited Grason into his office, a large room with white walls and decorated with vague, impressionistic watercolors framed in black.

Grason was in no mood for the small talk, the polite circumlocution of the real topic at hand. Tanaka was a lean, hard-eyed businessman, one hundred and thirty pounds, a little pretzel, but with a hot temper. Grason's intent was to make him respond and he got straight to the point. "What the hell's this forty-three dollars a pound crap? We'd agreed on forty-five. You stiffed me. I have a thousand dollars coming yet."

Tanaka stiffened. But then he spoke quietly, with admirable control. "I informed you of the new price."

"But I didn't agree."

"Your courier delivered the ivory. There is a great deal of supply right now. If you wish the delivery returned, it can be returned."

"You little sonofabitch," Grason snapped. He glared at Tanaka, a little shrimp of a man, strictly urban, a man who never argued, who always gave a reasonable out, who wouldn't stand up and confront you man to man. And yet the little bastard never relinquished his position of control.

He could argue, Grason thought. Tanaka would sit and listen. But nothing would be resolved. The price was set. He'd make the same offer as before, Grason could have his goods, five hundred pounds of fresh ivory straight from the Bering Sea. Grason stood. "I don't think I can do business at this price."

Tanaka looked up, staring at Grason's sealskin vest and broad, powerful chest. His voice was calm, easy, without hint of a threat, a man in complete control, a man who knew how to exact revenge. "The price continues to drop. Forty-two now, perhaps less if supply continues good."

Grason stilled a retort. He managed a polite smile. "How come you never go flying with me? I've offered a half-dozen times. I feel offended that you don't want to see the real Alaska, rather than just stay in Anchorage here."

"Too much business," Tanaka said.

"No, I think it's lack of guts," Grason snarled. He quivered with rage. He turned and departed. Julie stood in the hallway, drawn by the shouts, uncertain how to respond.

"Is that guy your boss or your master?" Grason asked. He brushed past, not waiting for a response.

He drove to downtown Anchorage. He'd never liked Tanaka, not from the start, using a Native front to trade ivory to Japan, using Oriental carvers to make family crests for rich Japanese families. Tradition demanded ivory, no matter what the price. He was certain Tanaka made thousands on each little crest.

He located the Rare Species Store on Fourth Avenue. It was a cool, breezy and sunny day. The sidewalks were crowded with a number of tourists. And of course there was the usual collection of derelicts, drunken Indians, Eskimos, white trash, minds fogged by booze, coordination lost between their minds and their legs. Pathetic dregs of human beings they should load into a cargo net and dump into Redoubt Volcano, more pollution for the earth, Grason thought. He parked his rental vehicle down the street, walked a block, and went into a combination warehouse outlet and pawn shop. The aisles were cluttered, goods piled on shelves from floor to ceiling.

"Terry Grason, how the hell are you!" Waite Hoyt said. He shook Grason's hand. He was a chunky man with a pale complexion and a close-cut crewcut. He wore baggy blue jeans and a black T-shirt. A hell of a pool player, Grason knew, although Waite wouldn't belly up to a table unless there was at least a hundred-dollar bill lying at stake. The more at stake, the better he played, the exact opposite of too many barroom types.

"What can I sell you?" Waite asked after they caught up on each other's lives.

"Information," Grason said. "What do you know about the Rare Species Shop down there?"

Morgan Zanke had been in Alaska twenty years, owned the Rare Species Store for ten years. In his early days he'd been somewhat of a world-traveler including Africa and the Orient. Word was he once had a lot of international connections. Not really community oriented, Waite said, but he did associate with some socially prominent types and was known as a law-abiding type. "Definitely not part of my social circle," Waite said with a laugh.

A year or so ago Zanke had a stroke, Waite continued. It was quite severe and took out much of his left side to include facial muscles and his arm. Since then a niece had moved in to help manage the store. But Waite didn't know anything about her, she hadn't been around that much. Reportedly she knew her business.

After he left Waite, Grason walked back to a tavern just down the street from the Rare Species Store. He ordered a beer and took a stool near the window. An hour or so later he saw a dark-complected woman with short black hair emerge. She wore a stylish blue and white polka-dot business suit. Nice enough looking, Grason thought, but too clean, everything too much in place, like a new house where no one had ever lived. Not built for the frontier rough and tumble of a place like Alaska. Reed was working class; if this was his girlfriend it wasn't a good fit. One look and Grason could see that.

But of course she'd be the source of money. She had that look, like a television reporter, always bright and perky so you never knew the truth about how they really felt.

Pewter went into a local restaurant just down the street. Five minutes later a woodsy type in leather boots, wool shirt and misshapen brown pants glided down the sidewalk, the thriving entrepreneur, Reed Goodnow. Tanaka wanted to jack him around on the price, well he could jack Tanaka around on supply. Once he found out what the hell this Reed was all about.

Forty-five minutes later Pewter emerged from the restaurant and returned to the gift store. Nice legs, average tits, Grason thought. And then Reed emerged from the restaurant. Grason paid his tab and walked out to his rental car. He'd just pick up a loose tail, see exactly what the hell this sonofabitch was all about.

How could two children from the same family be so different, Reed wondered. He stood in the corridor of the Anchorage International Airport watching people pass and waiting for the passengers of the DC-8 to disembark. If children could give purpose and hope to life, they could also generate doubts and despair. In Trish and Stacy he had both.

It was a mark of the passage of time, life changes, the gaudy cover of fashion that he barely recognized his own daughter. Stacy was seventeen, but she could easily pass for twenty-five. She had lush, curled hair down to her shoulders. She was a walking advertisement for the conspicuous consumer, one of the many points of light, multiple bracelets, huge earrings, rouge, eyeliner, shaped eyebrows, ruby red lips, tight black skirt, black nylons, gold silk blouse, all at seventeen for God's sake. Reed ground his teeth, struggling for the control he'd promised. Except for the hardness in her eyes, Stacy could have been a model.

Of course who wouldn't be hard? She already had a juvenile record for dealing drugs, a high school dropout, already escaped from home and living with a girlfriend, a boyfriend and working at a dress shop in a mall. That she'd been an active, straight-A student one year and a screaming, defiant dropout the next had rocked both him and Pam with the force of an earthquake. Sure it was drugs. But why drugs? The failure. Every parent whose kid escaped drugs had the same, smug, superior expression — they'd raised their kids all right.

The girls stood side by side, looking around, wondering where he was at, no doubt wondering if he'd let them down again.

Reed stood frozen, gaining control, almost too frightened to move. But then he focused on Trish. He had to smile at the pure joy. Fourteen-year-old Trish, slight freckles, ponytail, and covered with no more makeup than a residue of soap. Stacy had never taken to the outdoors. Trish took to it like a plains native: hiking, camping, canoeing, cross-country skiing. Young, positive Trish, the focused one, his jogging partner, a cross-country runner already on the varsity team, a volleyball player.

It was unwise to favor children, Reed understood, but over the past few years Trish was a joy, Stacy a pain. Thus he stepped forward and approached Stacy first, gave her a hug, a light, necessary embrace to which she responded in kind.

"Father. I see you haven't changed," Stacy said in amused reference to his dull clothes, brown shapeless pants, blue wool shirt, scuffed leather boots.

"No, but I did wash clothes," Reed replied. "You look, ah," he bobbed his head searching for the right words, "older."

Reed turned to Trish. She came to him without reservations, a wide, happy grin in a shiny face. If he'd ever seen her sad, he couldn't recall the day.

"Daddy, we went over the Wrangell Mountains like you mentioned. You could see the mountains, all the snow and ice. And then we went over, how

84   ESKIMO MONEY

do you say that, Chugach Mountains when we were coming in for a landing. It was so wild, mile after mile and nothing there."

The infectious tone in her voice brought a lump to Reed's throat. Such a promise of life, so many dreams, none of it yet battered by reality. Perhaps it never would be.

And then he noticed Stacy, looking while he stood there with his arm draped around Trish's shoulders. Reed dropped his arm. "Let's get your baggage. Then I'll tell you about our plans. There have been a few modifications."

"When haven't there been?" Stacy said. It was her combative tone. It had not eased at all, and Reed felt a familiar dread, the most case-seasoned undercover agent in Special Operations.

The first day went better than he could have hoped. They checked into a bed and breakfast, a classic frontier-style house with a big porch and a reputation for the best breakfast and company in Anchorage. They drove down the coast to Portage Glacier, standing by the icebergs, feeling the wind and chill, tasting the fresh air. That Stacy wore earphones and listened to a heavy-metal tape, Reed managed to ignore. On the drive back to Anchorage they saw mountain goats, and a cow moose and calf, all within a few hours of touchdown.

They proceeded to downtown Anchorage shopping, hitting the gift shops, although Reed managed to steer them away from the Rare Species Shop. They'd meet Pewter later when they went out to a supper club for an Alaskan comedy show, dining and listening to a band. In explanation of their changed plans, Reed explained part of his case, using the undercover last name of Goodnow. He mentioned his trip to Nome, out hunting with the Eskimo, he even drove past the apartment where he and Pewter lived, although he'd only explained that Pewter was an agent assisting him on the case.

They met Pewter at the club, a frankly tourist attraction with dark red siding and red carpeting and dark walnut interior. They dined and watched the show, a satire on Alaskan foibles and Alaskan politics. Afterwards, at Stacy's insistence she wanted to listen to the band, they sat in easy conversation, waiting for the room to clear and the band to set up.

"Do you have a boyfriend?" Stacy asked Pewter.

"I did. I think we're more or less finished. He's an environmental attorney. He wanted me to give up my job. I said no."

"My boyfriend would never say that to me," Stacy replied. She wore a tight fitting, short, pink jump suit.

"That's because your boyfriend doesn't have a job and needs you to pay the rent," Reed said. Stacy glared and he immediately understood there had been more of an edge to his tone than intended.

Twenty minutes later the band began to play, a good hard rock. Reed asked Stacy to dance. She hesitated, then relented. She was an unabashed dancer, Reed knew, and dressed and moved in such a slinky fashion he felt a sense of embarrassment that someone might think he was robbing the cradle, or know that in fact she was his daughter.

They danced two numbers and then returned to the table.

"You did a pretty good job," Pewter said.

Reed nodded his thanks as he wiped perspiration from his brow.

"Father always liked to dance," Stacy said. "Mother didn't like to dance, too primeval."

"Mother danced," Trish protested.

"Sometimes. But she didn't like it," Stacy said. "She wasn't primeval, not like Dad."

The band finished a number. A large figure loomed beside the table. Reed felt the nudge of Pewter's foot and turned and looked up. His heart lurched with all the force as if he had looked down the barrel of a gun.

Terry Grason grinned. "What the hell's a guy like you doing with three lovely ladies?"

Reed stood. His chair tipped backwards. He looked into Grason's massive face, the solid jaw, thick curly hair, the hard blue eyes. Could this be a chance meeting, Reed wondered, or had Grason followed him here?

"Hi, Terry," Reed said in what he hoped was a pleasant tone. "I didn't know they let you northern guys come south in the summer."

"We get around," Terry said in a tone that didn't allow for humor. He looked at the women. "Are you going to introduce me or make me introduce myself?"

"This is Pewter. She runs her uncle's gift store. And, ah, these are my two daughters, Stacy and Trish. They're just up from the Lower 48 for a short visit."

Stacy stood and held out her hand decorated with three rings. "Are you from Alaska?"

"Born in a trapper's line shack, raised by a pack of wolves," Grason said as he took her hand. He grinned widely, showing clean, straight teeth. He turned to Reed. "How about if I buy a round?"

"Ah, that's okay. This is the first day and the girls are a little tired."

"That sounds nice," Stacy said. "Why don't you join us, Mr. Grason."

"Terry," Grason said. As the band began to blast another number, he grabbed a nearby chair and slid in between Trish and Stacy.

When Grason's back was turned, Reed shot a warning glance at Pewter. Now what the hell was he going to do? One slip, a casual question, a name, a job. Already Stacy had turned to Grason, leaning close, talking with great enthusiasm. And above the throbbing music Reed couldn't hear a word. He leaned back, drained of strength, drained of resolve. He'd blown it with Pewter, and now he'd blown the case. He'd washed everything down to his job, and now he couldn't even handle that.

Someone pulled on his arm. Reed looked over, then out to the dance floor where Stacy was going wild with a man twice her age and twice her size. Pewter's fingers dug into his arm. She bent close, shouting into his face. "Warn Trish. When Stacy comes off the dance floor I'll get her to go to the bathroom with me. We have no choice now. Just play it out and see what happens."

Her dark eyes were intense, imploring. He could smell the faint lilac of her perfume, his favorite scent. He loved the line of her jaw, clean with just a slight bow. "Dammit, Reed," Pewter shouted. "You have to wake up, get with it. Be flexible, be ready. Remember the lecture?"

Reed glanced across the table. Trish was confused, isolated, his lost little girl. Priorities, at all costs he'd protect Trish and Stacy. The hell with everything else.

"Thanks," Reed said. "It's a good thing you came along." He turned to Trish, bending close, talking above the music. He explained that Grason was a possible target, that his undercover name was Reed Goodnow, a name he'd used before. The cover extended back to towns and jobs in Wisconsin. If Grason asked, Trish should use her name, her place of residence in Washington. If she had to give a last name use their real last name Erickson, and say it was their adopted name from their stepfather. Other than that, Reed's job, and the fact they hadn't seen their father for two years, they did not have to lie. And they wouldn't even have to do that unless Grason asked. "Understand?" Reed asked.

"Oh, yes," Trish said. But her voice was shaky.

Putting a lot on a fourteen-year-old girl, Reed knew. Besides, Stacy might have already given them away.

Grason and Stacy returned from the dance floor. Pewter rose, said something to Stacy and the two of them disappeared toward the bathroom.

"What brings you down to Anchorage?" Reed shouted.

"Business," Grason said and refused to elaborate. "Stacy and Trish are your daughters?" Reed nodded. "Hard to believe out of an ugly mug like yours."

"They take after their mother."

"Your ex-wife?" Reed nodded. "Where does she live?"

"Out East. I haven't seen her for ten years," Reed said. He waved a hand of dismissal. "Past history. I don't worry about that now."

"You can't escape your past," Grason said. "I don't care how you lie, how you try."

Reed nodded. There was an ominous undertone there. Perhaps Stacy had already said something, revealed that he worked for Fish and Wildlife.

Pewter and Stacy returned from the bathroom. The girls were alert, Reed thought. Now he could make a graceful exit, see Grason another time. The band began another tune. Stacy bent over Grason, talking in his ear. Grason smiled and rose and followed her onto the dance floor. He turned, "C'mon you two, get out here. Let's see what you can do."

Reed could barely contain his rage. Stacy knew what was going on and she started pushing. Didn't she understand the stakes? As he rose to his feet, Pewter held out a restraining hand. "I'm going to end this right now," Reed hissed. "I give a damn."

"You'll blow everything," Pewter shouted. Grason was dancing, giving them a funny look. "Stacy didn't tell him anything. Grason was talking about himself, what he does, his house."

"What the hell is she doing asking him to dance? We have to get away. He's more than twice her age. Jesus!"

Pewter pulled Reed onto the dance floor. "Just dance, take it easy."

Reed exhaled. He felt Pewter's firm grip, her cool touch. He tried to calm down, get rational, pick up part of the beat. Grason moved at his side, a towering figure who moved with surprising grace. "You're not having fun," Grason shouted.

Reed unclenched his jaw. "Stacy's only seventeen."

"We're just dancing for Chrissake." For a second, a brief blink of time, Grason's face reflected a meanness, like a horror monster, and then it came on with a smile as broad as that of a televangelist bringing people the faith. "Daddy," he said in a mocking tone.

Reed managed a wan smile. Somehow he finished the dance. They returned to the table. The band took a break. Now they could leave, Reed thought, the perfect opportunity.

"Terry said he'd take us flying in the morning," Stacy announced, "show us the real Alaska."

"I don't think we can fit that in," Reed said.

"I already said yes," Stacy responded. She glared at her father. "You said we had the morning free."

"Just a friendly little hop around the mountains and down the bay. On me," Grason said. "You're not going to deny your girls a good time, are you?

You don't see Alaska in Anchorage, that's for sure. I'll stop by at your apartment, pick you up."

Their apartment! He'd given Grason a business card with the address of the Rare Species Store, and he'd written the apartment telephone number down. But no address, Reed thought. Grason was checking. Grason was in the know. They had to get the hell away.

"We'll meet you. Where's your airplane, Lake Hood?"

Grason nodded.

"It's been a long day," Pewter said. "We don't want the girls to get exhausted the first day."

"I could go all night," Stacy said. "That's what you're suppose to do on vacation, right?"

Grason laughed.

They took their leave. As soon as Reed screeched out of the parking lot, he whirled on Stacy. "What the hell did you think you were doing in there?"

"Being just like Pewter said," Stacy hissed.

"Pewter said?"

"Yes. She said act normal, be myself."

Pewter laughed. She reached across the seat and touched Reed's arm in sympathy. "That's what I said. Be yourself. We got out of there. I think we'll be all right."

Reed's tension eased. God, Pewter was good for him. If only he could tell her, show it in a way that would not offend. No fighting. Perhaps they'd be all right. In the morning he would call Grason, make his apologies, another time. Of course he couldn't tell Stacy. It would result in a big fight. They'd have that tomorrow, when he was under control, when whatever she argued would be too late.

CHAPTER NINE

Pewter returned to the apartment. Reed spent the night at the bed and breakfast with Stacy and Trish. Pewter returned in the morning for a full-course breakfast. Reed called Grason and made his apologies. And then he informed Stacy and Trish. As they'd been informed the night before, Grason was a suspect in his case. He had a cover to maintain. He couldn't possibly take a chance and have them involved.

"You canceled without asking us?" Stacy said. "We have no say over our own lives?"

"I think you have a say over every part of your life, Stacy. We don't control you. But this affects other people and it's not something you can argue," Reed said calmly.

"No. I guess it's not," Stacy said. She picked up her purse and left the room.

The lack of vehement argument surprised Reed. "We'll leave in an hour," Reed called to Stacy's back. "Pewter will drive us down to the station and we'll take the train over to Whittier and pick up our boat." But Stacy was gone.

Reed turned to Trish. She'd been so quiet, her earlier excitement had been erased. Now she seemed apprehensive, perhaps confused. He unfolded a map of Prince William Sound and began to go over their plans. In a few minutes Trish was at his shoulder, leaning over the table, eagerly anticipating Columbia Glacier, seals and sea lions, perhaps a few whales, camping in the bays, hiking in the hills.

Fifteen minutes later a taxi pulled up in front of the house. Reed, sitting at the breakfast table and sipping coffee, watched as Stacy suddenly materialized and ran across the lawn. He jumped up and ran outside, waving the taxi down as it started to back away. He jerked open the back door. Stacy crawled against the opposite side.

"Where do you think you're going?" He tried to stay with reason, to keep the raw force of demand out of his tone.

"I called Terry up. I'm going flying."

"No you're not."

"Oh, yes. You don't run my life anymore." Her hands were up, nails painted black and extended like a cat fighting for its life. Her feet were raised, ready to kick. The taxi driver, an older man, in his fifties with gray hair and a paunch, sat looking straight ahead, waiting for the argument to resolve.

They were at it now, screaming in each other's face, bringing up old wounds, her dropping out of high school, her selling drugs, his absence in their lives, giving everything to his job and nothing to them, an unmerciful verbal kicking and gouging that soon gave way to raw physical force. Reed seized Stacy's arm, ignoring the clawing as he dragged her from the taxi. She kicked him in the shin. She raked long painted nails at his face and eyes.

Pewter and Trish were in the parking lot. Bob, the owner of the bed and breakfast came out, a thin, athletic man with a black goatee and moustache. They were circling, yelling, mostly at him, Reed realized. He had blood down one arm, a smidgen on one cheek, Stacy's wrists in his hands as she lashed out with her feet and repeatedly spit at his face. This was going nowhere. He let go of Stacy's wrists. "You bastard!" she screamed. "You lying bastard!" She turned and ran into the house.

"I think she's a little upset," Reed said lamely to Pewter.

"And you make a joke?" Pewter asked. "At least you have daughters, something to hold onto. And you could throw that away?"

"No, that's not what I mean."

"If I had what you had, I wouldn't do this," Pewter said with surprising emotion. She whirled and followed Trish into the house.

The vacation was ruined. The refrain ran through Reed's head. He stood unmoved, heart throbbing in a painful rhythm as if he'd sprinted beyond his capacity to run. What the hell happened? Why was Pewter upset? He'd explained to Stacy that Grason was a target of his case, there were dangers, not just to them, but to him and Pewter. And still Stacy defied him. He'd promised control, moderation. But that didn't work with Stacy. No matter how vaulted his control, Stacy always found a way to push him over the edge, almost as if she was pushing herself.

Reed paced the parking lot. The vacation was ruined. He and Stacy could never weather four days of camping, hiking and sightseeing cramped together on the same little boat. And they sure as hell couldn't stay in Anchorage, not with Grason, Kurth, Wynona and the motorcycle gang around. No, one accidental meeting and the time together as a family was shot.

Of course maybe Grason meeting them wasn't accidental. He had to consider that. Maybe he should end the case right here, take what he had, Kurth, Wynona, Vitus, the factory, get Grason another time.

In time Pewter came out of the house. She wore tan slacks, brown Gortex hiking boots, and a purple denim shirt. Her eyes were direct, hard. Reed felt himself turn crimson.

He'd wanted her to know him, to understand. But not this. What the hell could she think, fighting with his daughter like some adolescent out of control?

"I don't know how to explain the history, the family situation. There are so many influences beyond our control. Stacy has this wild streak, this urge to self-destruct."

"Genetics," Pewter suggested. "Don't be embarrassed. We all have our public face. My father and I have had screaming matches after I opted out of biology and into law enforcement. He called it a waste. He wants me to fail. He wants me back into biology, carrying his mantle, under his control, Professor Daniel Torbino's little daughter. We get away from ourselves. Stacy's just trying to get away from herself — but you're in the way."

The undercurrent to Pewter's words struck Reed as more personal than he'd imagined. But of course how was he to know.

"The situation now is that she's not going on that boat with you."

"Then I'll buy her a ticket and she can fly home."

"That's what I said. She agreed. Give her the money and she'll be gone."

"I'll have to take her," Reed said.

"You don't trust her?"

"What are you, on her side? You don't know her history."

"Don't snap at me, damn you. Your problem is you don't understand how people react when they're rejected."

"I wasn't rejecting Stacy. I invited her up here. I paid her way. I was reaching out. She pushed me into an untenable spot. She's good that way."

"Then it must run in the family," Pewter said. She spun on her heel and walked toward the house.

Pewter drove. Reed sat on the passenger's side in front, Stacy and Trish in the back seat. They sat in near silence. Reed had tried to apologize, tried to explain. Stacy had left the room. That he scarcely had money for a same-day, one-way ticket back to Washington DC, Reed kept to himself.

"Daddy," Trish spoke.

Reed turned. There was something small and wounded in her voice. That she hurt, he hurt. She could not look him in the eye, like a girl ashamed, like a girl who'd lost the trust in her father. Reed could barely talk. "Yes, Trish?"

"I want to go home."

The muscles across Reed's chest constricted, like a man having a heart attack, he thought. "Today?"

"Yes." Trish was very close to tears. "If Stacy won't stay, then I want to go."

"Don't be stupid," Stacy snapped. "You'll be doing everything Reed just loves, fishing, hiking."

The use of his first name, Stacy's ultimate revenge, Reed knew. "I'm sorry about what happened between Stacy and me. Don't let it affect our relationship."

Trish shook her head. She was resolute. "If Stacy won't stay, then I won't either."

"She's just trying to force me to give in," Stacy said. "The answer's no. I'm not staying. If Trish won't stay, that's her problem."

Reed turned to stare down the road and at the turbulent, muddy waters of Turnagain Arm. Trish had never stood against him like this, never. Should he simply acquiesce? Should he plead? Surely he could not resort to force. He glanced at Pewter and could see by the set of her jaw that she'd bowed out, just as he'd bowed out on her. He shook his head like a punch-drunk fighter, wondering how such hope and promise and carefully laid plans could evolve into such a state.

They turned down the International Airport Road. Reed turned and looked at Trish huddled in the corner of the seat. She looked so small, so frail. As a child she'd been quiet, watchful, always eager to go fishing or hunting or just hiking with her father. At eight she'd accompanied him back to Wisconsin to join Guy for their annual deer hunt. She'd trailed Reed through the forest and watched while he shot and then gutted a deer. He remembered her silent awe, touching the deer, poking at the warm, fresh blood, understanding the evolution of nature and man, the realities of life and death in the forest. It had been the last time he'd taken the time to hunt with Guy, Reed suddenly realized, one more tradition erased. Where the hell was his head?

He struggled to maintain a neutral tone. "Trish, I want you to stay. I think it's a great opportunity. You'd love Prince William Sound, the glaciers, the whales, the seals. I'd like you to stay more than anything in the world. But if you have to go, you can go."

"If Stacy stays, I'll stay. We're supposed to be a family."

Reed turned to Stacy. She gave him a half-grin, half-sneer. "All right, I'll stay, but only as long as we can go flying with Terry."

"If you ever go back and finish high school, you should think about majoring in psychology. You're a master at the job." Reed said tersely. He turned back to the front. He spoke quietly to Pewter. "Why don't you pull up in front of the terminal and we'll unload the baggage. Maybe then you can park. I'll have to wait until the airplane takes off."

"I like that," Stacy said, "the trusting father, right up until the end."

Reed whirled. He glared. Stacy sneered in defiance. He saw the fear in Trish's eyes, the tears. He spoke softly. "Thank's Stacy. You did well. I did well. Now look what we've done."

Stacy shrugged, but she looked away, and just for a second Reed saw a look of doubt.

But what good were doubts when nothing had changed?

* * *

Reed climbed steadily through the midnight gloom. He wore only a light shirt to ward off the nighttime chill. Exertion would do the rest. Already he was layered with a thin coat of sweat. He carried a fanny pack, a pint of water and nothing else. At times the trail zig-zagged up through pockets of brush, foliage that blocked out the light and obliterated footholds and hand-holds. Still he raced upward, slipping, muttering, giving not one thought to his safety should he fall.

In patches off to his left the turquoise blue of Exit Glacier gleamed like a neon light, a reminder of good times that someone else had experienced a long, long time ago.

He broke out onto a plateau to where he could see the glacier clearly, and stare back into the valley below, see the layers of clouds edging up the river like sheep too frightened to advance all the way. Reed perched on a tundra mound, turning all around, drinking in the scenery and filling his senses with all that was good and worthwhile. But all he could think about was the fact he was alone.

He turned up, facing the next steep rise that would take him all the way to the top, where he and Pewter camped, the Harding Icefield. It would be cold. He was not dressed. He had no dry clothes. He'd have to keep moving, he knew, or hypothermia would have him dead.

He foraged upward, sometimes sliding, feeling the burning in legs crying for oxygen, the buildup of lactic acid, arms and shoulders aching, coordination fading, his step not as firm as he rose up into the night.

They'd sat in absolute silence, like at a funeral, waiting on the airplane. When they announced boarding, he gave Trish a hug. Stacy moved next to him, smirking, waiting to see if he would hug her, not saying a word. It took all his willpower just to not say something incendiary as he gave her a perfunctory hug.

He dropped Pewter off at the apartment, said he was going for a ride. He'd just kept going south, like this was the only place he could go.

He topped the last steep rise and reached another open plateau of rolling tundra mounds that led up into glacial snow and over mounds of glacial gravel and on up into the icefield itself. A cold glacial wind blew at a steady pace. Reed moved on, enveloped by the wane light like an hour before true dawn, a light of revelation and concealment like being covered in the gauze of a cocoon.

He looked at the depression where he and Pewter had pitched their tent, where they'd felt the contentment of the mountain and slept side by side. Had he truly used her like she claimed?

He stumbled around and then walked to the edge of a steep slope leading down toward the glacier. It was a dying giant, tens of thousands of years old, impervious to animals that had stood here on its slope. Reed stood motionless, wondering on the lines of crevasses in the blue and white, deep canyons that could consume a man and make him one again with the earth. At least here, one man alone with nature, in a position where nature was dominant, there was harmony, a feeling of contentment, of being part of something good and whole. It was salve to his aching heart.

Reed shivered violently, teeth chattering. He peered up, stumbled and almost fell. He should continue, all the way to the top as he'd promised. Never quit, never back away, never give up, even if he died.

"Hey," he shouted. His voice echoed across the valleys. "Hey. Is anyone out there?" The wind swirled. His shirt clung to his body, a frozen shard. He could feel the trembling as deep as his bones. Reed Erickson freezes to death taking a tourist's 3,500-foot hike to the top of a glacier. Ego, it was always ego.

Reed turned. He slipped and fell, arms and legs splaying out to the side like a newborn fawn first learning to walk. Concentrate, he thought grimly, think. He crawled to his feet. Where the hell was the trail? He had to get down off this ridge, get out of the wind. He circled one way and then another. It was the best part of nature, he thought, the lack of caring, the lack of prejudice — the beauty was there for all, the cruelty as well. Human beings did not count.

ESKIMO MONEY

CHAPTER TEN

The day after his hike Reed slept until four in the afternoon. After her day of work in the gift shop, Pewter did not return to the apartment. Whether she had a date or was going to the health club she did not say, acting as perfunctorily as if he were a passing acquaintance.

Reed wrote a long letter to Trish. Perhaps they could work things out so she could visit Alaska later in the summer. What transpired between him and Stacy should not affect their relationship.

He even wrote Stacy, albeit a much shorter note. He'd been wrong to bring them up here in the middle of a case. She'd been wrong trying to get with Grason. Further contact would have jeopardized his and Pewter's lives. Somehow, someway, they had to achieve a truce. He had to learn to accept her, and she had to learn to accept him.

He called Doug and the two of them went out for a beer, like in the old days. Paperwork on the carving shop indicated the shop had been shipping one hell of a lot of goods to Japan. Doug casually surveyed the bar, making certain there was no one he knew. He wore blue jeans and a tan shirt that was pushed out by his protruding stomach. "You've been making some pretty good inroads, partner. I haven't seen you that much. How've you been feeling?"

"Fine," Reed said. That was one thing he missed about working with Doug. They were as straightforward as two men could be with each other, as open and honest as he wished he could be with Pewter. One thing with Doug, he always gave as good as he got. "I'm going to call Grason again and apologize for the mixup with Stacy."

"You were lucky as hell on that one. Grason might be tainted goods. Who knows what he learned from that incident."

"Then he'll push me off," Reed said. "At this point I don't have anything on him."

Two days later Reed telephoned Terry Grason in Fairbanks. "I'm sorry about the mixup on the flight," Reed apologized. "Like I said, Stacy's only seventeen."

"I appreciate your concerns. I told you she'd be safe, but I understand." Grason spoke softly, a soothing voice like a preacher setting his parish up for a thundering shock. "Like I said, I had a son. They become your life, your existence. You're always concerned."

"Yes, that's the truth."

"Of course that's gone now. I suppose that's part of why I'm talking right now. People need connections. I was down there checking you out. I knew you couldn't be an agent, bringing your children up here like that."

Reed waited through a brief pause. "Maybe we could talk business."

"I don't know about business. I don't know you that well. But you know how to handle yourself; that's something by itself. All I'm saying is that if you get up to Fairbanks, give me a call. We'll go out for a beer. Talk."

"I was thinking about driving up to Denali this week," Reed said. "I've never seen the place. I guess they're just opening up. Maybe I could swing on up to Fairbanks, say about Wednesday."

"You seem like a man in a hurry," Grason said in a tone that suggested a man easily irritated.

"I've got a lot of orders. And a lot of bills. I can't pay one without filling the other."

"I know that route. It gets worse every year. Insurance is the killer. I've instructed my guides that if they ever cripple a client, go ahead and finish the bastard off. It's a lot cheaper to pay off the dead than cover for some wheezing cripple they wheel in front of a jury. Come on up. I'll show you Fairbanks, although there ain't a hell of a lot left."

Reed appreciated the dry tone, without a hint of kidding.

He didn't know when he'd be back, Reed told Pewter. If Kurth or Vitus called, go ahead and place an order for more ivory, enough to keep them on the string. He was headed north. Pewter barely nodded. They weren't a team anymore, in truth they barely spoke. She was hurting, Reed understood, kept in the dark. And still he did not speak.

He did stop at Denali, part of his cover. He even rode one of the school buses back into the park, saw eight grizzlies, caribou, moose, foxes and lucked out and glimpsed part of the great killer mountain itself. It was part of the psychic of man; the more people the mountain killed, the more people there were who wanted to climb.

He met Grason in downtown Fairbanks. They started the night by making the rounds on Fourth Avenue, the dregs of a city Grason claimed had died ten years before.

ESKIMO MONEY

"There's no flavor to Fairbanks anymore," Grason said. He wore green workman's clothes and a grey sealskin vest. He leaned on the bar, a shot glass and a beer in front of him, a towering presence, like a prospector straight out of the hills. His voice was soft, filled with pain. "The old has been destroyed. What's left is a hodge-podge of strip malls, fast food joints, and freeways. Ever since the pipeline boom there's nothing about Fairbanks that's Alaska anymore. It's just like Anchorage."

"That's not good," Reed said with a self-induced slur. He'd been trying to dump as many drinks as possible, but with Grason tight on his arm and the bartenders watching, he'd still consumed much more than was prudent. "It's happening all over the world, everything's becoming the same."

The Fourth Avenue Bar was made for drinkers. At least the dozen or so patrons were beyond the point they could even fake being sober. The bartender, his black hair slicked straight back and his florrid complexion that of a drinker, moved with steady deliberation up and down the bar, dispensing drinks as they were requested. As soon as one man asked for credit the bartender took the man's glass. "Out. Now." The voice left no room for compromise.

Reed glanced down where Doug had taken a stool at the end of the bar. Entering a small bar with a dozen patrons was not his idea of a loose tail. But Doug had simply shrugged at his angry look.

Four younger Indians, mid-twenties, loggers with lean, hard bodies and intense passions circled behind Grason and Reed. "This is the great, tough Terry Grason," one man said.

"John Wayne, frightened of no man," another said.

Grason spoke over his shoulder. "Do yourself a favor, boys. Go on home to your wives. If you have a wife. If you don't this isn't the place to find one."

One of the men huffed, "The great white hunter. People say you're as tough as all of Alaska. People say you are Alaska. Then who are we?"

Grason turned. He stood, a towering figure with his head less than a foot from the ceiling. "The last of a dying population, just like me," Grason said sadly. He appraised his four targets. "Don't do this boys, I don't want to hurt anyone."

Reed sat with his elbows on the bar. His head buzzed. The thing would be to let the four of them take Grason on, clobber him if they could. But that would be the end of his relationship with Grason. Grason would never deal with a man who would not help him in a fight. And there would be a fight. The four men wanted a fight.

Reed looked down the bar and shook his head at Doug to stay out of it. Other patrons turned to watch the shouting. One man wore a black T-shirt with no sleeves. One arm was tattooed down to the wrist, the other was clean and as white as a sheet. He seemed amused, not the kind to get involved in someone else's fight. But if he did, the first thing to look for would be a knife.

"I can't afford trouble," Reed said quietly to Grason as he slid off his stool. The forlorn thought passed that perhaps a show of force, two against four, would be enough to forestall a fight.

"You don't need to get into this," Grason said.

"You killed a man in a bar with a knife," one man said.

"His knife," Grason said. "He came at me. Twenty years ago. Then we had a few men. He wasn't one."

A fist lashed out, catching Grason flush on the jaw. He staggered. "Good shot," he said calmly and moved forward.

A swirling, confused melee surrounded Reed. He stayed low, crouched, the towering lee of Grason's back at his back and the bar to one side. A fist touched the side of his forehead. He ducked. A midriff loomed and he snapped a punch up into a man's solar plexus. The man gasped and lowered his hands. Reed snapped a second punch and caught the man directly on the nose. Tears welled in the man's eyes. Blood flowed as he held his hand to his nose and staggered backward.

Something loomed in Reed's peripheral vision. He recoiled. One of the four Indians had raised a stool. But then someone seized the stool from behind and jerked the man onto his back. Doug. Reed nodded. The way the guy had that stool cocked he would have been crushed.

Reed turned. Grason had both his men down. "Let's go," Reed yelled. He grabbed Grason's arm.

Grason turned, fist cocked. The melancholy look on his face had been replaced by the wildness of an enraged bear. Reed cringed, but then the look was gone, like an illusion briefly emerging from a fog. Grason noted Reed's two men, one prostrate on the floor with his wind gone, the other cowering against the wall and holding his bloody nose.

"Pretty good," Grason said in admiration. "There aren't many men who can cover my back. And even fewer who I'd trust."

"Cops will be coming. I can't afford trouble with the cops."

"Oh, they'd like to get me too." Grason turned to the bartender. "I wasn't here tonight, Sully." The man nodded. "Send me a bill. I'll send you a check." Grason turned and surveyed the room. Stools were tipped over as were two tables. Those who hadn't been in the fight had retreated to the side walls. Only Doug and the man with one tattooed arm sat on their stools with drinks in hand. Grason spoke to his prostrate victims. "Sorry guys. I tried to warn you. Next time take the advice. There's enough fighting in this world. You don't have to start more."

Reed led Grason into the night. He blinked against the light. Of course it was light out. Ten-thirty at night and the sun had yet to sink. The makings of a gigantic headache began to pound.

"C'mon," Grason said. "I'll take you to a higher-class place just outside of town. Out beside the Chena River. It's an old galvanized shed on the outside, all red velvet and stuffed animals for the tourists on the inside. They won't let people fight me there, but we might pick up a couple of chicks."

It was the worst of evenings, Reed thought. Grason probably weighed two hundred forty pounds and could consume the alcohol to match his size. Finally Reed just quit drinking, no matter how Grason cajoled.

And then two college girls, adventurous backpackers who planned to spend the summer working in the fish factories in Valdez, were taken with Grason's sealskin vest and rugged Alaskan ways.

Grason became every bit as polite as a college professor with an eye-pleasing coed. He spoke quiet, gently, a self-confident man stating the facts. "Yeah, I was born and raised in Alaska. My father made his living panning for gold. Myself, I guide and fly."

"That sounds neat," the girl next to Grason said. She was a slight girl, the kind Grason preferred. Her hair was black and frizzed, her eyes green, intelligent, determined, ready for adventure.

"Listen, if you're looking for a place to spend the night, I have a spare room. Hand-scribed log cabin. Built with these hands." Grason held out two large, muscular hands for the women to admire. "Hot tub on the porch, moose in the front yard. In the morning I'll fix a big Alaskan breakfast. I don't have a client booked, I could take you up for a little flight."

"That sounds marvelous," the woman said. "I like to experience the real Alaska as much as I can. Not just these tourist spots."

"You're pretty quiet," the other girl, Penny said to Reed. She was a strawberry redhead with a lot of freckles and clear blue eyes.

Upper middle class, Reed thought, Pewter's level. The thought gave him a start. Reed looked long and hard at the girl. Her eyes had yet to be twisted by the trauma of hard living. College graduate. She'd marry her doctor or lawyer or business executive and get a job and raise her kids. Relatives would die, she might get divorced, but she'd never really know the hard side of life, not like being raised in a broken family in the slums, not unless she went with the wrong person and spent the night.

"I'm a quiet fellow," Reed said in response to the girl's question. She was young, firm, probably willing. He couldn't deny his urges, the attraction, man and woman, flesh against warm flesh, the way it should be. How long had it been since he'd really been with a woman? Even for a one-night stand. Fantasy was wearing thin. Of course then the issue might arise at a trial. Pewter would find out, although it sure as hell wasn't any of her business, he admonished himself. Might be a good thing.

He looked away from the attraction. This was getting hard to do. A man had the right to live and the hell with the department. More complications messing up his case, when it was far too messed up already.

When the opportunity presented itself, Reed leaned close, speaking so Grason could not hear. She looked so clean, so innocent, so desirable. Her naiveté enraged him. He went cold, a capacity he'd too long feared. His brown eyes were level, steady on hers, almost the equivalent of his predator's gaze. She became uneasy, just looking in his eyes. "Listen, when the big guy here says separate rooms he doesn't mean the two of you together. He's not purebred Alaskan, but he's a man who always gets what he wants. If you don't give it to him, he takes. Once you choose to go to that cabin, you lose your freedom for any other choice. Your friend there is a little enamored because she had a couple drinks and never saw a sealskin vest. Take her to the john and give her a little talk. Then get your packs and go sleep in the woods. It'd be the safest thing you could do." Reed was intense, hard, without a hint of kindness.

The girl swallowed. He'd frightened her, Reed thought. As always it was a shock at how easily he could give someone like her doubts, as if his behavior was more natural than an act.

They returned to Grason's cabin at two in the morning. Grason was still muttering about being dumped by two dumb college girls. "They go to the bathroom and then they don't even come back. What the hell kind of a deal is that? I've picked up a lot of chicks at that place. I treat them nice, keep my promises, give them a room, a big breakfast, a flight. Like I said with your little girl, perfectly safe." Grason's lined face turned soft with some memory. "You'd be surprised on how often they come to me. Once, one gal came to me in the middle of the night. A half-hour later her roommate shows up. They both stayed."

"They were just talkers," Reed said. He'd noted Doug's vehicle parked at a wayside a half-mile down the road. This late at night, with little traffic on the roads, Doug knew a single tail would be impossible. He must have figured they'd head for home.

102   ESKIMO MONEY

"Nice place," Reed said as he blinked against the lights. The place was maintained like he figured for a man like Grason, bright, airy and clean. The walls were varnished pine paneling, the floors tongue-and-groove oak. A five-foot spread of moose antlers decorated one wall while on the opposite three-foot-long walrus tusks and head hung above a shelf with two ivory tusks with carved figures of seals and bears. A large gun case covered one wall, a bay window the opposite. The girls would have been impressed.

"I built this place for my wife," Grason said. "Alaska's a man's state, hunting, fishing, flying, getting out in the wild. It's a tough place for a woman. Guys are mostly considering for themselves. Jeri was from Kansas City, the daughter of an attorney. Boy did that guy clean me out on the divorce. She came up here on vacation. She wasn't tough at first, but she got tough. I didn't think we'd last five years. And then after ten years I didn't think we'd ever part. But then those wardens ran Jeff off the road." Grason's voice caught. His rugged face became a twist of emotions, trying to hold himself together.

"It was never the same after that," Grason managed to continue. "Twenty years. Jeff's gone. Then Jeri's gone." He turned and peered down at Reed. "You know what it's like, being flayed alive. They just strip it all away. I don't blame Jeri. She hung on a long time. But then those damn wardens. And then her father. He was the cutthroat, the reason why America's going weak. A pencil pusher, a button pusher, charts and graphs. If we ever got into a real war, face to face, we don't have any men to fight."

"Yeah, it's all computers and buttons," Reed agreed. "I think the work ethic is getting away."

"That's right, that's right," Grason brayed. "You ought to see the jerks I take out hunting. They don't want to hunt, they just want to kill something and brag about it. I've had guys offer twelve grand and ask me to just drop the skin off at their motel and bring them a broad besides. Like I'm a god-damn pimp. Other guys want to hunt grizzlies from tree stands, so they can't be touched," Grason said in a high-pitched sissy voice.

Reed sank down on a heavy, wood-framed sofa. The trick here was to get onto ivory, polar bear, make a buy and get it on the Nagra, something they could take to court. "Hell of a moose rack there. You shoot that yourself?"

"Sixteen hundred pounds. Took three shots to bring that down."

"The only moose I ever shot was Canadian, twelve hundred pounds at the most. And the rack wasn't like that."

Grason squinted at Reed, judging. "You want to shoot a grizzly bear?"

The question caught Reed by surprise. He'd been thinking about walrus, ivory, perhaps polar bear hides. He shrugged. "Well yes, of course. Who wouldn't?"

"Yeah, tomorrow," Grason said as if making a decision. "We'll see what kind of a man you really are."

"I'll have to borrow a gun," Reed said.

"Oh, I've got guns," Grason said. He sat down on the sofa next to Reed. "The question remains. You've been after me for a long time. Just what in the hell is it you want?"

"I told you, we need large quantities of ivory. We have connections on Hawaii. The carving community out there is short on supply. Perhaps some polar bear hides. I have some Japanese clients that expressed a lot of interest. I'm sure I could make some sales."

Grason stood, a towering presence, bloodshot eyes peering out of a massive cranium and thick, curled hair. He wavered, about ready to fall, like a massive redwood being chopped off at the knees.

He was vulnerable, Reed thought. The alcohol and the mood made the situation ideal. Now was the time to take advantage. "I'm not talking a one-time deal here, Terry. Steady, reliable, long term. If you can fulfill your end of the deal."

"You sonofabitch," Grason breathed. "You're pushing. I don't like to be pushed. Friends don't push friends."

"Sorry," Reed said. "I just mean this wouldn't be a single transaction."

"Yeah," Grason growled. His doubts had returned. He shook his head and walked unsteadily toward the back of the house.

Reed exhaled and took a deep breath. He should follow him, he thought, but he'd taken chances enough.

Grason returned with a duffel bag stuffed with two polar bear hides and three wolf hides. Reed sat forward. He felt a bit suicidal. This was what he'd come for. "Damn, those are nice polar bear hides. You shoot those yourself?"

"Nah. I bought these from some Eskimo eeking it out on the subsistence dole. The mayor of a village, no less."

Reed spread a ten-foot skin out on the floor. A big male, ten or twelve years old. He touched the front paws, the short, thick claws for gripping ice, the complete furring between the pads. The ears were small to protect from heat loss. He ran his finger down the white, Roman nose. Another evolutionary marvel, one to two hundred thousand years from its grizzly ancestors. There'd been the days of aerial gunning, city-dwelling, big game hunters shooting polar bears from the air. Thousands more had been killed by set-guns attached to a piece of meat set on a platform. The bear would stand up, pull at the rancid meat and take a slug in the face. It had been only a few decades previous. The word conservation was not known — still wasn't in a lot of circles, Reed thought morosely.

"Nice skin mount. Who does your work?" Reed asked, one more target they could add to the list.

"Don't get too nosy on me. It doesn't make me feel good," Grason warned.

"How much?" Reed asked in a tone that ignored the warning. Grason's suspicions lay right on the edge.

"Three thousand."

"Two thousand. I have to make some profit myself."

"Hell, I paid a thousand dollars to have the damn thing mounted," Grason brayed with sudden anger. "I don't like this dicking around. Do you want the thing or not?"

"Twenty-five hundred and that's as good as I go," Reed said. The anger surprised him. Grason was having the same kind of mood swings as he was.

Grason nudged Reed with his toe. "You sonofabitch, I ought to kick your head off."

It was, Reed understood, Grason's way of saying yes.

Reed picked at the lush, multicolored fur of the wolf skins that had been tanned. "Did you get these from the same guy?"

"Nah, those I got myself. Last winter."

If the lab could inspect beneath the fur they'd find pellet holes, Reed would have bet. Wolves aerial gunned. Every year around one thousand of the seven thousand wolves in Alaska were legally trapped or hunted. In Anchorage a hip-length wolf-skin coat cost two to three thousand dollars. In recent years so-called prominent citizens such as surgeons and dentists had been convicted for aerial gunning wolves. In Denali the entire Savage wolf pack disappeared, the suspected victims of illegal aerial gunning.

"I don't know what I'd do with these," Reed said. He felt a little strange, aware he should be angered at Grason. But he was not. "Furs aren't big in Hawaii. Maybe I could do something with full mounts. Let me ask my Oriental clients. What kind of price do you need on a mounted wolf skin with head and all?"

"Six hundred. I have mounting costs, you know. It costs money to fly an airplane."

"I'll check around. If I get the customers, do you have more polar bear hides?"

"I've got a half-dozen in stock."

"Where do you sell them all?"

"What the hell are you, a federal agent?" Grason grunted. He sank tiredly into an easy chair and leaned back and closed his eyes.

"What about ivory? That's really what I came for."

"I'll get you all the damn ivory you want in the morning," Grason grunted irritably. His head lolled to one side.

Reed blew a sigh of relief. The tension, the long night had made him exhausted. He turned off the lights. The gray, musty light of an Alaskan night permeated the house. Grason had been gone a long time getting the polar bear and wolf hides. He should go looking, Reed thought, find his cache, but Grason might wake up. Maybe he was faking it right now.

In truth, as a mark he'd just started with Grason. He had yet to find out who he sold to, who he bought from. What village mayor was betraying the trust of his people? That'd mean time with Grason, playing at his level, like crawling into a cave with a maze of tunnels, no rope and his light was getting dim.

Or maybe he was losing his nerve. Take what you've got, he thought, and wondered if Pewter would approve.

Maybe he was just tired, Reed thought. He cast about for a place to sleep. The sofa looked good. But instead he lay down on the polar bear hide and pulled a wolf skin over his chest for a cover.

Reed turned on his side and, using the back of the polar bear head for a pillow, he slept. He awoke once to see a huge figure staring down at him on the floor, Grason, his eyes gleaming from the gray of night. And then the giant turned and stalked into the back bedroom to sleep.

Reed lay motionless and silently cursed. It'd take a half an hour to get back to sleep. His heart beat too fast. Grason could be a pleasant man. But he'd also heard the threats, the passion against conservation officers because of the death of his son. And he'd witnessed what Grason had done to those Indians in the bar, an unstoppable force. What would happen if he really got mad?

All part of the game, Reed thought. He stared into the yellow glass eyes and the jaws of the wolf whose skin he used for a cover. Remarkably intelligent creatures that had all but been eliminated from the Lower 48. He felt a deep loneliness and in his mind heard the howl of a lone wolf in a cold dark night. But that was wrong, he knew. Pack wolves howled, joining one another for the thrill of the hunt. Lone wolves stayed quiet, unseen, lest an unfriendly pack rip out their throats. In that way wolves and people were the same. Grason was a lone wolf, just as he was.

CHAPTER ELEVEN

Breakfast was delicious, fresh hashbrowns O'Brien with melted cheese, eggs, moose steak, fresh-squeezed juice, hot coffee and homemade bread, all served on the glassed-in porch overlooking a corner of the Tanana River. Down the small dirt airstrip that Grason had bulldozed, a moose cow and calf meandered across.

"I've damn near crashed into moose twice either landing or taking off," Grason said fondly. "The stupid bastards just don't know enough to move."

"They won't get off the tracks for a freight train, why the hell should they move for an airplane?" Reed said.

Grason laughed. "Used to be pleasant mornings out here, Jeff, Jeri, myself. That's why I hoped those girls would come. I like that pleasant ring of female laughter. It would have been an experience for them."

"That's for certain," Reed said sadly. It would have been the thing to have their shiny faces and innocent laughter. Lately he hadn't laughed enough.

"Where do you get this bread, it's delicious," Reed said.

"I make it. Sourdough special. Always have. Clients expect it, part of the frontier experience. They like to taste it, like seeing a grizzly from a bus down at Denali. But they don't want to meet one face to face. People just aren't tough. They want the adventure, but no danger. And damned if they'll give up any comfort."

There was that bitterness again, Reed observed, pleasantries one minute, wild ranting the next. Of course Grason had cause. He felt the same way himself. They'd just have to get themselves in sync.

He glanced at a small framed picture set on an end-table. It was a nice looking woman, even features, high cheekbones, straightforward, practical eyes, someone you'd look at and see stability. A lot like the way he used to look at Pam. Only the passion was missing, and that he'd mistakenly thought he could do without.

"Jeri," Grason said tightly.

"Nice looking woman," Reed said. "Is she still in Alaska?"

"Nope. She had her fill. Went back to the Lower 48. Said she wanted to see what reality was like."

They had a pleasant breakfast and talked of hunting, the severity of Alaskan winters, "Too long for a man to be alone," Grason allowed. And the highway to Prudhoe Bay and the prospect of opening the Arctic National Wildlife Refuge to oil exploration. Most Alaskans wanted it, Grason admitted, for the jobs. But opening the North Slope was what killed Fairbanks, brought in the development, destroyed the frontier atmosphere.

It was a pleasant morning. The two men did dishes, Reed washed, Grason dried and stored the dishes in the cupboard. Not one mention of ivory, Reed thought. But he'd wait, bide his time.

Grason abruptly turned on Reed. "Let's go get that grizzly you wanted." He donned his sealskin vest.

"Sure," Reed agreed. He kept his disappointment inside. He'd thought the talk of a grizzly had been alcohol-induced. He laced up his old, scuffed leather boots. He stood. Grason was watching. Reed met the man's eyes, a friendly gaze or a suspicious man. It was the measure of Grason that he could not tell. One thing certain, Grason viewed this as a test.

They took off in Grason's Super Cub, a slow-flying two-seater, one person behind the other. Grason's Beaver was in use for the morning, Grason said. Besides, for grizzly bear, the Super Cub was the thing.

They circled the low craigs of the White Mountains north of Fairbanks. The soft green of newly emerging summer foliage shone brightly under a clear sky and high sun. They crossed mile after mile of forest, no houses, no development, sparkling lakes here and there, gleaming rivers. Like the majority of Alaska, it took but a moment or two to leave all vestiges of civilization behind. It was, Reed knew, a country too vast to effectively patrol. If poachers were caught it was when, as they inevitably must, they returned to civilization with their wares. However, the method by which game was obtained was more difficult to prove. The laws forbade aerial hunting or even game spotting and same-day hunting after a fly-in. It was disheartening to think that a guide with the reputation of Terry Grason could be so crude.

Grason dropped the red and yellow airplane to five hundred feet. They passed moose, black bear, a small grizzly sow and early cubs. Eventually they spotted a nice grizzly, shaggy haired but with beautiful markings, brown legs and neck offset by a platinum blond back and rump. Grason circled, standing the airplane on the tip of its wing, giving throttle, a blood-wrenching spin that made Reed feel light headed. The bear looked up. "It's an eight-footer,"

Grason yelled over the roar of the motor. "You won't get much bigger up here. You have to go down near the coast to get the big ten-footers."

Grason circled away from the bear. He shouted back at Reed. "I had one guy up from New York. He wore a gray three-piece suit and Florshiem shoes while he shot his grizzly bear. Paid two grand extra so we'd videotape the damn thing. Said he'd show it at the next meeting of the directors. All kinds," Grason said, his voice fading in the throb of the engine.

A half-mile away he spotted a sandbar on a stream. He circled once, surveying the site from twenty feet in the air. With the deftness of a seagull riding the wind currents over the sea, he swooped in over the water, flaps down, seemingly on the verge of a stall. Reed felt a sickness in his stomach, a hundred yards or so of soft sand and then a screen of brush. Either Grason made it or they crashed. The ballooned tundra tires splashed water and then sand. Within scant feet Grason had them stopped. He taxied right up to the brush and spun the airplane to face the river.

Reed climbed out. He turned back to face Grason who handed him a short rifle still in its case. Grason shouted over the roar of the engine. "Head for that little sand knoll two hundred yards straight west. It's a two-hundred-and-eighty-grain bullet. That should be enough." And then he closed the door.

Grason revved the motor. Reed ducked from the sting of flying sand and sprinted to one side. The Super Cub bounced down the sandbar toward the water. The wheels touched water, skimming like skis and then lifted into the sky, drops sparkling in the sunlight as they fell. A show, Reed wondered, or was the margin that thin?

He uncased the rifle, a gun he hadn't touched or shot. It was a simple Remington bolt action .308. A bullet was taped to the stock with masking tape. Reed checked the breech, the chamber, the gun case. He looked to the sky. One bullet! "You sonofabitch," he said. And then he smiled. Yes, this was Terry Grason's idea of a test all right.

Reed loaded the bullet into the chamber. He checked the sights and made sure the safety was on. A half-mile away Grason dove his plane, throttling back. The distant *pop, pop, pop* of the engine backfiring carried through the forest. Reed knew of the maneuver, sometimes used by unscrupulous guides, men who guaranteed a bear to clients who paid ten to fifteen thousand for the job. Grason would dive to one side of the bear. The bear would move away from the diving airplane and popping noise. Already the bear would be headed in his direction.

Reed turned and faced a wall of scrub willow. He ducked inside, snaking through the limbs, ducking, squirming, moving as quickly as he could. At least on the knoll he could see a good twenty or thirty feet. Once through the thickets lining the stream, the brush thinned; however, he could only see a matter of feet. Grason dove again, a silent hawk out of the sky, and then the fire of the sputtering motor, a brief glimpse less than a quarter-mile away.

Reed's heart lurched. He raced ahead, rising now, scrambling upward. He knew the speed of a grizzly over a short distance, fifty yards in about three seconds. But even just rambling a bear could cover a lot of ground. He neared the top of the rise and turned, surveying the tops of scrub willow and dwarfed birches. And then he saw it, the tops of brush swaying, marking the progress of the bear passing off to one side. At the best he'd have a glimpse. Dared he take a shot? Or could he plead no shot and spare the bear?

Would Grason lose faith?

And then Grason dove again, a whistling red and yellow devil dropping from the sky. The brush movement stopped less than fifty yards away. In spite of the coolness of the day, beads of sweat had formed at Reed's temples. His mouth was dry. Muscles tensed. As he raised the rifle he flicked the safety off with his thumb.

He heard what he could only describe as a loud, irritated grunt. Again the brush began to move, tracking up toward him with all the force and speed of a locomotive. And he was directly in the path, a tiny figure in the middle of a vast wilderness, sun beating down, a red and yellow airplane circling overhead. He glimpsed brown and blond, a blur of eight hundred pounds hurtling through the brush with surprising agility. And then he saw the hump and the thick massive head that could so easily deflect a misplaced bullet. He'd read too many stories, a dozen shots to down a bear.

And then the small, wide-set eyes seemed to focus on him and the bear adjusted its path. In such circumstances most men just saw the bear and shot. Reed focused on his sight picture, an instant to align the bead, the vee and place it just below one eye, and then the quick squeeze. The bear collapsed as if poleaxed from above, the massive head and gaping jaws less then ten feet from Reed's legs.

Grason swooped over and waggled his wings. Reed stood motionless, legs trembling, chest aching. He struggled for breath. His heart hammered like a man facing a firing squad. Now, with the bear lying at his feet and without any ammunition, he could not bring himself to move lest the bear was just wounded and would suddenly rise. The sunlight bathed him like a spotlight framing a sports hero on the podium. The acrid odor of cordite and the sickly sweet smell of blood combined with the musky stench of the bear. So freshly dead, vibrant, a paw still twitching, blood still oozing, spreading into the earth.

He could not escape the notion that, at least in this little corner of the forest, the world was a lesser place.

* * *

"I don't have any quantity of ivory in stock," Grason said. They'd skinned the bear, salted the hide and returned to Grason's house on the Tanana River. They sat on the porch overlooking the river and the airstrip. Grason sipped a scotch and sat with his feet propped on a wicker footstool.

Reed sat nearby and drank his third beer. The first two had gone down rather fast. He felt a light buzz, and a deep tiredness, like after combat. You couldn't push the body that high without paying the price. It was the thrill of the hunt, what men paid thousands of dollars to do.

"They should make that a law," Reed said. "You get one bullet and you stand there all alone. Like I always used to say, sometimes you get the bear, sometimes the bear gets you. It's the way life should be."

"Yeah, but it ain't," Grason growled. "You did that pretty good, last minute. If that bear would have got you I would have just turned around and flown home."

Reed shrugged. "That'd be all right. I'd rather get eaten by a bear and shit back into nature than covered with makeup and dumped into some hole in the ground."

Grason laughed. "My sentiments exactly. We're born of the elements, we die of the elements, and that's where we should be buried. If you have a few days and you have the cash, we can get some ivory."

"Yeah," Reed said. "I have to call Pewter. She expected me back yesterday."

"She's quite a looker, although I can't say you two looked that close."

There wasn't much Grason missed, Reed realized. He had to get back in the game, realize where he was at. "We're a bit on the outs lately. I've been doing a little too much fishing and seeing the country. Like visiting you. Pewter's been working for her uncle." Reed gave a nervous laugh.

"Jeri was that way the first couple of years," Grason said. "Although she liked the outdoors. But you have to do what they want once in a while, make some accommodations. That's the only way a marriage will work."

"If you're certain I can get some ivory, I can take a few days. Just let me make a call."

"Telephone's at your elbow. Just dial direct," Grason said.

Like he expected to listen in, Reed thought. He dialed the Anchorage gift shop. Pewter answered the telephone.

"Busy?" Reed asked.

"Reed? Where are you at?"

"I'm in Fairbanks, visiting Terry Grason. If you don't mind, I might take a few more days."

"A few more days?" Pewter questioned. Reed could read her doubts. How did he expect her to play this? Was Grason listening in?

"Now don't get mad. I'll have some goodies when I get back. Guaranteed."

Pewter picked up the cue. A real professional, Reed thought. The telephone volume was rather loud and he wondered if Grason could hear snatches from her end. "You've been gone quite a few days," Pewter snapped.

"Just a few more. This will be worth it. Then we can take that cruise on the sound like you wanted."

"We better. Where are you going?"

Reed looked across at Grason. "Where are we going?"

Grason just smiled. Reed shrugged as if he couldn't care less. "I don't know, honey. Big secret, I guess. I'll talk to you in a few days."

"I miss you," Pewter said.

A lump lodged in Reed's throat. Part of the act, or did she mean it? That he was unable to distinguish the difference was part of his instability. He spoke with real fervor, almost in anguish, "I miss you too."

Reed gently cradled the receiver.

"A man isn't a man without love," Grason said. "After Jeri left, twenty years . . ." He shook his head. He clambered to his feet. He turned, towering over Reed. "I'm just going to say this once, make certain there are no crossed lines, no miscommunications. I'm going to be opening myself up to you. That's my choice. My mind says I can trust you. My bones say the same. Our philosophies aren't that much different. But every once in a while I get a twinge of doubt. If you're a bureaucrat, you're a rare breed. I'm going to take you out and introduce you to some people. But you'll never deal with these people without going through me. That would be a betrayal."

"Oh, hell no," Reed agreed.

"This is fair warning. I've lost too much. There's not much left. Every year my gross goes up. And every year my debt does the same. If you're an agent, the time to leave is right now. Nothing will be said."

"What are you starting on this now for?" Reed demanded.

"Fair warning," Grason said easily. His voice held no malice. "If you're an agent and I find out later, I'll kill you. It's just that simple. If you walk now, no problem. We can argue about that grizzly, but of course that was no charge, something you wanted to do."

As he knew he must, Reed spoke without hesitation. "Terry, I wanted to buy some ivory for shipping to Hawaii. I don't know why you're suddenly going on like this now."

"I just don't want people to say Terry Grason was never fair or didn't give adequate warning. Come on, let's get some things together. It's going to be cold out there on the ice."

The silver de Havilland Beaver droned west, following the expanse of the great Yukon River, 1,500 miles long, starting in British Columbia and crossing the entire state of Alaska and flowing into the Bering Sea. The main channel might run a half to a mile wide, but other areas such as the Yukon Flats had meandering channels that covered a width of fifteen miles. There were a few scattered boats, and a smattering of log cabins, mostly fish camps for when the salmon run began to peak. It was rugged terrain, Reed observed, a mixture of cliffs, cut-banks, tangles of fallen trees, mud flats and large expanses of wetlands mixed in with the rocky shoreline.

"I knew a sixty-year-old woman from Minocqua, Wisconsin that canoed the entire Yukon by herself," Reed said. "Sounds like the kind of adventure I could like."

"Once upon a time," Grason said. "Now there are too many boats, too many fishing camps, too many people, period. Although there's still only one bridge across the Alaskan Yukon, that's something I guess."

Grason glanced into the second seat of the rumbling Beaver. Altona Mosby sat quietly, her squat, rotund form slightly tensed like a person who'd never become comfortable in the air. "Altona and Brian have a fish wheel, a big three-basket job. What'd you say you took out of there one time last summer?"

"Three hundred pounds," Altona said.

"That's where that smoked salmon is from," Grason said. "Brian's working for me. She tends the camp. Cuts the salmon into strips, dips them in brine, hangs them out to dry. Chases off the bears. Beat one black bear with a walking stick." Grason laughed.

Altona showed the hint of a smile. Her face was round with puffy cheeks. Her black hair was cut in bangs straight across her forehead and fixed in back into a crude bun. She wore rubber boots with felt liners, lined blue jeans, a flannel shirt and a blue down vest. One tough woman, Grason had said, a fact Reed had witnessed when they loaded the airplane. Altona handled heavy duffel bags without a hint of strain.

"She may not look like much," Grason said. "But she's the kind of woman a guy needs in Alaska, an Alaskan original, not frightened of anything much except flying. I don't make any sharp turns when Altona's on board. Don't want to get her mad." He smiled, like a man suddenly enjoying his life.

But why bring her along? Reed had asked. Grason explained. Altona was an Inuit from Barrow. He needed her to make his transactions. The men he dealt with, the Keelachuck brothers, would never get caught in a violation. They only sold fresh ivory legally, Native to Native, even if Grason was standing there with money in hand.

"These boys are tough. They don't much like whites. And I can't really blame them for that. There are times I feel the same. You have to know how to play the game. They'll test you, just like they tested me, just like I tested you. Then they'll decide if you're all right."

"And then we get our ivory?"

"Not us, Altona. She's the only one."

"I doubt they could top your test," Reed said.

Grason shot him an amused glance. "I wouldn't bet on that."

CHAPTER TWELVE

Sissy was yelling. Vitus Inokenti searched the dirty dishes clogging the sink, located his mug, dumped the old coffee, rinsed the cup and poured fresh coffee. He did not notice the sour stench of spoiled food caking the dishes. Alicia needed braces, twenty-five hundred dollars.

"Stevie needs them also," Sissy said. "But he can wait. A girl needs her smile. Although for what is beyond me. She'll just attract some man and then he'll ruin her life." Sissy spoke out of puffed cheeks. Her brown hair hung in a stringy ponytail. She wore black slacks, a white blouse and a red vest, her uniform for working the checkout counter at a convenience store on Highway 3.

"I'm talking to you," Sissy snapped as Vitus started to exit the room. He turned back and briefly met his wife's eyes. She was getting bigger, a hundred and eighty pounds. But he knew better than to mention her weight.

"Alicia has an appointment next Friday, but I have to pay five hundred dollars down. And I don't have it. And if we don't pay the light bill by Friday they're going to turn off the lights. Don't you have any money?"

Every time he turned around someone needed money for something, Vitus thought. He needed gas for the airplane to make his rounds of the villages. And Kurth . . .twenty thousand dollars Kurth owed him. He was going to have to do something about Kurth. "I'll stop by today and pay the light bill."

"Both months?"

Vitus shrugged, he'd pay what he could afford. Sissy knew that, and still she yelled, her North Dakota shrill. Straight out of high school, her father an unemployed farm implement mechanic, and she and a friend hitchhiked all the way to Alaska. Her first husband worked the pipeline. But when that ended, the marriage ended. They'd had money at first, Sissy used to reminisce. Now her ex drove taxi and her new husband, half Eskimo, flew charters and sold ivory — whenever he could.

Right to his face she'd refer to him in the abstract, like he wasn't a real person, a Yupik, Vitus thought as he walked into the living room. He pushed aside a pile of clothes and sat on the clear plastic covering their sofa. Twelve hundred dollars he'd paid for this sofa and other than the first couple of days no one ever touched its surface.

The beeps and buzzes of a Nintendo game made Vitus frown. Their youngest, Stevie, playing his game. If you didn't take it away from him he'd never go outside. It was just as destructive as drugs, only people did not see. Stevie had no interest in going out to the villages, no interest in flying, no interest in hunting, no interest in people. Not like Samuel. Samuel was true Yupik; Samuel lived for the hunt. Stevie . . . Stevie did not care.

Sissy's lumpy form blocked the doorway. She looked at her husband, then her son. She sighed like a woman carrying the weight of the world on her shoulders. "I'm going to work. I'll see you tonight. You'll be here, right?"

Vitus nodded. He'd called Anchorage. The gussuk Reed said he'd buy more ivory. Vitus planned on flying to the villages that afternoon, but he couldn't tell Sissy. He'd leave a note, Vitus decided. Pay the light bill and leave a note. Sissy could yell when he got back.

"Goodbye, Stevie," Sissy said. The boy quickly waved. But his eyes never left the screen and he never missed a stroke in playing his mindless game.

He should make him stop, Vitus thought, but the boy would just start again as soon as he left. He heard Sissy pull out of the yard. Samuel never played those video games. But then Samuel never mixed in school. And last semester he'd gotten two failing grades. Nevertheless Sissy had finally granted Vitus's wish, Samuel could go live with his grandparents on St. Lawrence. "He sure as hell doesn't fit in here, he might as well go out there," Sissy said while Samuel stood and listened.

"He can learn to be a goddamn Native," Sissy yelled. "Just like you, Vitus. Isn't that what you want? He'll never get a steady job either. Just like you."

"I make good money," Vitus protested to his wife in front of his son.

"Here and there, from time to time," Sissy yelled. "But you're not eight until five, day in and day out, year after year. Steady work, that's where it counts."

Vitus turned away. He couldn't live like that. No man should live like that. It wasn't living. It was dying, inch by inch.

"You go to St. Lawrence," Sissy had screeched to Samuel before he left. "I know what'll happen." She repeated the saying Vitus had heard the first day they'd met. Then she said it with a hearty laugh, like a woman who could cope no matter what she faced — not anymore. "I always expect the worst from life. And I've never been disappointed yet."

"Where's, Samuel?" Vitus asked his mother, Lulu. He'd just flown into Gambell, bucking a strong headwind all the way. If fog had settled it was doubtful he would have made it back to land. Lulu worked over the gas stove

116   ESKIMO MONEY

where she was canning jars of walrus meat in a large pressure cooker. Vitus chewed rhythmically on a hard piece of reindeer jerky.

"Out on his four-wheeler. I warned you not to bring one. That's all he does, run around with those Keelachuck boys. They're like gussuks, too strong in the mouth. Samuel likes to hunt. He does not like to work."

"Is Jake hunting? I saw the boat on the platform."

"The ice is too far north for the smaller boats. They are having a meeting. Some of the elders turned in Joe Stevens and his sons for head-hunting. They killed nine walrus and only brought back the tusks and the meat from one calf. Some of the younger men think the elders did wrong." Lulu was short, stocky and wore black-rimmed glasses. She'd lectured Vitus many times that she had lived in both worlds, but the material comforts of the gussuks could not compare with the spiritual ease and purpose of living she found in the village.

"Wasteful hunting," Vitus snorted. "Because now the courts say so against the Yupik. The gussuk hunt grizzly bear and wolves just for their skin. The meat goes to waste. At the turn of the century they sail into our waters and wipe out the whales and sea otters and almost destroy the walrus. And they invite us to headhunt and then it is all right. But now, when we must pay cash just to live, and ivory brings us cash, they tell us it is wrong."

"The gussuks make the laws," Lulu said with a resigned tone. "It is not something we can fight."

"You are wrong, Mother! That is why the elders lose power. That is why father is no longer on the council. He will not fight."

"Your father accepts what is. If you tell him you buy ivory to sell to Native carvers in Anchorage, he believes you. But if he knew the truth he would never hunt with you again, or invite you to join us at fish camp."

The thought brought a painful lump to Vitus's chest. Truth be known, the hunt and flying his airplane was all he had.

Weber Peowok's house was falling down; at least one corner sagged badly as if the foundation had been washed away. Various parts of four-wheelers and snow machines littered the gravel yard. An over-dried sealskin was tacked on one wall just over what appeared to be two fresh walrus skulls that were minus the tusks. Maybe he'd get a load of ivory yet this trip, Vitus thought. He knocked on the door that had a crack in the window and brown paint that curled in small flakes.

Weber Peowok opened the door. Weber was short, driftwood-thin with a pockmarked face. Behind his black-rimmed glasses his dark eyes were glazed, the lids half closed. As Vitus stepped inside the smell of unwashed bodies, drying skins, fish, and the unmistakable smell of marijuana smoke stopped him. The Peowok boys were lost, Vitus thought. There were getting to be too many in the villages who were lost. And the gussuk took advantage, feeding the addiction, all the while laughing at those who cared — the Substance Abuse Councils, the peer groups, the many socially responsible members who died as their people died in front of their eyes.

Pete Peowok, Weber's cousin, was also present, along with a towering figure who brought Vitus up short, Terry Grason. Another man peered past Grason, Reed. Vitus felt the flush of alarm. What was Reed doing here with Terry Grason? He'd promised Reed all the ivory he wanted. And he knew Reed also bought through Kurth. Something was not right.

Grason spoke. "You're late, Vitus. The Peowok boys already dealt."

Reed nodded a friendly greeting at Vitus, picking a moment when Grason's head was turned. He could see the questions in Vitus's eyes. If Grason knew he dealt with Kurth and Vitus those same questions could be magnified. He stood silently, part of the background. Clearly Grason and Vitus knew each other, but how well?

Weber waivered uncertainly as if unsure what protocol demanded. Pete sagged on a sofa, his posture every bit as worn as the springs.

"Want a beer?" Weber finally asked.

"No," Vitus grunted.

"You still buying for Breismeister?" Grason asked. "I heard he stiffed you a few times."

Vitus shrugged. It was not a question to which he had any reason to reply.

It was the way business was conducted, Reed thought. He had his Nagra reel-to-reel tape recorder fastened to his chest, taking it down as Grason traded marijuana for ivory in this smoky, foul-smelling little house out in the middle of a small village. It'd been a real disappointment to see Grason stooping to dealing drugs. But some Natives would only trade for drugs, Grason said. That way they knew they weren't dealing with an agent. Besides, what cost two thousand dollars on the streets of Anchorage could purchase ten thousand dollars worth of ivory in the remote villages.

Grason hoisted the heavy duffel bag and they took their leave. As Reed trailed Grason out, he passed within a foot of Vitus. He touched Vitus's forearm in greeting and again nodded, but said not a word. The heat was on. No, Vitus had his suspicions. And in a small village like this it didn't take long for word to get around.

They locked the ivory in the airplane and then proceeded to the Keelachuck's house. The village houses were small, some HUD built, stud and plank shacks that had been blistered and weathered by salt spray off the ocean and constant winds that swept unchecked from the Pacific, Arctic and nearby Siberia. A few houses had drying sealskins nailed to the walls. Here and there huskies rested in deep, cool hollows dug out of the gravel and rock base. One dog was tied to the huge rib of a whale that had been thrust into the earth. The ground was littered with excrement and gnawed animal bones. And not even the constant wind could erase the odors of dung, rotting meat, blubber, fuel oil, salt spray, and boggy tundra.

"Winters must be hell," Reed said.

"Long, dark and cold," Grason said. "It'll check your psyche." He pointed at an ordinary looking ranch-style house that had a relatively fresh coat of dark-green paint. "Nothing special, but you ought to see their gun collection. They must have sixty or seventy Weatherby rifles."

"And you think they'll deal?"

"Not with me. At least not directly. And certainly not with you. But if I say you're all right, they'll check you out. You can bet your butt on that. Gordon's a big guy, looks me eye to eye. Not short and squat like most Eskimo. He was in the marines. Still wears a crewcut to prove it."

If Gordon Keelachuck appeared mean and surly, Delvin looked traditional Siberian Yupik and acted reserved. The warm, smoky house was crowded with men, women, children and belongings. The two were cordial and offered Grason and Reed strong black tea and smoked salmon. They talked, speaking of the hunt, admiring the glass-covered case of guns that all but covered one wall of the dark-paneled living room. For the most part Reed stood silent, his Nagra working against the buzz of conversation. The tape recorder was his one danger, he knew, with Grason or anyone else.

After a good hour of conversation, Grason conveyed the message, Reed was an ivory buyer and had contacts in Anchorage and Hawaii. But of course the Keelachuck brothers had no ivory to sell, either fresh or fossil.

"This afternoon we're going scuba diving for fossil off one of the haulout areas," Gordon said to Grason. He looked across the oilcloth tablecloth at Reed. "Have you ever scuba dived?"

"Some," Reed allowed.

"Maybe you'd like to go diving in the Bering Sea?"

"Sounds pretty cold."

"Delvin has a half-inch-thick Farmer John wet suit. You're about his size."

If Gordon's tone was hard, his dark, glittering stare left no room for doubts; this was not a friendly invitation.

"Sure," Reed said. He dived in the dark waters of Wisconsin; he'd dived in the Keys; he'd dived in Hawaii, and wreck-dived in the freezing waters of Lake Superior. How bad could it be in the Bering Sea?

The Bering Sea was an unforgiving beast. The two-hour ride down the coast had been an experience in itself. Twenty-nine-degree salt spray broke in stinging sheets over the deep-V-hulled, open, aluminum boat. A black two-hundred-horsepower Mercury motor slammed them wave to wave, a constant jarring compressing Reed's vertebra to the point he didn't feel he could safely sit.

At least the wet suit and parka covering helped keep him warm, although his gloved hands were little more than clubs and a thin sheet of ice had formed on the sides of the boat and on the outside of Grason's parka. Grason grinned and Reed smiled back — this was the life.

He'd taken his Nagra recorder off in the Keelachuck bathroom. As he'd struggled into the skin-tight black wetsuit, he'd tucked the recorder under the front edge of the jacket. When no one was looking he'd dropped it into the water, combat loss, government property. Peter could write it off.

They stopped near a small island that was little more than a rocky shoal a couple hundred yards across. The island was black, without the benefit of one touch of green. The rocks rose sharply on three sides. Only the northeastern side had a shallow pitch. Delvin bore in close to shore where a small herd of sea lions lay warming under a pale sun. He cut the motor. The boat swung, pitching mercilessly in the three-foot-chop.

Reed straddled a seat, balancing precariously as he donned his fins and then more than thirty pounds of weights. Grason screwed his regulator into a battered steel tank. Delvin threw him an old-style buoyancy compensator, a barely serviceable one he had to inflate by mouth. He could feel his breath shorten, and forced himself to take longer and deeper breaths.

"Why the hell don't you guys have dry suits?" Reed yelled over the whistle of constant wind and the slopping of water against the lurching aluminum boat.

"If you're cold, take a piss; that'll warm you up," Gordon said. He pointed down the island. "The current runs strong. Hug the bottom. Put the ivory in the net. Surface near shore, wave your hands and the boat will pick you up."

"Sounds like a piece of blubber to me," Reed said. He jerked the neoprene hood over his head and began to tuck it inside the top of his wetsuit. He smeared Vaseline on the exposed area around his lips and cheeks. Gordon donned his tank.

"We going to buddy up?" Reed asked.

"If you move along," Gordon said.

ESKIMO MONEY

Grason set Reed's tank on the seat at his back and helped thrust his arms through the shoulder straps and then handed him the waist strap. Reed was sweating profusely. He spit into his mask and tightened the strap. Last, his dive gloves, one-quarter-inch neoprene. It was going to be a bitch. Abruptly Gordon tipped over backward into the water. Reed grabbed for his mesh net and put the regulator in his mouth. He sucked air. The regulator seemed labored, although his pressure gauge read more than three thousand pounds of air. Perhaps the valves were old, in real danger of freezing in water such as this. He laughed.

"What's so funny?" Grason asked.

"The way life goes. Some tourist dives on a thirty-foot reef in clear water with the most expensive equipment in the world. We come to the Bering Sea and dive with stuff invented before Jacques Cousteau."

"It's called justice," Grason yelled.

Reed pulled his mask over his face. It instantly fogged. The boat lurched. He felt himself tipping like an ungainly knight in rusted armor who'd lost his balance. Grason caught his arm. Reed nodded at the blur through his mask and tipped over backward.

He felt a spasm, almost like going into shock as blood flow to his extremities closed up as every available drop went to fight the cold knifing into his body core. He had too much air in the BC and bumped up toward the lurching boat, fending it off with one hand while he raised the airtube and released some air. As soon as he began to sink, he tipped his mask and rinsed the glass. He spun around, searching in all directions. Visibility was not as much as he'd hoped, twenty or thirty feet. Gordon was no where to be seen.

Reed mentally shrugged. Get to work. Controlled emotions even in the face of extreme danger. He'd known the faculty as a young boy, and proved it as a rifle platoon leader in Vietnam. When the firing started everyone went down. But he had to raise up, figure out what was going on, deploy his men, talk on the radio, direct artillery, direct gunships. That any second a bullet might knock you dead, you put to the back of the mind. If you died, you died.

He looked up. The boat had disappeared. And then, as he turned to kick toward the dark bottom, he felt the force of the current zipping him along like being caught in a river at flood tide. If he paddled up current as hard as he could, he still lost ground. But at least he'd lost the ungainliness of a beached walrus. The weights and tanks were equalized. He could maneuver, albeit not with the darting grace of a walrus or a sea lion.

He neared the bottom, thirty feet, but more filled with silt. He worked into the lee of rocks, the undulating bottom breaking up the current. He took Gordon's advice and urinated into his suit. The localized flood of warm urine felt good.

His breathing slowed. He could hold himself against the current by gripping a rock. He began to search among the crags and rocky bottom. At one time, Delvin had said, this had been a prime haulout and feeding area. But the last few years walrus had been scarce.

He spotted a piece of white and darted over and triumphantly picked up a foot-long piece of a tusk. Score one piece of fossil ivory.

He began a systematic search, looking in the canyons between towering rocks, hugging the bottom, staying out of the current. He found more pieces of treasure, Eskimo money, currency in the villages, a piece of nature just to survive.

Perhaps it was a sixth sense, although he did not believe in such things. Or perhaps it was displacement in the water by a massive force, or maybe a gigantic shadow blotted out part of the sky. Whatever, the shock hit him with as much force as the twenty-nine-degree water when he'd dropped over the side. He rose up, whirling around, cursing the limited visibility of his mask.

The current caught him and he suddenly slammed into a rock and knocked his mask askew. He fumbled blindly and was swept around the rock. He kicked mightily, trying to hold his place. He fumbled with the mask, unable to feel with his gloves, trying to get it seated in his hood. His elbow smacked a rock. Ice water flooded his face and leaked into his nostrils. His vision blurred. He tried to purge. A shadow blotted the sky. Reed turned, one direction and then the other. The black of a four-foot tail disappeared from view.

Reed clawed for the bottom. Or was that just an illusion, his mind playing tricks? He sank to the bottom and seized a rock to hold him against the current. He purged the last bit of water from his mask. He laughed. Nice little world down here, out in the middle of the Bering Sea where no one could see and no one cared.

But at least he was warm. The cold pervading his entire being had dissipated.

He checked his pressure gauge, less than a thousand pounds. And he had maybe twenty-five pounds of ivory, a thousand dollars at Hawaiian prices. And that wasn't paying a middleman.

He glanced toward the gleaming underbelly of the surface. On a drift dive like this the boat was supposed to follow their bubbles. But he and Gordon had split. The surface was a gray, tossing cauldron with bubbles from waves crashing in on themselves.

And then a tank appeared out of the gloom, a broad, black beam five-feet across and coming at him with the force of a careening bus. His heart barely had time to stop. He scarcely could duck. The white markings beneath the jaw and just behind the eyes, a towering black fin, a body as long as a house. Reed rolled against the bottom. And then it clicked, killer whale. Orca!

Killer whales weren't known to attack humans. But they did eat sea lions and walrus, literally chasing them right up onto shore. The creatures roamed the world ranging all the way from the Antarctic to the Arctic, independent, wild and free. Clearly this was a hunting ground and this big fellow was on the prowl. A scuba diver and a sea lion were about the same size. Hadn't a killer whale ever made a mistake?

Oh yes, life was a joy. Once he escaped the bottom, the current would have him cold. What if they couldn't see him from the boat, sitting up there, framed in black outline against a silver sky, kicking, thrashing, a nice little piece of prey.

Besides which he was running out of air. Naughty boy, Reed thought, he hadn't been conserving these past few minutes. And still he waited, wondering if the whale would make another pass. That was one thing about blackwater diving, whatever came to get you, you didn't see it coming. Like a grizzly hurtling out of the brush.

Maybe the Orca would recognize him as a human being. Its brain was much bigger than human's. And they were incredibly smart. While some Orcas stripped black cod from long-line fishermen, others circled at a distance in order to decoy fishermen with rifles in the boats. Long-liners brought up their lines and had nothing but a bunch of heads.

One last circle, one last look in an area so restricted by visibility that he could not see either end of the creature when looking at the middle. He removed his regulator and tentatively blew a couple of breaths of air into the buoyancy compensator, something to account for the ivory. Then he let go of his perch and kicked toward the surface, keeping his arms out to his side, legs wide, anything to avoid looking like a sea lion. Once away from the reference of the bottom, the current seemed to ease, an illusion, he knew, just like the whale.

He surfaced, looking at a wide expanse of endless and tossing ocean. He was really dragging for air. He circled, bobbing. The island lay two hundred yards away. And there, not fifty yards away the aluminum boat. He bobbed beneath the surface. The tank was dry. He kicked as hard as he could, trying to get his head above the churning top, grab air and blow into his BC. One leg began to cramp. Water sloshed into his lungs and he began to cough and hag. He could barely get a breath to live, much less inflate his BC.

Weight belt, he had to dump the weights. A failure. They'd see it that way. He kicked harder. Another breath in the BC, and then another. It was puffed, all but inflated and still he rode low in the water. But he could breathe.

He waved his hand over his head. Delvin was standing in the boat, looking in his direction. He turned to the motor. Reed lay back, for the first time feeling the exhaustion. He glanced around, searching for a high black fin, dropping four feet into a trough, rising up, washed over by the slop, and then sinking down again. Just breathing was a struggle. He really should dump his weights, gain a little altitude at least.

The boat circled and then it moved away. Reed blinked and was blinded as a wave dumped over his head. He struggled in a trough, kicking up, straining to see. But the boat was sunk between waves. He could not tell. Two, three times, he rose up. There was no doubt. They were a quarter-mile away and he was steadily being washed out to sea.

The distance quickly increased. He spotted a third body in the boat, Gordon. They seemed to be just drifting, not even looking around.

He rose up on a crest. Salt spray, driven by the wind, blasted the back of his head like flying sand. He saw it clearly, a high black fin slicing the frothy ocean like the periscope of a submarine. Bessie, a prehistoric monster, a creature in its element, going about its business, a predator on the prowl. The fin passed between him and the boat. Reed kicked hard up on a crest, sending vibrations through the water, waving and shouting as loud as he could, useless noise dashed away by the wind.

And then he lay still, a tiny speck on a vast, tossing ocean. The fin had disappeared. For two waves in a row he could not see the boat. He'd freeze before he would drown, if he wasn't eaten before he froze. He giggled. Hypothermia, he knew the signs. He really should dump his weights, but that would be cowardly. He would not pass the test. Not even the bad guys would accept him then.

He was buried by a wave. A high-pitched whining filled the water. In Hawaii he'd heard whales sing. Did killer whales sing before an attack? New scientific discovery. He'd have to write a report. Maybe take up a new line of work.

A silver monster loomed. Reed whirled and kicked out like a mouse attacking a fox. The aluminum boat coasted to a stop. Grason reached down and grabbed the top of Reed's tank.

"I got you there, partner. Where the hell are you going, headed out to sea? There's a killer whale swimming around, or didn't you know."

"Here," Reed muttered. He coughed as water slopped into his mouth. "Take my weights. I saved my weights."

"Who cares about weights," Grason said. "Did you get any ivory? Gordon got a hundred pounds." He took the weights and set them into the bottom of the boat.

Reed handed Grason the net full of ivory and then his tank. He'd been liberated, unshackled, freed to move about with the ease of an eel. He took off his face mask and rinsed his face in the sea, momentarily savoring the blessing of even this icy water washing away the stickiness and clamminess that had gathered under his mask. He looked up to see that Gordon and Delvin were watching. The surliness of the two had disappeared. He'd joined the fraternity and, bobbing like a cork in the sea, he basked in their acceptance. He reached up his arm. Grason took him in his powerful grip and heaved him from the sea.

Reed crumbled in the bottom of the boat. He looked up and grinned. "Thanks, bud. Guess what? I got to touch a killer whale."

CHAPTER THIRTEEN

Even with an inch of neoprene wetsuit over his body core, Reed could not get warm. The hour ride back to Gambell took forever. His lips were blue, teeth chattering. Delvin and Gordon were amused. But he could scarcely concentrate on them. The war with the elements had taken its toll. His fixation was on his own misery, his own survival.

As soon as they beached the boat on the rocky shore, Grason took Reed in tow and they headed for a small ranch-style home where one of the Caucasian teachers rented out a room.

"The Keelachuck boys weren't looking too hard for you," Grason said. He held Reed's elbow, steering and holding him up. "If I wouldn't have been watching the fin of that killer whale I wouldn't have seen you out there either, just a tiny speck in all that glare. That current must have been terrific."

"You saved my life," Reed mumbled. His lips were so numb he could barely speak. He followed Grason into the teacher's home. The teacher, a dark-haired, athletic man named Dave Svacina, was immediately concerned.

"Just brew some good hot tea," Grason growled.

Reed sat down on a kitchen chair and, with Grason's assistance, struggled to peel his way out of the wetsuit.

He toweled off and slipped into dry shorts and a sweatshirt. After two cups of hot tea, Dave showed him to the bedroom where they had an electric blanket turned up high. Reed crawled under the covers. Almost instantly his shaking and battered body began to relax. He curled into the fetal position and put his hands over a stomach that was still cold to the touch. In the darkened gloom of the closed room, he glanced up at Grason's towering form. Grason's anguish was his anguish, destruction of the land, erosion of the pioneer spirit, a fixation with technology and materialism, a time of togetherness and family and a purpose in life somehow lost in his past. They were kindred spirits.

When he awoke a huge body lay tight against his side on the tiny double bed. Grason. Reed rolled. He stared at the wall. The shades were drawn and the room was bathed in a sickly yellow light. What the hell did he have here? Was Grason a major ivory poacher? Nothing seemed to fit.

He dozed.

Light flooded the room. Reed turned and blinked. Grason, fully dressed and wearing his sealskin vest, stood over the bed. "Well sunshine, you've had your ten hours. I took a little flight north. The pack ice is about thirty miles away, but I spotted a couple of nice herds of walrus. We're headed back out on the balmy Bering Sea. If you can stand it, I told the Keelachuck brothers you're coming along."

"Sure," Reed said, the instantaneous response, just as his instinct was to rise, to feel the tearing at worn muscles. He stifled a groan. A nauseating veil of black clouded his vision, lack of blood to his brain, almost enough to make him faint. He sat back on the edge of the bed. The memory returned, icy fingers of water eating into the marrow of his bones, salt brine clogging his lungs, a dark shadow blotting out the light. He leaned forward, elbows on his knees and inhaled deeply. At least he had the Keelachuck's trust; he had to build on that.

Reed stood and faced Grason. "I'll tell you one thing, I'm going to dress damn warm."

But not warm enough, Reed thought as they slammed over the icy waters. Spray flew, coating his parka, his face. Tiny rivulets ran their icy fingers down inside his neck. There were four of them in the boat: himself, Gordon, Delvin, and a man named Andrew. Grason rode in a second boat with three other Yupik. They were out of sight of land, two open boats boldly slamming out across an icy sea. One thing the Yupik did not lack was courage, Reed had to give them that.

It took almost two hours to reach the pack ice. The boat carried the latest in marine radios as well as a Loran satellite navigation system that Delvin used to home in on where Grason had spotted the walrus. And then they allowed for the drift of the pack ice.

They moved in among smaller cakes of ice and near the cracked and open edges of the pack. The two boats slowed, moving more than half a mile apart as they searched along the ice. Reed sat quietly, feeling Gordon and Delvin's mistrust, like the scuba dive had never taken place. It didn't make sense. The way these guys acted it would take years to gain their trust. Perhaps forever. Grason indicated he'd been dealing with them for three years. There was no sense of the camaraderie of the hunt, not like with Vitus and Jake.

Once Gordon stood over Reed. He was as tall as Grason, but not as muscular. He'd spent four years in the United States Marines. He knew the world. He'd returned home to Gambell and never left.

Reed looked up. When he moved the thin coating of ice cracked. He ignored the surliness, the unshakable attitude of a prejudiced man, and tried for an easy, friendly tone. "I'm damn sure glad I'm inside the boat instead of out. I can tell you that."

"What are you doing out here? You go hunting with Vitus and Jake, and now you come by us."

"Just enjoying myself and doing a little business," Reed said in a perfectly neutral tone. Gordon stared, just as Vitus had stared, unconfirmed suspicions.

Delvin responded to a voice on the radio. The others had located a herd of walrus. Gordon sat down and Delvin increased throttle.

Sure he was vulnerable, Reed thought, but the trick was not to let it show.

The walrus had hauled out through an interior lead with no direct access to the open sea. They pulled the boats up onto the ice and began a three-hundred-yard trek toward the waiting herd. Reed carried a 30-06 bolt action rifle and moved near the rear of a single file of eight men. With Delvin in the lead, they circled gray pools of rotten ice. In the pressure ridge to either side, the azure-blue edges of old ice presented startling contrast to surrounding grays and whites. The ice trembled and two hundred yards away a thin gray water-fog formed as a marker over the new lead. The wind blew steady, a constant rustling across the snow and over the ice.

Reed could not escape the dread, the sickness in his guts at the slaughter he knew would follow. He trailed ten feet behind Grason's broad back. That Grason carried a Kalashnikov AK-47 fully automatic rifle with a thirty-shot banana clip he could not fathom. He'd even mentioned it as they unloaded the boat. "Plenty of firepower, Terry."

Grason hadn't taken offense. "Strictly business here," Grason explained. "Forgetting the pretend, expediting the end. You go with what gets you the most. This isn't hunting, so why pretense. The walrus are dead, we're just taking ivory before it rots on the bottom of the sea."

"That's what I'm after," Reed said with an upbeat tone.

Of course there were rumors that walrus herds had been machine gunned. Nothing confirmed, stories of the North, once told and repeated a hundred-fold until the repetition gave them the basis of fact.

A bellowing, like that of an enraged bull, thundered from just beyond an ice ridge to their front. The bellow echoed across the hard ice and snow like a foghorn booming a warning in the night. Reed opened his parka. The hike had built up plenty of warmth.

Fifty yards away the walrus came into view. Ayvek, the brown earth. Walrus, normally gray when in the water, usually turned brown and even slightly pink when hauled out and their thick hides and inches of fat were exposed to even moderately warm sunlight and air. The men spread into a line, a single wave like a rifle squad making an assault. They crouched, approaching close to fifty walrus.

Step by step, fully exposed, the men moved across the ice, crouched, rifles held cross arm and ready to shoot. The herd stirred. A massive two-thousand-pound bull, with thirty-inch tusks and with hide on the wrinkled neck two inches thick, rose on his front flippers and gave a thunderous bellow. The herd shifted uneasily but not one walrus tried for the water.

Thirty yards away, point-blank range. Reed willed himself to be cold, mechanical, look for the end, the ultimate goal, stopping the slaughter once and for all. The big disappointment was Grason. The man's behavior just didn't make any sense.

Gordon raised his rifle. The others followed in line. Eight rifles roared, two on full automatic. Instant pandemonium swept the herd, lunging, grunting, bellowing brown, mists of blood spraying into the air, the hard splat of bullets, some misplaced and unable to even penetrate the hide. In the midst of the melee, Reed picked out a bull, aiming for the pockmark of the ear behind the eyes. The rifle bucked even as the bull's head slammed sideways and he slumped onto the ice.

Within a second some walrus, some wounded and some unscathed, were splashing into the water and further confusing the scene. A huge bull bolted in panic, slamming over everything in its path, crushing a confused yearling and following gyrating and panicked bodies into a frothing sea.

Within seconds it was over. What walrus could had escaped into the sea, surfacing here and there, angrily looking back at the lifeless forms of members of their herd. Some moved in with the wounded, one on either side as they shepherded them along the closed lead. A large bull surfaced nearby and stared at its attackers. Its tusks gleamed against the dark water, the bristles on its snout seemingly stiff with rage. Gordon raised his rifle and fired, encasing the head in a frothy, pink spray. He turned to look at Reed, but Reed had seen the move and casually looked away.

He felt a trembling, the raging of his blood. A few more shots exploded, unnatural thunderclaps in a silent world of white, tiny lead projectiles finishing off those wounded lying on the ice.

And then it was over. The ice ran red with blood. The acrid odor of cordite flared the nostrils, memories of Vietnam, human beings slaughtered thusly, human beings upon human beings. The men moved in, adding up the count. They had thirteen dead, a nice day's work, but easily that many more had been killed or wounded and sank into the sea. Head hunting, a travesty to wildlife, an abomination on nature and the outdoors. And he'd been a part.

"Damn, only thirteen. I thought we'd have that entire herd," Reed said to Grason. He sounded disappointed and noticed Gordon shrug and turn away. Perhaps, just perhaps Gordon was buying the act.

They began the process of cutting off the tusks. A small chainsaw made the bloody work easier. To Reed's surprise they cut off several flippers and dragged two dead calves back to the boats.

"We'll send villagers back for the rest of the meat," Gordon pointedly said to Reed. "No wasteful hunting here."

The suspicions never ended, Reed thought. He shrugged. "Hey, I just want the tusks."

But of course the Keelachuck brothers would not sell Reed the tusks. Nor would they sell Grason the tusks. Altona had flown a small commercial airplane from Nome to the village. Grason talked to Altona who walked back and forth from the gravel yard to the kitchen and negotiated a price. And when the sum was agreed, Reed handed the money to Grason, who handed it to Altona who then paid the Keelachuck brothers for the ivory, one Native selling raw ivory to another Native, all perfectly legal under the guidelines of the Marine Mammal Act. The criminal here was Altona, mother of three, selling to Grason, and of course Grason out killing walrus, buying from a Native and then selling to him. All nice and clean, Reed thought. But he had none of it on tape.

Eventually they loaded the ivory into wooden trunks and used an ATV to drive to the single-runway airport. As was too often the case, St. Lawrence Island had been enclosed by fog.

"I'd wait but I have some clients I have to ferry out to the fish camps," Grason said. He turned to Altona in the back seat. "At least you don't have to close your eyes, Altona, there's nothing to see anyhow."

"How are you going to follow the runway?" Reed asked. "You can't even see the end of the wings."

"Do I detect a note of fear?" Grason kidded. "No, this is just like being in the air, just follow the compass, instrument takeoff all the way. Besides, there's nothing much to hit, one tower."

"Bastard," Reed said and Grason laughed.

"Actually it isn't the fog that will get you, it's the icing." They hurtled down the runway, completely blind. Grason eased back on the stick and without Reed fully realizing the difference, he understood they were in the air. Twenty miles out they broke into brilliant sunlight. They climbed and were soon gazing at the top of carpets of clouds and an occasional glimpse of a dark-blue sea. It had been quite a few days, Reed thought. Into the throat of the whale, as it were. He leaned back, sitting in companionable silence.

"I'll be busy this afternoon and tomorrow morning," Grason said. "But if you want to stay on a few days we could fly out to where you can catch a four- or five-pound rainbow every other cast."

"Sounds like a deal. Pewter will kill me, but the ivory will take care of that, give her shopping money."

Reed glanced at Grason, a fading icon of the North. The man filled the cockpit, huge hands, solid craggy jawline, thick curled hair, a man bigger than life. But somehow sensitive, somehow aware. Even participating in the slaughter, Grason was aware of his role, the exploiter, expeditiously giving in to that which he loathed.

The Keelachuck brothers were the ones, Reed thought, the real exploiters. Grason knew that. They could work as a team, plea bargain Terry and get him on the team.

Reed felt the hollow pain inside his guts when he pictured himself revealing his identity to Grason. That'd be a trick. How the hell does a man turn on his friend?

CHAPTER FOURTEEN

That Pewter came to Grason's house made Reed furious. They'd made no plans, no contingencies. Who the hell had authorized such a move? He stood in the varnished, open-air living room and watched as Pewter climbed out of a taxi. His hands were covered with fish slime from the several king salmon lying on the kitchen counter.

"Looks like your gal came chasing," Grason had said. "Sometimes that's good. It shows they care. Then again it could be bad, shows they're possessive, a good thing to know before you tie the knot. A man needs his space. Jeri understood that with me from day one. That's why we got on so good. She knew she had to adjust."

Reed glanced at the filet knife and his hands.

"Go wash off. I'll get the door," Grason said. "Fresh grilled salmon and a glass of wine will be just the ice cube she needs."

Reed quickly soaped and rinsed his hands. He even glanced in a mirror and ran a comb through his hair. He needed a shower and it had been a few days since he'd last shaved around and trimmed his beard. How to play this, he wondered, for Grason's benefit or Pewter's? She shouldn't be here. She had to know that.

"Beautiful place," Pewter said to Grason. Reed entered the living room. Pewter crossed the tongue-and-groove wood floor, her sloe-brown eyes looking dead into his. Reed could not read a thing. "Hello, honey." She embraced him warmly, a genuine hug such as he hadn't felt in ten years. Her lean, athletic body pressed into his and in spite of his irritation he felt a stirring in his loins. Pewter stepped back and looked at Grason.

"You two talk," Grason said. "I'll get at those fish, get a couple of salmon steaks going on the grill." He strode into the kitchen.

Grason understood, Reed thought; he knew what life was about. Reed turned on Pewter. He spoke in a low hiss. "What are you doing up here?"

Pewter did not lower her voice. "You've been gone ten days and not a word. If we're going to be a couple you better start acting right."

Reed stared, searching for some signal, some indicator to show her game. All he saw was anger, brought up after such a nice warm hug. He spoke a little louder. Perhaps Grason could hear. "I told you before, you don't tell me what to do."

"No, I don't. But you can't ignore me and expect a relationship. And forget about your ivory also. Those are my contacts, my friends."

"Dammit, I'm having a good time. Is it a crime for a man to enjoy life?"

"It is if he hurts others in the process. But then you should know all about that."

The bitterness was real and Reed could only wonder wherein came the act. "Maybe I have been a little selfish," he allowed. "Grason knows Alaska. He was showing me a good time. I've got almost three hundred pounds of ivory. Maybe later you could take a look. You might want to hold out a few pieces for yourself."

"And then we're heading out," Pewter said in a neutral tone.

"In the morning," Grason said from the kitchen door. "Salmon steaks and wine tonight. You guys can have the master bedroom. Great place to makeup. In the morning I'll fix you the biggest breakfast you've ever seen. Then I have to pick up some clients at the airport."

"Sounds good," Reed said. He glanced at Pewter for confirmation.

"Sure," Pewter replied with perfect modulation. "Just don't think one kiss and a glass of wine makes everything all right."

Grason turned his head, concealing a smile.

By nine o'clock the next morning, Reed and Pewter were driving south. Reed was exhausted. It had been a long, tense night lying next to Pewter and not being able to touch her or to at least talk freely, get to the bottom of her visit. But she'd seemingly slept like a baby, barely stirring for the entire night. When he had leaned close and tried to talk, she'd simply placed a hand on his chest and pushed him away. "Later."

It was infuriating, she could be so warm and so much in control it was almost cold. But the anger was genuine. How she actually felt toward him Reed did not have a clue.

They drove in silence. She'd gotten him out, but now what, Pewter wondered? How could she feel any attraction to a man who infuriated her so much? He was so damn self-assured, practical to the point of boredom, without a hint of romance. And yet he could seem so warm, so talkative, although now he'd turned to stone. He was the most experienced agent in Special Operations, a man without a hint of fear. What she couldn't tell him, what she, the rookie, couldn't tell anyone, was that she didn't trust his judgment. He'd gone off, and no one seemed to know.

Get out, her mind screamed. Even if Reed was solid, undercover wasn't for her. He was right about that, yet he was the guy who invited her in. The only problem was, he needed her help.

They were twenty miles south of Fairbanks before Reed felt compelled to speak. "You came on awful strong."

"We had to get you out of there."

"Did something break?"

"We thought so."

"What?"

"You."

Pewter's hands shook. Her voice quavered. Reed was shocked to see such fear, at him. He tried to be easy, but already the anger was starting to build. "That's a bunch of bull. Who put you up to this?"

Pewter kept her hands on the steering wheel, eyes straight ahead. "No one."

"No one? You decided this on your own, the rookie operative."

Pewter whirled. "Don't pull that rookie crap on me. It wasn't entirely on my own. It was all of us. But I concurred, wholeheartedly. You're hanging with Grason like he's your only friend in the world."

"He is," Reed shouted. He looked away in embarrassment. Why did he say that? She'd take it out of context, the wrong way. He had to explain, he knew and spoke in a softer voice. "In a way. That's the only way you get in with these guys, be one of them."

"But maybe you've gone too far. Maybe you don't really see the slaughter that's going on."

"I saw the slaughter, I was there. I even participated."

"And what do you think of Grason now?" Pewter demanded.

Reed stared out the window. It was a bright, clear and sunny day. They were nearing Denali and he could see some of the foothills of the Alaska Range. He spoke softly, "Grason's had some tough times lately. Getting at the Keelachuck brothers is just about impossible. I don't know if we could make a wasteful hunting charge stick or not. I'll get Grason to cooperate, plea bargain him and maybe we can get the Keelachuck brothers that way. We just have to give it a little more time."

"You know what the state troopers said about Grason after his son was killed. He was a wild man."

"That was his kid for Chrissakes! Grason knows the wholesale slaughter of walrus is wrong. With what's gone on in his life he's lost his perspective."

"He's lost perspective, what about you? I haven't been kept informed. I've been alone. I've been ignored. Doug is curt at best. You pretend I don't exist.

What happened to your promise of fair play and teamwork?"

"I was making progress."

"And you couldn't keep me informed?"

"The situation didn't permit it. It's not that black and white out here."

"And now what? You want to plea bargain Vitus and then Grason? You wonder if I have the capacity to kill. How about you? Can you arrest Terry Grason?"

Reed responded hotly. "Look, if you want out of this goddamn case, go ahead. It might be for the best."

"You bastard. That's your reply? Kick me away. Pull rank because I pose a question or two. No, I don't allow that any more. I've got my life. It isn't much but it's mine. And I've got my career, my job. Or at least maybe I had a career. Now I don't know. Maybe I can't go out on the ice slaughtering walrus left and right. I admit that. But I have a role. We could be a team. I have needs. Maybe I couldn't admit that before. But no, you pick Grason instead."

"I didn't pick Terry," Reed said tiredly.

"No? Then just what the hell have you been doing the last ten days?"

"Go to hell," Reed said. "Just go to hell."

"Yeah, good reply," Pewter said. She fell silent. They drove in silence down the long straight road. Dark green foliage covered both sides, the Alaskan Range gleamed off to their right. She didn't understand. He'd given his life to the department, case after case. Sure they weren't all orthodox and didn't end up getting the arrest teams together, heading out at dawn and making dozens of simultaneous arrests. The more complicated the case, the messier it could be. Besides, the bottom line was that he got the job done, never mind the method. Peter knew that, which was why he got free rein, why he called the shots. Doug and Rich knew that as well. They just had to be reminded as to who the hell was in charge, Reed thought grimly. If there was going to be a break in ranks, he'd lead the damn charge.

* * *

Classical music boomed through every corner of the house, Beethoven's Fifth Symphony, music with power and anger, unrelenting highs and lows that played to the human spirit. Or what used to be the human spirit, Grason thought. He sat on his sofa, martini in hand, a large wolf skin rug at his feet, one of the Savage wolf pack out of Denali, a touch of revenge after they'd murdered Jeff.

He'd run the pack in deep snow, using the Super Cub and buckshot. He'd taken all but the last one, watching it run, tearing along the top of a ridge with sheer sides. He could see the ridge ended. There was no place to go. Still the wolf tore, breath billowing in the frigid air, huge bounds even though he'd been running for half an hour. Grason crabbed the airplane into the wind, all but hovering a hundred feet above the wolf.

There was no hesitation, not even a look. The wolf reached the cliff and leapt right off the end, pawing at the air, snow and wolf falling through a clear, bright sky. It disappeared in the drifted snow below. Grason circled back. Amazingly the wolf struggled up out of the drift. He laid the shotgun out the open window. And then he pulled it back. It'd be a shame to kill an animal that made a run and then a jump like that. He watched as the frightened creature disappeared into the spruce forest, the last of his pack.

He hadn't killed a wolf since, Grason thought. Such intelligent creatures. You could watch and see them figuring, just like bears. But they were doomed, just like the Eskimo, just like the walrus, just like the Alaska of old. There were no more pioneers, just fat cats from down south with lots of money to pay three thousand dollars for a carved walrus tusk or twelve thousand dollars for a bear and then pretend. Which was why they should quit the charade, Grason thought. Put all the animals in a zoo, Eskimos as well. Hell, it was during the twentieth century that they'd put African pygmies in an American zoo, just so people could gawk.

Grason glanced at the clock. Clients were landing at the airport in ten minutes. He'd be late. Or maybe he wouldn't go at all. He sipped his martini. Maybe he'd give them a few thrills on the flight out to the fishing camp, a few bumps, some wing-over turns, a sharp drop down to the water. Or delay takeoff like he sometimes did, barely clear the trees, maybe pick up a couple of limbs. They came to Alaska to experience "The Last Frontier." He'd show them the last frontier.

The telephone rang. Grason sat motionless. He stared around the empty room. Music boomed. He had all the material possessions in the world, everything Jeri loved. He stood, turned off the music and picked up the telephone. "Yeah?"

"Grason, this is Gordon Keelachuck."

"Yeah. You get more ivory?"

"We've been thinking about your friend. Did you know he was out here earlier in the year hunting with Vitus Inokenti. He bought ivory from Vitus."

Grason stood silently. What the hell was he supposed to make of that? He knew Reed was shopping around.

Gordon continued. "We've seen all this before. Remember Operation Whiteout. Agents set up a gift shop in Anchorage. They bought fresh ivory.

It's only been a few years and already people forget. The young men get blinded by drugs and greed and forget to be careful. You are not a young man."

"You're getting on there yourself," Grason said. "I checked Reed up one side and down the other. Even called out to Hawaii to check on his gal. She used to carve out there. You can't fake that attitude. No agents I know are that tough. Besides, they know what would happen if they sent an officer out with me. I've told state troopers."

"It's your life. But next time come alone."

"Yeah, sure," Grason said. He hung up the telephone. He stared at a framed black and white picture of him and Jeri standing in front of a Cessna 170, the first airplane he'd ever owned. He'd had everything a man could ask for, the wilderness, a home, family. For ten years there he'd never touched a drink, not even with clients who came to Alaska and stayed drunk the entire time.

Kurth Breismeister and Vitus had dealt together for years. He placed a long distance call. Wynona answered the telephone, a milk-white looker with a mouth, he recalled. He hadn't liked her much. She was suspicious, evasive. Kurth was up in Nome.

Grason gently cradled the telephone. His clients had been on the ground ten minutes now. The hell with it, he thought. He'd dump them at the camp. Brian Mosby could handle things from there. It was time to make a flight.

* * *

Vitus Inokenti and Kurth Breismeister drove up to the yellow-painted post office in Nome. They walked around and Kurth opened the back of the Bronco. It was a bright, sunny day and a raw wind whipped dust and a fine salt mist down the wide main street. A blue and white bus filled with tourists, mostly older people, pulled out of the Nugget Inn and passed down the street headed for the gold dredging field north of town. The two men manhandled a heavy box to the back of the vehicle.

"You won't regret this, Vitus," Kurth said.

"I already have," Vitus mumbled.

"Hey, I gave you the extra thousand, up front."

"And you still owe me nineteen thousand," Vitus said. "Some of it for two years now. My family has to eat also. My daughter needs braces. All this money goes for that. I keep nothing."

A huge shadow blotted the pale, northern sun. Vitus recoiled like a rabbit from the shadow of a hawk. He all but lost his grip on the box as he turned to look up at Grason's grim face.

ESKIMO MONEY

"Heavy load. Must be shipping a little ivory, eh, boys."

"What are you doing here?" Kurth asked in a harsh voice. He nervously glanced up and down the street.

"Don't you think you're being a little bold here? There's a fish and wildlife agent right downstairs. She might come up and nab your ass."

"You can't open the mail without probable cause," Kurth said. "Besides, she's out flying patrol. One agent within nine hundred miles. People know every move she makes."

Grason leaned over the box as if to check the label. "I thought you were buying for yourself these days, Vitus. After all the times Kurth stiffed you, I'm surprised you're still dealing with him."

"I pay my debts," Kurth said. His blue eyes flashed and his tanned face twisted with anger. But he kept his tone neutral.

"What the hell is this?" Grason asked. He pointed at the address on the box. "The Rare Species shop? You're shipping to them?"

"You know them?" Kurth said.

"Word is they've been trying to do business with a lot of folks."

Kurth set the box back in the vehicle. He glanced at Vitus, questioning, and then Grason. "These are the same. But I had a connection in Anchorage check them out. That shop's been there ten years. The gal has a history doing scrimshaw. I had them at my house, got them in the hot tub. We went through their things. There were no recorders. I'm sure they're clean." But his voice lacked conviction.

"What about you, Vitus?" Grason asked. "Have they been after you direct or have you just been going through Kurth?"

Vitus mumbled without looking Grason in the eyes. "We went hunting. Reed is a very good hunter. I sold him some ivory as well."

"And I'll bet he asked to buy from other people as well. And he hinted around asking who supplied you."

Vitus did not reply. He looked past the yellow building and at the nearby Bering Sea. A half-mile offshore a ferry anchored while supplies were transported onto shore by a launch. There were no outside roads to Nome, or many other villages of the north. During the short-lived summers, ferryboats carried in bulk supplies. A sea gull dove into the water and surfaced with a small fish in its mouth. Kurth had called, begging for ivory, promising extra payment on old bills. And now this.

"Just like I thought," Grason growled. "We've got a problem, guys. The question is, what are we going to do about it?"

"I checked them up and down. I'm sure they're clean," Kurth argued. He walked in a small circle, put one leg up on the rear bumper, took it down and repeated his circle.

"Well, I guess we'd better verify that, don't you think?"

"I already did. I told you," Kurth said in a voice with little conviction.

A green, dust-covered Suburban taxi passed. Old Joe Pasterwald waved at Vitus. Joe was from Gambell, a sometime walrus hunter and ivory carver. Joe had moved to Nome to find more steady work. Joe was a cousin to Lulu. He once hunted with Jake. He might mention seeing him, Vitus thought, standing on the street with Kurth Breismeister and Terry Grason. Jake wouldn't say anything, Vitus knew. But he would have his thoughts.

Down the street, near the gray walls of the Board of Trade Saloon, Dan Jenkins leaned unsteadily against the wall and brayed unintelligible shouts at the passing world. Vitus turned his head in shame, why couldn't Dan keep himself in his little, dark hovel of an apartment where tourists could not see? With some people Dan would be the only man they'd see, the only man they'd recall.

"What do you think?" Grason yelled at Vitus. He seized his coat and jerked his arm.

Vitus jerked away. "Reed is a very good hunter. He understands animals, the hunt. A good hunter is honest, a man you can trust."

"Jesus Christ, Vitus, most fish and wildlife agents are good hunters. That's the way they were born. They just think they know too much and they've gotten too good. I know you don't have much, Vitus, but they'll take every damn thing you have. Of course maybe that will be good. You'll make the papers. Out in the villages you'll be famous, especially with your elders, those holier-than-thou old farts hanging onto the past."

"We can't stand here like this," Kurth interrupted.

"Let's go back to your room," Grason said. Kurth looked at the heavy box. "Well don't ship it for Christ's sake. Bring it back. You can use that as bait."

Kurth frowned. He exchanged a glance with Vitus. But Vitus simply shrugged as if there was nothing he could do. Kurth pushed the box back into the vehicle and closed the back.

Vitus climbed into the Bronco beside Kurth who was nervously jerking his head from side to side and talking at a rapid pace, wondering on Grason's accusations, wondering on how much dealing Vitus had done directly with the Rare Species Shop, wondering on how Vitus could betray him and take one of his customers behind his back.

Vitus let Kurth talk, just as he let Grason talk once they reached the small hotel room. The argument raged. At a minimum they should entice

Reed and Pewter back up north, promise them the ivory and a couple of polar bear hides, Grason said.

"What good will that do?" Kurth asked. He was whining, clearly uncertain of how to save himself.

The first man to abandon a sinking ship, Vitus thought, but then he'd always known that about Kurth.

Grason shouted as if at a child, "If they're coming to make a buy they'll be taped. If we have to strip them naked, we'll strip them naked."

"I did that with the hot tub," Kurth said.

"They knew what you were up to. If they had a recorder they hid it. Or maybe the first time or two they didn't have one. If they know they're making a buy they'll be bugged. Those bastards are sneaky as hell. They don't hesitate to lie and cheat. Honesty isn't part of their name. That's why they work for the government." Grason did not grin at his joke.

"So what if they're agents? There's nothing we can do."

"You get someone up here in deep Alaskan wilderness and there are a million accidents waiting to happen. Damn near a hundred tourists a year lose their lives to accidents up here — bears, falls from cliffs, drownings, airplane accidents. There are a lot of ways you can die."

"Are you nuts?" Kurth demanded hotly. "You'd murder someone over ivory? Pay the fine. Jesus, if they're agents other people will know they came to see us, accidents or not."

"I'm just kidding, Kurth," Grason hissed in anger at Kurth's tone. "The point is if we know these guys are agents we can save ourselves a bundle. When they raid us we'll be clean. We can transfer assets, your bank accounts, your boat, my airplane. Otherwise they confiscate all that. Every time these guys buy they add more charges. You're not going to get a two-thousand-dollar fine like some drunken Eskimo selling ivory in a bar. You're looking at jail time. Five years. And they won't just break your piggy bank, Kurth. They'll break your back."

"It's not going to prove anything," Kurth argued.

"You going to keep selling to them?"

"I don't know."

"Well, there you go then. If they're not agents we keep on selling. Apparently they can use the ivory. If you have a secondary market you can hold the line on price. We've all got a good thing going, as long as we don't undercut each other on price."

Kurth looked at Vitus. "What do you think?"

Vitus shook his head in the negative. "No. It is not a good idea."

"What the hell would you know, Vitus?" Grason roared. "Don't you understand that you're losing everything? These people are taking your life away just like they took away mine. So your answer is what, bury your head in the sand?" Vitus shrugged.

The argument raged for more than an hour. Kurth slowly came around; he would like to know so he could transfer assets, fix his records, dispose of as much incriminating evidence as possible. Eventually they agreed. Kurth would invite Reed and Pewter north for a promised Bering Sea ride on his boat. He'd take Vitus to help collect fossil ivory along the beach. There would be time. They'd go through everything Reed and Pewter brought with them.

It was dishonest, Vitus thought. A betrayal. But if they were agents, and if Jake learned of his transgressions he'd never be invited on another hunt. It would be the end.

Vitus looked at Grason. There was something about the man, the way he carried himself, the quiet force in his voice, something serious, deadly, like a man with an absence of fear.

"I just want the news," Grason said as if reading Vitus's mind. He spoke without threat, without malice. "I'll be on standby. Ideally you don't even want them to know you're looking. That'll give us the most time to react. It'll take them a couple of weeks to set up a raid. Just don't take anything illegal on the boat. That way they can't make a case to confiscate that."

"Yeah. You're right there," Kurth said. He sounded pleased and relieved at the course of action. "At least then we know, one way or the other. Otherwise, well hell, we just couldn't go on."

Vitus nodded agreement. Reed had been his friend. He'd taken him hunting with his family. He'd been so polite, silently taking his place as a guest, fitting in like a man who had been on many hunts. Was it all a ruse? Perhaps Grason was right, Vitus thought. A man to whom he'd given his trust had betrayed him. And suddenly Vitus felt sad. But he also felt rage — he, Vitus Inokenti, a man who never felt rage.

142   **ESKIMO MONEY**

CHAPTER FIFTEEN

The first inkling that things were not right came when Reed and Pewter stepped onto Kurth's thirty-eight-foot boat in Nome. *The Escape* was a ten-year-old Viking convertible with twin two-hundred-forty-horsepower diesel motors. Duel-control consoles were located in the main cabin and on an overhead bridge. "If you close her down tight she can take a lot of water," Kurth said. He was eager to show them around, like an adolescent with a new automobile. "She has an extra heavy keel so she can roll a good sixty degrees and still come back right. Of course I don't know how the people inside her would do."

For running the windy and stormy Bering Sea it appeared barely serviceable, Reed thought. He briefly wondered at Kurth's seamanship. Kurth grew up the son of a fisherman, but there was a lot of difference from being a deck hand to running a boat on waters potentially as dangerous as the Bering Sea.

Reed greeted Wynona, painted as usual with rouge, eyeliner, and bright red lipstick. She wasn't dressed for the icy ocean as she wore thin black slacks to match her black hair. Her clean, long fingers were cool, almost bloodless. Her eyes were direct, probing, and there was a discernable bitterness to her attitude. Perhaps from being out on the boat, Reed thought. And then she stepped aside and Vitus Inokenti emerged from below deck.

"You know Vitus?" Kurth said.

"Sure," Reed said easily. "We went walrus hunting together." Except for Vitus who did not seem to want to look him in the eye, they were watching his every move. He did not glance at Pewter. She was on her own. They'd continued their argument in Anchorage with Doug and Rich. It was him against three, him against the world. Taking on Stacy and Trish and of course Pam as well. Pewter, Doug and Rich were all for closing down the case, taking what they had. Reed flatly refused. It was painful, having to pull rank. He'd never pulled rank on Doug, never before. And Pewter, he'd expected more support.

Kurth continued, "If we're going to cruise the coast searching for beached carcasses, I thought an extra hand would help. Besides, it's legal for Vitus to take and sell all the beached ivory he wants."

"The more the merrier," Reed said. "I've seen Vitus work. When it comes to walrus, he knows what he's doing." He took his handgrip, Pewter her suitcase, and they trailed Kurth and Wynona into the main cabin.

"This is really nice," Pewter said. She spun around with the easy movement of a woman without a care. Only Reed could see the tightness in the lines at the corners of her eyes, the way she clenched her purse. She took in the brightly polished brass fixtures, the teakwood-trimmed Formica countertop and table, the white leather seats in the booth. The interior was paneled in light-colored sen wood. A touch of greenery in the form of clean, silk flowers and plants added to the decor. "This is just like home."

"This is only the second time we brought *The Escape* north," Wynona said. "I like it better down south in Prince William Sound. You're protected there."

"Honey, I know this ocean," Kurth said.

"There are six-foot swells out there," Wynona said.

"Four to six," Kurth corrected.

"Six-foot," Wynona said. "You want a Dramamine patch, honey?" she asked Pewter.

"I should be all right," Pewter said.

"I'll take one," Reed said. "Can't afford to be sick on a great trip like this."

Pewter's eyes flashed at the lecturing tone.

"What's that cooking?" Reed asked. "Smells great."

"I'm baking some halibut. A few weeks ago Kurth caught one that weighed one hundred and eighty pounds."

They trailed Kurth down the narrow hallway where he showed them the head and then their bunk. "It's cozy," Kurth said suggestively, "that's what makes it fun. Why don't you store your gear in the drawers under the bunk then come on out for a beer and some halibut, and then I'll show you my electronics and the powerhouse."

"Sounds great," Reed said with a note of excitement. "This is a great layout. A boat like this must really cost."

"I got a deal," Kurth said with the eagerness of a man obliged to describe his every conquest. "Heck, you get down the coast in Florida or California, boat thievery is big business. Especially for drug runners. They use the boat one time and then dump it. But they do steal for retail also. They get fake titles. If a boat's wrecked, they buy a salvage boat of the same type and switch papers. It happens a lot."

"So this is a hot boat."

Kurth shrugged and winked. "Not according to the paperwork the guy gave me. And I sure as hell wasn't going to call him a liar, not at that price. Of course you have to know what you're doing, or they'll just take your money and run."

As Kurth departed their cabin Reed looked at Pewter and frowned. Was Vitus' presence a reason for alarm? Or was Vitus along just to make the gathering temporarily legal and to assist in cutting tusks off bloated carcasses? It did make sense to have some help. Reed touched the small box of the new Nagra recorder taped to his chest. Pewter understood, if they found the recorder they were finished.

The room was narrow, one bunk where they could squeeze together and barely enough room to turn around. Reed knelt on the floor and pulled out a drawer. Pewter placed her suitcase on the bunk and knelt beside him. "What do you think?" she asked.

Reed whispered in her ear. "It could be legit. Play the role to the hilt. If we have to take them, well," he shrugged. He lingered, smelling her perfume, her clean washed hair. From less than six inches away Pewter looked in his eyes. He was the experienced agent. He knew the ropes. Now, up here on the high seas, far from any possible backup, far even from the eyes of witnesses, she could not conceal her doubts.

Reed rose. A moment before he'd been excited, keyed. Now he was filled with unease. They were supposed to be a team.

They cruised north, headed for the Bering Strait, the fifty-six-mile stretch of water separating the United States from Russia. By late afternoon they'd cruised as far north as the Diomede Islands which were all but astride the International Date Line. The dark line of what had once been the Soviet Union lay clearly visible to the west.

"The Russians have tens of thousands of pounds of walrus and mammoth ivory just waiting for market," Kurth said. "They've already tried to smuggle ivory into the U.S. Hell they even process walrus meat commercially. If things keep opening up, one of these days I'm going to put in over there and establish some contacts. I wanted Wynona to learn Russian, but she isn't keen on that."

"You learn Russian," Wynona retorted. "They put you in a jail in Siberia and you'll stay the rest of your life."

Kurth laughed. "Wynona worries too much."

"I've got a lot to worry about," Wynona said vehemently. She glared at Reed.

Something was not right, Reed thought, a notion that would not leave.

After they passed the Bering Strait, Kurth turned northeast and bore in toward the barrier coast of sand and gravel beaches that sealed off interior lagoons and northern tundra. "If all goes well, tonight we'll anchor on the Arctic Circle."

"Sounds good," Reed said. While Kurth drove, he and Vitus stood on the bridge, bundled against the cold wind and braced against the rolling of the boat while they glassed the beach looking for walrus carcasses that had floated ashore. Now, as the pack ice receded north, the walrus hunting season was winding down. Those walrus that had been struck and lost in the ocean depths built up gases and eventually came to the surface. If winds and currents were favorable the carcasses would be pushed to shore. Carcasses like those they'd taken with Grason and were unable to recover before they sank.

There were more walrus that ended up this way than people realized, Reed knew. In 1988 one Fish and Wildlife aerial survey that extended from Wales to Point Barrow spotted 418 walrus carcasses, all but three of which were headless. A 1989 survey spotted 227 carcasses. Villagers in four-wheelers drove the beaches looking for carcasses. Others with Super Cubs searched from the air. And of course there were those in boats, men like Kurth Breismeister.

Time passed. The relentless lurching of the boat up and down the waves began to wear. Thin sheets of ice formed on the white deck, on railings and windows. The freezing spray, wind and cold worked underneath their layers of clothes. Reed and Kurth made frequent trips into the warm sanctuary of the cabin for cups of hot coffee. Only Vitus seemed impervious to the elements.

They began to spot the occasional gray mound of a walrus carcass on desolate beaches. Most times they could tell if the head had been harvested. On occasion they spotted a grizzly bear working a thick-hided carcass for a meal. Sea gulls and jaegers soared on the icy winds searching for a meal. Small flocks of fast-moving eider ducks barreled past low over the water. For hours on end they moved up the coast and did not see one sign of human habitation.

Once, toward two carcasses, they launched the small Zodiac hard-bottomed rubber raft that had been secured across the bow. Vitus started the fifteen-horsepower motor and crossed over shallow sandbars and quickly saw that the tusks had already been harvested.

"I hope there isn't another boat in front of us," Kurth muttered, "or I'll have to sink the sonofabitch." He checked his radar. "It only has a twenty-mile range. I don't see anything. Mostly I use it for navigation, as long as I'm close to land."

Two hours later, after passing several more headless carcasses, they spotted four carcasses spread the length of a barrier island. At least two of them had tusks. "Four-wheelers can't get out here," Kurth chortled. "We're going to hit it now. I can feel it in my bones."

They anchored *The Escape* with bow into the wind and waves. Reed, Pewter, Kurth and Vitus crowded into the Zodiac and headed for shore. Kurth was elated. "Say ten pounds of tusks on each walrus. Fifty dollars a pound. That's two thousand dollars laying there."

"Who said we're paying fifty dollars a pound," Reed said.

"Asshole," Kurth said with a grin. He ducked from an icy spray. "Sixty degrees down in Nome. You get up here near the ice fields and on the Chukchi Sea and the temperature drops twenty degrees."

"That's why I wore my red flannels," Reed shouted.

They bore into the beach. Kurth, wearing hip boots, jumped into the water and hauled the raft up onto the chewed rock and gravel.

"Boy, that's a beaut," Kurth said. They stood beside the two-thousand-pound carcass of a bull walrus. The thick skin was wrinkled and gray like a collapsed dirigible. "Nothing's touched this baby."

"Thirty-six-inch tusks," Vitus said. He held a small chainsaw at the ready.

"Better watch out, flesh will fly," Kurth said. "I'll go look at this other one up the beach. Reed, you and Pewter can walk down and check out those other two. If a bear comes let him have the carcass. Vitus can run him off with the chainsaw."

"Yeah, right," Reed said. He and Pewter started down the beach, which consisted of millions of rocks worn flat and rounded by waves and crushing ice. They leaned forward into the blistering wind.

After several minutes Reed felt obliged to speak. "This is great. This is what I like about this job, walking a beach on the Chukchi Sea up near the Arctic Circle. Virtually no one around. This is what life is all about, out with nature, being a part."

"It should be fun," Pewter said. "This is why I took this job, for minutes like this." She looked at Reed with a critical eye. "So where's the fun?"

"We'll be all right."

"You don't think something's wrong? You don't think there's an attitude there?"

"Kurth prattles on just like always."

"Wynona can't look me in the eye. Vitus hardly says a word."

"That's his nature. Just like I know violence isn't part of his being."

They stopped beside a walrus carcass. It was partially covered with rocks and sand that had built up in the lee of the carcass. Clearly it had been beached long before the others. The head had been removed, out to sea when it was killed, or on the beach they could not tell.

Pewter squinted into the brilliant glare of the pale Arctic Sun gleaming on the sea. "Vitus can do this kind of killing. Why not more?"

"Listen, I have some misgivings. I'm not saying I don't. Maybe there is something here. Whatever, we have to be together."

"Oh yes, back to teamwork."

"Back to teamwork. We're a hell of a long way from any help. Your instincts here are the same as mine. All we have is each other. There's no where else to turn."

They turned back down the beach, going with the wind. Pewter looked across the beach, turning the side of her face to the cold wind. "Maybe later I'll look at this and think I was having the greatest time in the world, out with nature, feeling like I was part." She paused and looked at Reed. "I know you're tough. I know you can do these things I've never done. I'll be there. I promise you my best. But think on this, you've changed. You're looking at these guys like you're one of them. But you're not. They know that. You don't."

By late afternoon they'd harvested the tusks from three more walrus. They'd crossed the Arctic Circle and rounded Cape Espenberg. Using his depth finder and riding a high tide, Kurth nursed *The Escape* into the protected waters behind the barrier islands and dropped anchor.

"At least now we can walk without staggering," Wynona said.

Kurth seized her around her narrow waist and kissed her on the mouth. "That's my honey, the last of the great explorers." He grinned at the others. "You should have seen Wynona last time we came north. We got into a little storm. Ten- or twelve-footers. Wynona was as white as if you'd covered her with a bucket of paint. Said she'd never come up here again. And here she is."

"Somebody has to watch you," Wynona said. "Otherwise you get going where you shouldn't be going." She patted Kurth's fanny. "And I have an investment I'm not ready to leave."

Kurth pointedly directed his smile at Pewter. "I'm taken, what can I say."

They sat down for a supper of baked salmon and wine and later, after Pewter and Wynona went to bed, Reed, Kurth and Vitus downed several beers. The conversation was strained, Reed could see it in Kurth's eyes. Vitus barely talked and would not look him in the eyes. Kurth was evasive, without the usual nonstop chatter. Something was up, Reed knew, he just couldn't decipher what — way up here in the middle of nowhere.

Long after midnight, with the sun hovering on the horizon, Reed headed for the bunk where Pewter already lay asleep. He'd consumed a few beers, a couple glasses of wine, just enough for a gentle buzz, he thought; not enough where he would be impaired.

Reed sat on the edge of the bunk and removed his pants and shirt and pulled on a clean T-shirt. A heavy curtain over the small porthole blocked most of the light from the midnight sun. The incessant Arctic Wind howled over the cowling and the boat rocked gently as it yawed back and forth on the bow anchor. Kurth had carefully picked a spot so that as the tide receded the boat would not be stranded on the bottom.

The long hours fighting the swaying of the boat and bracing against the cold and wind had taken their toll. But it was a good kind of exhaustion, earned. Kurth, the fisherman's son, the striving entrepreneur. And Vitus, just trying to get by, making it in two worlds. Reed felt his stomach tighten and knew what the look in their eyes would be once they made the arrest.

He closed his eyes and was thankful for the exhaustion, the beers. He crawled into the narrow bunk and lay on the edge, trying not to crowd Pewter. The covers were warm and she smelled of soap and sleep. His sadness grew deeper. He clenched his eyes tightly and wondered how he'd messed that up so bad.

Pewter stirred. She turned toward Reed. He could see the gleam of her eyes in the gloom. "Sorry," he apologized. The sound of Wynona's giggle carried from the captain's berth down the hall.

"Do you have enough room?" Pewter asked.

"Yes."

Pewter rose up, leaning over him to check. He lay on on his side, his buttocks over the edge of the bunk. Her arm reached around his ribs. Her breast brushed his chest. "You've got less than a foot. I won't get upset if we accidentally touch."

"I'm fine," Reed said.

"All males are fine," Pewter said. "They just can't tell the truth. I have gone to bed with a guy just for the fun of it. Although most males don't like it that way. It's only when *they're* doing it for the fun of it. I'm not a prude, Reed. We can touch. I just didn't want to be used. I don't want to be used just to fulfill someone's need. All right?" She bent and briefly kissed him on the mouth.

Her warmth consumed him. It took every effort to keep himself in check, to stop the passion welling up in his chest. He returned the kiss, softly, warmly, not pushing.

Pewter quickly pulled back. "You smell like beer," she said. "Here, slide over." She gave him room and then turned and snuggled with her back against Reed's chest. She took his arm and held it across her stomach.

"Good night," Reed whispered. His lips touched the top of her head. He savored the warmth, the vibrant touch of her being. He felt her shake, like the deep inner trembling of a volcano. His doing. He could have cried. He felt like a kid, all pumped up and filled with hope and joy. Was this an invitation to a more involved relationship, or did she just want him to be comfortable? He'd strayed so far from reality he wasn't sure he knew.

When Reed awoke Pewter was already awake. He patted her shoulder and she turned into him for a brief, hard hug. But no kiss. He felt as confused as a teenage boy on his first date, him a grown man. What the hell did it all mean?

"Did you hear an airplane last night?" Reed asked.

"No. I slept pretty sound. Must have been a dream."

The low murmur of angry voices carried from the main cabin. They lay holding each other, heads cocked.

"Something's up," Reed whispered. He checked the Nagra tape recorder he'd placed under the mattress.

Abruptly the curtain covering their door was thrown aside and a huge form ducked through the low opening and loomed over the bunk. Eyes gleamed out of a mat of curled hair that butted up against the ceiling. "Well looky here, two little ivory-buyers all snug in their bed."

"Terry Grason," Reed said with just a hint of surprise. He felt Pewter stiffen, her muscles going as tight as wire, Terry Grason! The empty feeling hit him like a sledgehammer to the stomach. Nevertheless his voice became as flat and calm as lagoon water on a windless day. "What brings you up to the Arctic Circle, in the middle of nowhere on a day like this?"

"Research," Grason said in a sad, whimsical voice. His brow was furrowed, eyes twisted like a man in deep pain. "Someone ventured a theory of deceit and betrayal. I said no. Friends don't betray friends. But then certain facts came to light. I felt obliged to check this theory out, determine the truth, seek justice. You know the tale."

A huge, painful lump blocked Reed's ability to speak. Against rage he knew how to respond. But this, he might as well have placed a dagger in his brother's chest.

Grason nodded, as if Reed's silence confirmed the lie.

150 ESKIMO MONEY

CHAPTER SIXTEEN

There'd be an explanation for this, Reed thought. "It'll be all right," he whispered to Pewter as they crawled from the bunk. She looked at him as if he was mad. Lost faith in his judgment, he thought. He climbed to his feet. For some reason his arms and legs felt encumbered with heavy weights. His mind buzzed as if inebriated. The Arctic Desert, with five to ten inches of annual precipitation lacked moisture, but he'd never felt anything like the paste coating his mouth. He'd dreamed he heard an airplane. It was no dream; Grason, out here in the middle of nowhere. It just didn't make sense.

They walked into the main cabin. "What are you doing out here, Terry? You take a wrong turn somewhere? What's going on?" Reed demanded. He was the center of a gathering that filled the tiny cabin, Vitus, Kurth, Wynona, Grason. Even Pewter, her face drained of blood, was watching for his response. Play it loose, easy, he thought. Don't push too hard. Grason would come around.

"We'll ask the questions," Grason said in a soft voice. "If you don't mind." As usual he wore his sealskin vest and blue jeans. An expensive green parka lay on a chair. His towering bulk filled one side of the cabin by itself.

"Would you mind if I got dressed first?" Reed asked. In shorts and T-shirt and weighing one hundred and sixty pounds, he appeared absurdly small next to Grason's six-feet-four inches.

"Yes, I do mind," Grason said.

Vitus ducked into the hallway and then into their cabin.

"You're making a mistake here," Reed said. His voice seemed to come from a distance. His stomach fluttered when he thought of Grason's reaction when Vitus found the Nagra recorder and pistol stuffed under the mattress.

"I'm going to get a cup of coffee. I'm not much good early in the morning without my coffee," Reed said, an actor speaking to a rapt audience. It was almost as if they expected him to provide a show.

He brushed past Grason, unable to meet his gaze lest Grason see his sense of guilt, and feel the dryness, the bitter bile that caked his mouth like dried flour. What the hell did they expect? You had to get in with these guys. You had to be friends. Besides, his intention had been to plea bargain the man, let him keep his airplane, get the Keelachuck brothers. But now the timing was all wrong.

Vitus emerged from the cabin. He carried their two pistols and Reed's leather belt with the zippered money pouch. "Just these," he grunted toward Grason. He did not look at Reed or Pewter.

A shot of hope flooded Reed like warm urine in a cold wet suit. Vitus had missed the Nagra. He spoke with just a touch of sarcasm. "The money is to buy ivory. The pistols are to protect the money from crooks. Where I come from the two go hand in hand."

"But right now they're not in your hands," Grason said. His voice was tight, an octave lower than before. "Take off your shirt."

"What happened to trust?" Reed said indignantly. It was hard to control the flow of adrenaline. He glanced at Pewter and she shook her head. He was overacting. But he could not stop, not here on a roll. "I'll tell you people once, I won't do business this way." He set his cup down then whipped his shirt over his head.

"For a scrawny sonofabitch you handled yourself in that bar pretty good," Grason said. "Now the shorts."

"Sure, why not," Reed said. He grinned, an unknowing neophyte hanging on a cliff. "We'll all get naked and have a good time." He pulled off his shorts then turned around. "Good enough?" he tersely asked. "Or did you want to look up my ass?" He pulled his shorts and T-shirt back on. "What the hell do you think you're going to find?"

Grason turned to Pewter. "Take it off."

"Go to hell," Pewter snapped.

"Absolutely not," Reed said. He stepped forward.

Grason also moved, standing in front of Reed, pistol touching his chest. Reed looked up, holding Grason's eyes.

"What are you doing here, Terry? You're ruining everything."

For a second Grason looked away, a man with a shadow of doubt. "I hope I'm wrong. But we've come this far. We have to see. Wynona can take her in the other room. There's no other choice."

"There's the choice of trust, doing business like we did in the past. That's going to be hard if you continue this."

Grason's lips seemed to curl, like a dog showing a snarl. He jabbed the pistol for emphasis. "I don't want talk. Do it."

Reed turned on Kurth. "Are you the captain of this boat or what?"

"We have to do this. Either Wynona does the search or let Grason do it," Kurth said angrily. His voice was unnaturally high, his eyes bright, and his body seemed to vibrate like a struck tuning fork. "It's your only choice. Look, we just have to clear this up and then everything will be all right. I promise."

"Everything will never be all right," Pewter said. Her tanned face was pinched, a woman who clearly understood what they faced. Grason loomed, a force beyond comprehension. She looked at Wynona and snarled as bitterly as she could. "Come on then, dammit. What you people are doing here is beyond me. The paranoia is enough to make me sick."

Reed moved back against the counter while Wynona and Pewter went into the back room. The questions loomed: What happened to the Nagra? How could Vitus miss it lying next to the guns? What brought Grason here in the first place? His suspicions had been raised someplace in order to make him set this up with Vitus and Kurth.

"You guys went through a hell of a lot of trouble to get us out in the middle of nowhere like this," Reed said with an upbeat tone. "Whoever's been feeding you stories hasn't been telling the truth." No one replied. Vitus leaned against one wall, legs crossed, head down, looking at the carpeted floor. Kurth sat on the edge of one of the booths, one leg jiggling up and down as if it had gone out of control. Grason sat on the edge of a stool, his face dark and brooding. The pistol looked like a little toy in his massive hand.

"You know how people like to talk," Reed said to Grason. "I never looked at you as a man who believed gossip."

Grason glanced briefly and then away. There was still a shadow of doubt, and in that doubt Reed found hope.

Wynona and Pewter returned to the room. Pewter crossed over to stand near Reed.

"There's nothing," Wynona snarled at Grason. "I told you. We checked before. They have a big operation. They need a lot of ivory. I think it's as simple as that. Now look where we're at."

Grason grumbled, "There's something too clean about these two. They push too hard, especially Reed there, milking me along. Did he want a polar bear hide from you, Kurth? For a Jap customer?"

"Yeah."

"And what about you, Vitus? You took him on a hunt. Did he want a polar bear hide from you also? For a Jap customer?"

Vitus had backed across the room, as far away from the others as he could get. He appeared uneasy, like a man who wanted to be somewhere else. He shrugged as if to say so what.

"It's a pattern, don't you see," Grason said. "He's adding up counts, adding up charges. It's called entrapment. Here, let me see those pistols."

As Grason reached, Vitus took the two pistols from the pockets of his black-and-white checked vest. The flesh colored end of an elastic bandage came out with one of the pistols. Grason took the pistols and seized at the elastic. "What the hell is this?"

Vitus pulled back. But a wad of elastic was jerked free and with it the Nagra recorder dropped onto the floor.

"You too, Vitus!" Grason cried. He turned on Reed, his face a splotch of purple rage. His hand shook with anger. His teeth were clenched, his lips curled in a snarl like a wolf confronting a bear over a kill. "Who the hell do you think you are, coming after me? Couldn't you see who and what I am? Do you think I'd stand by and let you go without consequences? How the hell would that look?"

The shouts cracked through the cabin like thunder after a nearby lightning strike. People cringed, cowering against the wall. Grason was on edge, ready to kill. A minute or two and he'd calm down, see reason. Reed waited, giving Grason time.

Grason's voice dropped, a low whine of despair. "I thought we were friends. You said we were friends. I trusted you."

"That part's real," Reed said softly. "You got caught up in the changes, guys making demands for a bear no matter how, the bills, insurance. The walrus can withstand normal Eskimo harvest, but not head-hunting. The toll's too great. We'd go easy. Plea bargain. All you have to do is help me get the Keelachuck brothers."

"Become the betrayer just like you," Grason shouted. His face contorted like a man in severe physical pain. He leveled the pistol at Reed's chest. Pewter and the others recoiled. Reed held his ground. At the last instant Grason forced the muzzle up and fired a shot just over Reed's head. In the closed confines, the shot thundered. Everyone ducked and turned away. Only Reed did not flinch.

Grason seized a chair to throw at Reed, but the low ceiling caught the legs and the chair smashed to the deck. Grason kicked and the chair flew, banging past the spot where Reed stood and clattering into the counter. Dishes flew. "No one sets up Terry Grason. No one." The shouts raged as loud as the pistol shot. Grason's eyes were wide, gleaming.

Grason seized Reed and slammed him up against the wall, his feet dangling in the air. Grason's hand pushed into Reed's throat, cutting off his air. Reed tried to kick but Grason was too close and slightly turned. He clawed at Grason's arm but it was as futile as if raking his fingers over cold steel. Pewter jumped at Grason's back but he swung a backhand and easily knocked her to the floor.

Reed croaked, unable to speak. A blackness clouded his vision, the first look at death. He was powerless, overwhelmed, only dimly aware of shouts and people pulling at Grason's back.

And then he was free and crumpled on the deck. Pewter knelt at his side. Reed gagged and gripped her hand, hanging onto something warm, soft.

Grason was shouting, "My son was everything. Everything! And you bastards took him away." He again raised the pistol and leveled it at Reed's face.

"Jesus, Terry, no," Kurth cried. "We were just buying time, remember, buying time."

Grason's anger seemed to ebb. He lowered the pistol, eyes unfocused, casting about like a man lost. "Buying time for what?" he asked Kurth in a sad, barely audible voice. Kurth could not reply. And then Grason bellowed, "Time for what?"

"Cover ourselves, get things in order," Kurth said in a small voice. He gingerly circled Grason and picked up the recorder. It was thin, half the thickness and approximately the width of two packs of playing cards. His hands shook uncontrollably. His voice sounded somewhere between hysteria and rage. "Where'd you get this?" he asked Vitus.

Vitus jerked his head toward the front rooms.

"Why didn't you say something?" Kurth asked. "Why?" He seized Vitus by his vest.

Vitus inclined his head toward Grason.

"And you said Vitus was as dumb as a rock," Grason said to Kurth. "Why do you think I said, don't tell him I would be here?"

"What are you talking about?" Kurth demanded. He was red-faced, visibly shaking. "Wynona and Vitus can fly back with you so we can take care of some of our affairs. I'll bring these two back in the boat. You know, like we planned. That'll give us a couple of days to get things in order."

"You planned?" Vitus asked. "You planned, but you didn't tell me Grason was going to be here. You said we'd search ourselves. If we found ivory it was mine, all legal."

"Plans change," Grason said. "I'm surprised. These people are destroying your people and you stand with them."

Vitus did not respond.

"Your choice," Grason grunted. "A man has to stand up for himself. Not blame others. We've gotten away from individual responsibility. Get a lawyer.

Not out here, Vitus. You make your choice, I make mine." He motioned with the barrel of the pistol. "Now get over there and stand with those two, seeing as you like the government so much. What'd you expect, Vitus, that I would just say, oh, too bad. I've been fooled, taken advantage of. Just go home and cry in my beer? You forget, Vitus, I have no home."

"What are you talking about?" Kurth whined. He stood in the center of the room like a little boy throwing a tantrum. With Grason it was all he could do. "We agreed. You're just making things worse here. We go cover ourselves, we pay a few thousand dollars in fines. Maybe we spend thirty days in jail. But then we're out."

"Please, Terry," Wynona said. "I know you're angry. I'm angry. But we have to think this through. If these two are agents, other people will know they came out here with Kurth and me. If something happens, they come straight to us."

"Nothing's going to happen," Kurth yelled at his wife. Cords stood out in the neck of his red, contorted face. He began to plead, "Now come on, Terry. Wynona will get dressed and you take her and Vitus and leave. If you want, take my radios. That way they can't radio ahead."

Grason spoke in a deep, sad voice. "I'll tell you what, Kurth, you and Wynona are sleazy enough. I'll let you stand with me. Either that or you can go over there and stand with them."

Kurth glanced at his wife. His face was a mask of fear and panic. His voice rattled nervously. "What are you talking about? We agreed."

"Others know they went out with us," Wynona argued. Her voice quavered. "We'll be the first ones they come to."

"Your boat sank," Grason said. "You were on deck. The others didn't have a chance."

"No," Kurth cried. "Jesus, think what you're doing here."

"Maybe no one had a chance," Grason snarled savagely. "I don't give a damn." The amused expression evaporated as if it had never been. His eyes were fixed with the cold intensity of a lynx stalking a rabbit frozen in its tracks. "Do you think I'd stand for the damn government interfering with my life? I do what I do, living off the land, living on my own terms. This is Alaska, dammit. The government has no business coming in here interfering with people's lives. I put the government on notice once and you didn't listen. Now you pay."

"Terry, you've got room here," Reed croaked. He struggled to his feet. "You won't lose your business, you won't even have to go to jail."

Pewter jerked Reed's elbow. "Wake up. It's over. He means to kill us. Can't you understand."

"Smart girl," Grason said. "The two of you were an act, huh? You follow his lead? That was a mistake. He doesn't know when to quit."

"I know that now."

"I'm sorry it has to be this way," Grason said. "But you see, as he doesn't, I don't have any options here."

They stood in silence. Reed glanced at Vitus and nodded a thanks at Vitus's effort to hide the transmitter. At five-foot-five, Vitus was eleven inches shorter than Grason. But he was stocky, his short arms and legs bowed and strong. He'd add something to any fight — if it came down to a fight.

"Are you with them or are you with me?" Grason demanded.

"Ah, sure," Kurth managed to croak. Dried lines of saliva had collected at the corners of his mouth.

"We're with you, Terry," Wynona said with some confidence. She shot a dark glance at her husband, imploring him to see the situation. "You can count on us. We have more to lose than you. But I'm telling you, this is still a bad idea. How are we going to hide our boat?"

"You're not. You're going to sink the sonofabitch."

"Oh," Wynona said in a small voice. She glanced at Reed, Pewter and Vitus. Her thoughts were plainly written on her face.

"We're not going to kill them," Grason said easily. "You could even take a lie detector test, tell the authorities the last time you saw them they were alive and healthy. They might be suspicious, but what the hell are they going to do? A couple years ago an airplane with a couple of biologists on board disappeared over the pack ice. They had a massive search, never found a trace. Then they had an idea where to look. It's a tragedy, but life goes on. This is Alaska, if you have a problem, you fix it." He stared at Reed.

"That's the way things are up here. If you recall, I gave you an opportunity to back off, my word on what I would do if you were an agent. Did you forget? Terry Grason is a man of his word. Everyone knows that."

Grason had calmed down, Reed saw. In fact his rage seemed to have totally dissipated. "Terry, let's you and I go into the other room and have a talk, man to man."

Grason stepped forward and then stopped and surveyed the spread circle of bodies. "Talk with a betrayer. Why would I talk with a betrayer?"

"You have to understand the overall situation, the reports . . . " Reed said.

"Dammit, Reed," Pewter hissed. "Grason's not mad. He knows what he's doing. He's going to do it."

"A man needs a mate," Grason said. "I didn't fully realize that until after Jeff was murdered and then Jeri left." He moved a step closer to Pewter. His voice was soft, inviting. "You and I could have been good. Still could."

"Sure," Pewter said.

Grason smiled. "I wish I could believe you. Circumstances call your sincerity into question."

"Oh, but I love the outdoors. That's why I took this job," Pewter said.

"I'll give you your fill of the outdoors," Grason said.

"You're not making any sense here," Reed said. He studied Pewter. First she loathed and feared Grason and now she came onto him as if she had an interest. He shook his head, understanding he'd lost his perspective, common sense. But there was the matter of truth; he and Grason weren't that far apart. He had to build on that.

Grason turned and addressed Kurth. His voice was mild, like talking to one of his guides in front of clients he was taking out fishing. "The first thing we want to do is get some adhesive tape on that mouth. Kurth, why don't you get some adhesive tape. Just do it lightly at first. We'll get them dressed one by one. Wynona, why don't you scrape up a breakfast. It's cold out over the ice. I need my daily fare."

Ice? Grason's warning flight, Reed thought, and was jolted by a sense of alarm, a look in the mirror, a sense of life passed, life lost. A man drowned. A man reached out. Any hand would do. What the hell had he been thinking? Not even the hand to his throat had been enough to wake him up. Grason was a man of his word, the basis of his pride. Ice!

Where the hell had he been? Reed wondered. Everything became lucid, as if he'd just been plunked down in the middle of the case and told to go to it. "You killed Abe. Your other warning."

Grason merely stared.

"You're right, Terry. You gave me your word. I didn't listen. I apologize. My mistake. Not these other people, not Pewter. Just take me. I'm the one."

Grason spoke to Pewter, "Now he becomes noble. Touching, isn't it, the male ego. I got rid of mine a long time ago."

"Good move," Pewter said with empathy. She and Grason locked eyes.

Abruptly Grason looked away. He licked at dried lips. "You're too good. You lie as good as him. I didn't think the two of you worked as a couple. I was wrong. You're a perfect match. Tape them, Kurth. First get it on their mouths."

While Grason stood guard, Kurth lightly taped their hands. Kurth's hands trembled and he pointedly avoided meeting their eyes. "If you get a chance, jump him," Reed said. "He'll double cross you also. You can count on it."

"I said put one across his mouth," Grason snapped.

158   ESKIMO MONEY

Kurth immediately put a strip of tape across Reed's mouth. He'd get no help there, Reed thought. Kurth was thoroughly cowed, jumping at every instruction Grason gave.

After Vitus and Reed had their hands taped, they moved over and sat down against the wall. Kurth grabbed their clothes and threw them at their feet. Pewter dressed first, pulling on long underwear over her white nightshirt. She picked up Reed's foot nudging at her clothes. Grason mentioned ice. She should dress as warm as possible.

After Pewter dressed, Kurth taped her hands and removed Reed's tape so he could dress. Reed removed the tape from his mouth. "Not one word," Grason warned.

Reed nodded his understanding. You got along with a man like Grason by agreeing, not arguing. He pulled on long underwear, a double top, a wool shirt, vest, and then a parka. Kurth securely taped his hands, this time behind his back. Grason wasn't taking any chances.

The first part of the plan emerged. They were all going to shore. Kurth and Wynona dressed for a windy hike down the beach. Careful as ever, Grason permitted them one at a time into their room.

"We're on your side," Kurth argued.

"That's the problem," Grason said. "Last week Reed there was giving me the same story."

They used the Zodiac to run shuttles to shore. Kurth took Reed and Vitus first, with Grason manhandling them into the raft. "Don't rock the boat. It's a little hard to swim with your hands behind your back." Grason hissed into Reed's ear.

"This isn't you, Terry," Reed said. "Too many people know we're out here. There's no chance you'll get away."

Grason manhandled Reed so he was looking him in the face. "That doesn't matter. Or don't you understand? In some ways you're doing me a favor. I should have gotten out of the business years ago, taken to the woods, get way the hell out where you never see anyone. I used to run a trapline. Lived in a one-room cabin all by myself for two winters in a row. There's only one person there that can let you down."

Abruptly Grason tossed Reed to the bottom of the boat. "You sit together like good little boys on shore there. If either one of you makes a move, I'll put one through the little girl's head here."

Reed remained silent. He caught Pewter's dark look of fear; she and Wynona would be alone on the boat with Grason. His fault, and there was nothing anyone could do.

A steady wind whipped small ripples on the lagoon behind the barrier islands. A thin white haze covered the sky from horizon to horizon. The slate gray waters of the Chukchi Sea stretched for one hundred and eighty degrees. Rocky beaches and distant lines of treeless tundra covered the opposite horizon. It was beautiful and it was bleak and there wasn't a hope anyone would come to their rescue, Reed thought.

He glanced at *The Escape*. The inflatable rubber kayak Grason must have used to get to the boat was tied at the stern. Pewter and Grason stood on the back. Wynona must have gone inside. If only she'd seize a gun.

All the way into shore Reed badgered Kurth, setting seeds. Kurth could help Grason now, but in the final analysis Grason would double-cross them, too.

"Shut up, just shut up," Kurth yelled. "You don't see me with a rifle, do you? What do you expect me to do? You've seen Grason. He handled you like a rag doll. You want me to grab him? A guy pulled a knife on him in a bar. Grason took it away and killed the guy."

"If you get a chance, no matter how slim, take it," Reed said. "That's all I ask. The life you save will be your own."

"Jesus!" Kurth shook his head. "How do you do it? Your life's at stake here and you're making jokes."

"It's not a joke," Reed said. "It just came out that way." He looked at *The Escape*. Grason and Pewter had disappeared inside the cabin. He closed his eyes against his helplessness and his pain.

Kurth drove the Zodiac up on the beach, stepped into the water with his hip boots and pulled the boat up further so Vitus and Reed could get out without getting their feet wet.

"Just get back out there fast," Reed said. "We'll wait right here on shore, no problems."

Kurth read the desperation on Reed's face and in his tone. "Hey, man, I'm sorry. I didn't know Grason would be like this."

"Just get back there," Reed yelled.

"And you go to hell," Kurth said. "The last guy to yell at me was my old man. And I swore there'd never be anyone else." Nevertheless he pushed the raft into the water and quickly sped back to *The Escape*.

Reed and Vitus, their hands still taped behind their back, squatted side by side on the gravel beach. The wind blew steadily in their faces. Reed's face was gaunt, hollowed, covered by a light beard. Vitus's face was broad, smooth skinned with high cheekbones and a tiny nose. They both stared out at *The Escape* and the sea.

"I'm sorry, Vitus. I take it Grason was a surprise to you also. I appreciate what you tried to do out there."

"I trusted you, Reed. I took you hunting with my family and they trusted you as well. Now I am dead. I sold ivory to the gussuk. Jake will hunt with me no more." Vitus spoke softly, evenly, in a voice heavy with sadness.

Reed looked away. Tears filled his eyes. Pewter, Vitus, boy he'd done it all this time.

But there was really nothing he could do. He sat in the middle of a desolate and isolated beach far north of the Arctic Circle with his hands tied.

Grason, Pewter, Wynona, and Kurth crowded into the Zodiac and came into shore. Immediately Kurth turned the raft out and sped back to the boat. Wynona silently sobbed.

Their attention swung as *The Escape's* motor loudly coughed to life. White exhaust spewed out the stern. The boat swung as Kurth winched in the anchor. Moving at a slow idle, Kurth pointed the boat toward the outer reef and the sea beyond. After a few minutes he emerged from below decks with a small suitcase, tossed it into the Zodiac that was bobbing in the prop wash. He was a small figure more than a quarter-mile away. He suddenly jumped and the raft separated from the larger Viking. The Zodiac sped toward shore. *The Escape* slowly chugged out into the gray waters of the Chukchi Sea.

"They'll be looking for us. They'll find that boat," Reed quietly observed.

Wynona shook her head. Dark lines of mascara streaked her cheeks. "Kurth opened the seacocks. A few miles out to sea and it will sink. Storm or iceberg people will assume. The bow just caved in." She looked at Reed; her eyes were hard, bitter. "It was a good thing Kurth and I were on deck otherwise we never would have survived. There! There, do you see what you've brought? And for what, a few dumb walrus. The Eskimo kill them by the thousands. The Russians kill thousands more. What difference does a few more make? Is it worth risking human lives?"

As soon as Kurth reached shore he turned the Zodiac around and, while standing thigh deep in the icy water, engaged the outboard and let the raft idle out into the bay. When the boat was fifty yards Grason raised his pistol. The first shot hit the water ten yards short. The second hit the raft, spinning it off course. Within seconds it began to sink. Further out to sea *The Escape* rode lower as if disappearing over the horizon. The Zodiac sank. Gulls and jaegers and terns rode the wind currents down the shore. The six people stood or sat silently as the wind-rippled waters of the lagoon closed up as if nothing had ever been there.

Grason checked Kurth's handgrip, patted him down to make certain he hadn't picked up a weapon, then turned with the stoic attitude of a lumberman going through the forest and cutting down his trees. It was little more than a job, food on the table, a roof over his head. "Let's go flying. Ever since I met him Reed's been bugging me about taking him on a polar bear hunt. Now that's not something I'd normally do on my own. But when the government asks, well, I figure nothing's too good for my country. Isn't that right, Reed?"

The bitterness crept through, as deep-seated as pitted rust. Reed had no response.

"Wynona and I can walk from here," Kurth said. "We should be able to make Kotzebue."

"Are you kidding? Do you know how many marshes and rivers there are between here and there? You'd die of hypothermia after the first stream crossing. I'll drop you off ten miles out of Nome. That'll make you look worn enough and make the time frame right."

Kurth opened his mouth to protest. He sought help from the others, but no help was forthcoming. He tried to meet Grason's stare. "Sure, we'll walk the ten miles to Nome."

Grason, hands on hips, pistol in one hand, surveyed his brood. "C'mon, Vitus. I'll untape your hands. You can fly. Can't be more than fifty or seventy-five miles to the pack ice this time of year. We'll go find us a bear, a big bear. I'll put it right in Reed's lap."

CHAPTER SEVENTEEN

The six of them walked over a spit of gravel to a one-half-mile-long, barrier-island thaw lake. The wind blistered their skin, a non-stop, abrasive presence filled with so much salt and sand it created a light, spume fog. The landscape rolled in a series of gentle mounds of gravel and rock worn round by ice, wind, and storms. The terrain was as desolate as the moon, unrelieved by trees, tundra, or even mosses and lichens. There was no place to run, no place to hide, not even a boulder large enough to conceal a human being.

"If you want to run for it, you're welcome," Grason said to Reed.

Now that he was bound and all but totally helpless, Reed's anger had begun to build, as much at himself as at Grason. Pewter, Doug, Rich, all had tried to make him wake up. But no, he'd been bullheaded, certain he was in control, just like he'd been in control with Stacy. Who the hell was he kidding? People didn't control other people, not without a gun and the force. And then you never controlled their hearts. The question nagged. Where had he gone wrong? Where had his head evolved? Had he been that much in need he failed to see? Well, no more. If Grason wanted war, he'd give the bastard a war.

"Run with my hands tied behind my back? You're a hell of a sport. Just like blasting those walrus with your semi-automatic as they lay there on the ice. Of course your first pistol shot missed the Zodiac by ten feet."

Grason jerked Reed's arms up his back and all but lifted him off the earth. "I wouldn't miss you, asshole. In fact that's where I'd put one, right up your ass."

Reed grunted from the pain and the strain. He managed to keep his voice even. "A nine-millimeter enema, that I can do without."

Grason dropped him and Reed staggered forward, did a half somersault, half roll and came right back up on his feet. He trudged on, a coiled bundle of energy all tied and contained.

"Your timing is something," Pewter said. "Grason could line you up and shoot you and you wouldn't show any fear, would you?"

"He wouldn't have any fear," Grason said. "That's how he fooled me and we got on so good. He just doesn't have any morality either."

"I've got enough morality to know when massive slaughter is wrong," Reed snarled.

"No, you just don't have enough sense to see the end," Grason said.

They rose to the top of a small mound of rocks and gravel. In the midst of plantless desolation, sitting on the dark water, Grason's silver de Havilland Beaver drifted on pontoons, anchored securely to shore by a yellow nylon rope tied to a claw grapple. They loaded through the side passenger and cargo door. Kurth and Wynona took the back seat, Reed and Pewter the middle, Vitus the pilot's seat and Grason the front passenger seat. Grason sat with one pistol in hand, one in the map pouch at his side and a rifle between his legs. Vitus started the stub-nosed airplane, taxied down the shallow thaw lake and turned back into the wind. He turned up full throttle. The cacophony from the Pratt & Whitney motor vibrated through the cabin.

They skimmed down the lake, picking up speed. Reed looked in Pewter's eyes. Her face was drawn, lips pinched, youth erased. She'd aged ten years. He turned away. Pewter leaned and spoke in his ear. "It's not your fault."

Reed shook his head. No pretense there. Such incredible melancholy, a woman fully anticipating her death. He never would have guessed she'd be so calm. Even going so far as trying not to give him blame. But he knew the truth.

They lifted free of the water. The usual sensation of freedom and flight did not follow. There was only dread, a sense of foreboding.

With Grason giving directions, Vitus turned the aircraft north and west over the Chukchi Sea. After a few minutes Vitus tipped the wing so they could all peer out. Moving at little better than idle speed, *The Escape* had covered almost a mile. Vitus circled low. Water lapped almost to the gunnels. It appeared the motor had flooded out and stopped.

"It won't be long," Grason said. "It must be a hundred and fifty feet deep out there. They'll never find that one."

Kurth and Wynona strained to watch. Kurth's eyes were filled with tears. Wynona's eyes were mostly concealed behind narrowed lids.

"Too bad you didn't have hull insurance," Grason said. He sounded upbeat, positive. "But like you say, hull insurance is expensive. Especially in waters up here. Don't think I carry insurance on this plane. If she crashes I'm out a hundred grand."

"That boat was worth more than that," Kurth muttered.

They continued out to sea. In the far distance a line of white that all but blended with the cloudy sky showed the edges of the retreating polar pack ice. Reed shifted uncomfortably. The tape cut his wrists and his fingers were numb from lack of circulation. He was grim, bitter. What would Stacy and Trish think? Their father would have simply disappeared. Would Stacy care? Would it even impact their lives?

And now there was nothing. Just Grason, the drone of the Beaver, the six of them huddled in silence as they approached the line of the pack ice.

As they approached the icepack they entered near-whiteout conditions where the horizon line between the white sky and white ice was not readily discernible. But they did have reference points below, the leading edges of rotten summer ice, millions of tiny ice cakes, speckles of white flakes on a black glass bed. As they drew closer they could see larger icebergs and then the more solid pack, four- and five-mile-wide floes separated by zig-zag rivers of black leads. The scarline of pressure ridges, twenty- to forty-foot-high mounds of ice thrown up by ice floes grinding together, lay scattered in random, riverlike patterns across the floes. Here and there salt-free, melted ice water had formed cobalt blue ponds in hollows in the ice beneath a pressure ridge.

Reed strived to maintain his bearings. He'd been watching the compass, the airspeed, figuring their time. Traveling across a single ice floe on foot would be difficult enough. But then to cross the leads to another floe might take days. One brief immersion in that twenty-nine-degree water and hypothermia would quickly follow. Besides, even if they could transfer from one floe to another, for the most part the pack ice had detached itself from the mainland. It would be an exercise in futility, something to pass the time, a quick whittling down of their strength before they died.

"Take her down to two hundred feet," Grason instructed Vitus. "Follow that lead. Let's see if we can find a nice big polar bear. Reed knows firsthand, I can put a bear right into his lap." Grason briefly glared at Reed then turned to watch out the window.

"I trust this time you won't even give me one bullet," Reed said.

"If I give you a bullet it will be right in the head," Grason said easily.

Reed studied Grason's profile. The massive cranium was perfectly proportioned, a strong, manly jaw, solid nose and cheekbones, wide mouth, thick eyebrows, and hair as curled as if done by permanent; a man who lived with nature, but not a man of nature. A man who used and justified that use, just as did a rancher, a logger, a farmer, a fisherman, any one of thousands who made their living from the land. As the Eskimo said, their garden was the sea. Grason was little more than clear-cutting the land. And out of that people should die?

One game warden was shot and killed for issuing a citation for fishing with an expired license. Another was killed while taking a man out to pick up roadside litter. Countless other wardens had been shot by poachers shining deer at night. Simple game violations and people ended up dead. You just never knew.

He felt Pewter's presence, the life between them as keen as the cut of the wind; she, a rookie agent, he the experienced pro. He knew the business, some people would give her the blame.

Still, somehow, he had to get through. "How come you're being such a coward about this, Grason. You've got damn near a hundred pounds, take me on man to man."

Grason lunged and snapped a backhand across Reed's face. "I told you I'm sick of your lip."

Reed shook his head against the sting. Grason didn't have much room to move, but such was the force of the short blow the entire side of his face was numb. The warm, salt-taste of blood oozed from a cut inside his cheek, moisture for his soul. Blood into blood, wet upon lips too numbed to feel. But of course he'd expected the blow — the price he'd paid to keep Grason on edge. He managed to speak, "That's what my daddy always told me, you give lip, you give blood."

"Smart old man. Too bad he didn't pass it on."

"There's a bear," Wynona said.

A large, somewhat yellowish colored polar bear stood on hind legs and pawed at the air as the airplane roared past.

"You're just a real doll helping out like that," Reed said over his shoulder. "Why do you think I was distracting Grason? Do you think you know what's going to happen here? You and Kurth are going right out on the ice with the rest of us."

Wynona looked at Kurth who turned away, just as he'd turned away from thoughts he dared not face. Who could say with Grason?

"Set her down in that lead over there," Grason said. "I want to show you how good I can drive bear with my airplane. Just like that guy down on the mainland, used his Super Cub and drove thirty-eight Boone-and-Crockett size grizzly bears to rich city hunters waiting on some knoll."

"And what are we suppose to do with him?" Reed asked.

Grason grinned. "Whatever you wish. Make a blanket, have a meal."

Vitus flew low, surveying the landing site, a two-hundred-yard lead between two large floes. Small tendrils of fog had formed over the open water. "There are a lot of ice chunks," Vitus said.

"Well, you better not hit one," Grason said, "or we'll flip over and all drown."

Reed spoke, "As the world goes, Vitus, that might not be a bad idea."

"If there was ever a chance for these other people, you're ruining it," Grason said.

"There never was a chance. Someone else would know your story, they might plea bargain, they might talk. Who are you kidding, Grason?"

"I could like you," Grason said. "I just can't stand to be around you."

Vitus stood the airplane on one wing, giving it throttle and giving himself maximum time to survey the landing area before it disappeared under the nose. He leveled off. He throttled back while increasing flaps. The aircraft settled. The black water and white ice seemed to rise up to meet them. Reed closed his eyes in momentary sorrow. If they hit an ice chunk it would be over in a matter of seconds, especially for him and Pewter with their hands taped behind their backs.

The pontoons skimmed the water. The aircraft settled and then quickly slowed. Reed roused himself. No matter how slender the chance, he had to go.

They taxied next to a main ice floe. "Climb outside there and anchor the airplane," Grason ordered Kurth. Ever obedient, Kurth opened the passenger's door. They were greeted with a wave of cold air, a bitter and mind-numbing reminder of what they faced.

Kurth climbed outside and took the grappling hook and rope out of the storage bin inside the pontoon. As Vitus nursed the airplane next to a solid looking piece of the main floe, Kurth jumped onto the ice and pulled the airplane fast. Vitus shut down the engine.

"You're next, Vitus," Grason said. He pointed the pistol at Vitus's chest. "This will give you a chance to see if living down in Anchorage has eroded your skill. Remember the legend of that Eskimo woman, stranded on the ice. She ate her husband and then her children just so she could survive. This'll give you a chance to see how Eskimo you really are."

Vitus gave no sign Grason's words were heard. He worked his way out of the pilot's seat and climbed out onto the pontoon.

"Help those two out back there," Grason angrily ordered. "When you get them on the ice you can untie their hands. Just don't drop them in the water. They won't get to have that much fun."

"I'm just sorry I'm not going to have some leg-of-Grason," Reed said. "I know it would be bitter, and tough, but I'd like to try some just the same."

"I'm going to miss your ass. I have a little bit of gas, maybe after I move that bear up this way I'll stick around to watch the show. I can always refuel at Point Hope. If you make it to winter the ice will reconnect over there."

"Put a six pack on hold, I'll be there," Reed said. As Vitus reached up to hold him, he stepped down on the pontoon then up onto the ice beside Kurth and Pewter. As soon as they were on the ice Reed turned so Vitus could free his hands. "Get Pewter," Reed hissed at Kurth. Kurth hesitated. "Grason said it was okay," Reed growled as if to a child.

Screaming carried from the airplane. Kurth looked up in alarm.

"Get the hell out of there," Grason yelled.

Wynona, her voice edged with panic, screamed back. "No. You promised. We'll say our boat sank and they sank with it. We'll take the blame. You have our word. There's nothing to fear."

"Get out of there," Grason yelled. He leveled his pistol.

Wynona shrieked and curled into a tiny ball.

Grason uncoiled like an angry spring, forcing back between the two front seats and into the rear of the six-passenger airplane. He seized Wynona who continued to wail and remained coiled in her fetal ball. "Out!" Grason snapped a hard punch into her face. Blood flew. Wynona screamed louder. Her hands and arms covered her head. Grason jerked her over the seat and half out the door where Kurth stood tensed on the pontoon.

"You can't leave us like this. It's inhumane," Kurth yelled. He helped his sobbing wife up onto the ice.

Reed, Pewter and Vitus had backed away from the edge and stood near the crushed ice of a ten-foot-high pressure ridge. There'd been melting, some settling, and then apparently fresh upheavals as shards of ice lay in a moraine. "Try to free some of these chunks," Reed said as Grason struggled with Wynona. He kicked hard at one big chunk but it had refrozen and he simply hurt his toe.

"This one gave," Pewter said.

"Keep working on it, but don't let Grason see."

"Stop," Vitus grunted.

"What are you guys doing over there?" Grason asked. "I'm not going to hurt you. I promise. They can give me a lie detector test. I'll tell them, the last time I saw them they were alive and well. In perfect health."

"You couldn't spare a rifle, a flare gun and a radio?" Reed asked.

Grason laughed. "Yeah, right."

"Vitus said he burned the gas mixture as rich as he could. You should make it about halfway between the ice and the shore."

Grason hesitated. "Ah, nah. I was watching. There's plenty of fuel." He turned to where Kurth held his sobbing and bleeding wife. "Hand me that grappling hook."

"Go to hell," Kurth snarled.

"I'll shoot you," Grason said with a smile.

"Go ahead."

Grason threw up both hands in mock defeat. "Ah, he called my bluff. What's a man to do? I'll have to get it myself." He stepped up onto the ice, picked up the hook, placed it and the rope back into the pontoon storage bin and then pushed off. The airplane drifted free into the lead. "I'll go take a look at that bear, turn it down here in the right direction, then I'll come back and give you a wave."

Reed and the others stared.

"No last remarks?" Grason's voice echoed across the ice floes, carrying in the stillness of the arctic ice. "C'mon, Reed, let's see your wit, one last wisecrack. Get in your digs, I can take it." Reed simply stared. "You sonofabitch," Grason angrily called. "I'll get your obituary, pin it up on the wall." He waited for a rejoinder. Getting none he climbed into the airplane and slammed the door.

"Quick, everyone get a big chunk," Reed ordered. He kicked furiously, trying to find a piece that was loose. Pewter picked up one the size of a brick. "Bigger, bigger," Reed yelled. A chunk gave. He bent, pawing at slush with his hands, furiously rocking the chunk to and fro. Vitus picked up a piece the size of a basketball and looked at Reed for directions. "Smash it on the tail, try to break the rudder or the tail wing. If Grason can't get out of here he has to radio for help."

With Pewter's assistance Reed wrestled a four-inch-thick by two-feet-long piece out of the moraine. They each held an edge and trailed Vitus across the snow-covered floe. Kurth stared in bewilderment. Wynona watched without comprehension. Tears streaked her cheeks and mingled with blood flowing out of her nose and mouth. The propeller turned over, but the engine did not catch. They closed in.

Grason looked out the side window and saw their approach. He grinned. The wind blew, drifting the plane back toward the ice, turning the tail until they could almost reach out and touch it. The motor turned over again. This time it caught. The roar reverberated across the ice.

Vitus threw his ice chunk. It rattled onto the tail section and then off. The airplane lurched.

"Ready, together," Reed panted to Pewter. "Back and then throw. Back, throw." They heaved for all they were worth. The chunk half turned in midair and crashed into the rudder and then fell onto the tail wing. The airplane pitched violently.

"You got it," Vitus said. "The bottom end of the rudder is broke out. The tail wing is bent down. If Grason tries to take off he'll crash for certain."

Grason revved the engine and attempted to taxi away. But the rudder was jammed. Almost immediately the airplane turned in a gradual circle back in toward the ice.

"Let's get out of here," Reed said. "He'll be after us sure as hell. Kurth, Wynona, let's move." The two stood uncertainly. Reed jerked at Kurth's arm. "Come on, dammit. He'll be out with his rifle in a minute." He took Wynona's arm on one side, Kurth on the other. They ran toward the pressure ridge. Slipping and sliding in the wet slush and ice, they clambored over the top.

They paused to catch their breath. The airplane engine quit. Reed peeked over the ice. "He's down a hundred yards. He's securing the airplane to the ice. He has his rifle out."

"What now?" Pewter asked.

"He can look over the damage and see if he can fix it. If that's not possible he'll have to radio for help or activate his Emergency Location Transmitter. If he has fresh batteries in it. With Grason you can't be certain. Of course first he'd have to hunt us down and dump our bodies in the water. But to do that he'd have to leave the airplane. And I don't think Grason's going to do that. Either he fixes the airplane, or we have a standoff. But he has food and shelter. We're not even adequately clothed. A couple of cold nights or one good storm and we'll be gone. Grason knows that. He'll just wait."

"So what the hell good did all that do?" Kurth demanded.

"It kept us alive," Pewter said. "At least Reed's given us a chance." She moved over and stood near Reed.

Reed flushed with embarrassment. He touched Pewter's arm and closed his eyes, feeling her presence, the warmth of her being. At the moment it was the entire world.

CHAPTER EIGHTEEN

In the distance, slanting shafts of sunlight illuminated white spires of ice. Deep within the massive, chaotically piled blocks of the pressure ridge, shades of the hard ice evolved from white into deep azure blue. The snow-covered ice stretched out in an uneven carpet with the frozen eruption of pressure ridges jutting skyward every few hundred yards. If they weren't dressed for the pack ice, they were at least dressed for a cold and windy arctic beach. Except for Wynona, they all wore boots with thick felt liners. The wind was negligible, the temperature in the low thirties, Reed estimated, enough to chill, but not so much they could not fight, as long as they could keep from sweating, and as long as they could slowly move about. It was a desolate landscape, beautiful, harsh, and he accepted and understood that nature gave not one damn about the antlike human beings struggling on its floes.

"Wynona's not well. I think her jaw's broke. She's cold. What are we going to do?" Kurth asked. He stood with both arms around Wynona's shoulders. His normally ruddy complexion had paled. The pupils of his blue eyes were pinpoints and he could not seem to focus. He shifted in small circles, looking one direction and then another.

Abruptly the ice trembled beneath their feet. They staggered for balance. A distant rumbling carried across the vast, white wasteland. In subtle fashion the spires of ice seemed to bob against the white sky, seven-foot-thick sheets of ice responding to distant collisions and powerful currents from the black water below.

"The ice lives," Vitus said with a teacher's simple explanation. "You have to be ready. Sometimes a floe will crack open without notice. It could happen while you sleep. We could be separated from each other, from Grason and his airplane."

"Oh, God, what is this?" Kurth wailed. His voice seemed to come from a great distance, like a man lost in the wilderness and talking to himself. "I did not ask for any of this, I swear."

Wynona sagged against Kurth's hip. She was lightly dressed with simple fur-lined boots and a thin parka. The one side of her face was puffed beyond recognition. Veins had burst and the white of one eye glared blood red. She giggled and spoke in a slurred voice through cold and puffed lips. "Why do you cry, honey?"

"Get the hood on that parka up," Reed said coldly. "Every little bit of warmth helps. We'll wait here a minute and see what Grason does. He's anchoring the airplane right now and then I expect he'll survey the damage. If he comes for us we'll split up. If he gets far enough away some of us can try for the airplane and try to get a radio, try to activate the emergency beeper, maybe smash the rudder worse if there's nothing else."

"What if he gets it fixed right away and starts the motor? Run out with more ice?" Pewter asked. She'd crawled up on top of a block of ice so she could peer over the edge.

"We might have to try," Reed said. "Although that could be a trap. Grason could jump out with his rifle and get us in the open."

"Why bother? We're going to die," Wynona mumbled in a thinly hysterical voice. "If it isn't the cold, then it's that bear. He isn't very far away. It's all a joke."

Kurth wrapped both arms around his wife. "She's freezing."

"Here, I'm warm, she can borrow my coat for a while," Pewter said.

"No," Reed snapped.

"What's with you?" Pewter asked. She looked at Reed as she would an intrusive stranger.

"I said no. You never sacrifice the many for the few. Because then you lose everyone. I need you and Vitus warm and ready for action. If we don't make it, Wynona won't make it. It's up to you, Kurth. Trade your coat back and forth, keep her moving. Get your core temperature up and your extremities will feel all right."

"We can all trade off helping her," Pewter insisted.

"I said no." Reed spoke softly but with an undeniably hard undertone. He tied a blue handkerchief around his head in pirate fashion, something to help retain his warmth. He met Pewter's glare with a steady, uncompromising look.

"Now you're taking on the appropriate look."

Reed ignored the pointed remark. He turned to Kurth. "I want the two of you to go over on the other side of that next pressure ridge. Look for some massive blocks of ice that form a bit of cave, someplace we can squeeze into if the wind comes up."

Kurth studied Reed as if judging his motives. His normally ruddy face had turned pasty. Bags had formed under his eyes. A twisted and frightened look had narrowed his blue eyes into darting little beacons that could not seem to focus. He nodded as if to acknowledge Reed's leadership. Then, without another word, he turned and set off across the ice, Wynona leaning on his side like an invalid.

After a time, Pewter hissed, "Did you have to say that in front of her?"

"Yes." Reed looked away from Pewter's anger. But she had to know the truth. "Kurth has to know the facts. And Wynona's not comprehending much right now. She has to know the score. It's going to take every ounce of fiber she has to survive. I'm not sacrificing anyone for her. If Grason comes after us, her only chance is to hide. The options here are limited. You go with what you have. That's all nature allows."

Reed glanced at Wynona and Kurth. Wynona stumbled and almost went down. He swallowed and muttered, "If the wind comes up or the temperature drops, she's gone."

Pewter stepped after Kurth.

"No," Reed ordered in a voice that made Pewter stiffen with anger. "We have to get that airplane or at least a signal out or no one goes home. And that's the bottom line here."

Tears brimmed in Pewter's dark brown eyes. She was bitter. "I don't really know you at all, do I? You're probably right. But I'd never decide to be like you. I couldn't."

Vitus spoke from his perch near the top of the pressure ridge. "Grason has his rifle. He's coming this way."

As if appreciative of the chance for physical action, Reed jumped up on the slippery ridge and peeked over. "All right, we must have done some damage to the tail. We'll have to move fast and split up here. I'll go up this way and see if Grason will follow. Pewter, you and Vitus go down the other way. If he follows me over to the next pressure ridge, one of you stand lookout and the other make for the airplane."

"He locked the doors," Vitus said.

"Well try to break in. Try the pontoon storage bins for a raft and emergency radio. If nothing else smash the rudder a bit more or take it all together if you can wrench it loose. Now go, and be careful."

"And what, you're going to offer yourself as a target?" Pewter asked.

"Just get moving down along this ridge," Reed hissed angrily. "We don't have time."

"Kurth, Wynona?"

"Dammit, Pewter, go," Reed snapped. He saw her anger. He glanced across. The two were struggling to climb the next pressure ridge. "They're on their own."

As Pewter and Vitus started down alongside the pressure ridge, Reed peered over the top of the ridge. This time he rose a little higher, his head from his nose on up, enough so Grason might spot him, but not enough so Grason might think he was leading him on.

Grason unshouldered his rifle, turned and headed his way. Reed dropped down and began jogging toward the next pressure ridge. He had two hundred yards. Grason, walking steadily, had about fifty. Here and there in patches of snow, Grason would see his tracks. And those of Wynona and Kurth, and Vitus and Pewter headed in the opposite direction.

Reed jogged steadily. He might get caught in the open. With a rifle and a scope Grason would have him dead. He jogged faster. He unzipped his coat and pulled the handkerchief off his head. He was warming up, beginning to sweat. And everyone who ever went on the pack ice knew that sweat was the beginning of death.

He glanced back, fully expecting to see a figure rising up over the pressure ridge. Pewter and Vitus moved at a jog-trot down beside the ridge. If Grason altered course slightly he could rise up and come down right on top of them. Or, with the jumble of spires, Reed might not see him. He could be lined on his chest this moment. Reed stepped to the side, setting up a zig-zag pattern, one direction and then another, very much like his life.

He neared the opposite pressure ridge. There was no set pattern to this strange and beautiful world of white, gray and blue. In places along the ridge wind-blown snow had drifted into impenetrable ridges. Other places gray patches of older ice that had melted and refroze multiple times lay rough and bare and would not show his tracks. In the open, rippled ridges of wind-drifted snow had formed hard crusts that broke through under his boots and left him floundering as helplessly as a walrus on the shore.

He paused, looking back and then up at the huge blocks of ice tumbled in a twenty-foot-high ridge that was at least thirty feet across. Other ridges were much larger. Some were older and worn and filled with snow. Others, like newly formed mountains, had sharp, jagged crags rising forty and fifty feet into the air. The forces were beyond imagining.

Reed picked out an opening in the ridge and climbed up onto the top and moved to place a large block of ice between him and Grason.

A shot rang out, an echoing thunder that sliced like an icicle into his heart. Reed whirled. Three hundred yards away Grason's head and torso rose above the ice, rifle pointed down the ridge. Pewter and Vitus ducked into a bay in the ice, peeking back. Grason started down the top of the ridge, moving with great difficulty, but staying high so he could watch both sides. Two hundred yards away, Pewter and Vitus edged along tightly against the ridge. Sooner or later Grason would see them in the open, sooner or later he'd get a clean shot. And he would, Reed realized, shoot to kill. Grason had no other choice.

Reed clambored down the ridge and moved out into the undulating ice field. The wind blew against his right side. Tiny ice crystals scraped across the snow. Twenty yards, then thirty, the safety of the pressure ridge falling behind. He cupped his hands. "Grason, you sonofabitch, come and get me."

Grason turned, looking one way and then the other. He abruptly snapped the rifle to his shoulder, the movement so fast a part of Reed saw it as a dream. But then he moved. A bullwhip sizzled through the freezing air. Thunder clapped. He sprawled into crusty snow with the ungainly lack of control of an animal that had been shot. Reed gasped for breath. He'd forgotten Grason's experience, the years of hunting. Even at three hundred yards and snapping a shot, if he would have stood still he would have dropped dead.

Reed bobbed up and back, a rapid peek, enough to glimpse Grason standing with the rifle to his shoulder. His chest ached and he felt the return of air into his lungs. He looked at ice crystals of snow covering his gloves, beautiful little spires, cones and pellets, a world unseen within the greater world around. And then Reed noticed the dampness, the cold seeping into his stomach, sucking the warmth out of the core of his being.

His mind clicked, as intense and focused as a man walking a corridor to his death. Had Grason seen the first bob? Was he lying there with the scope centered on the spot?

Reed gingerly crawled to one side, picking up more snow, becoming more damp, feeling the chill. He bobbed up. Grason was in the open, moving steadily across the ice in his direction.

He was a dead man, Reed thought. As soon as he stood it would be like walking in front of a firing squad. Or to lie here like a wounded animal and wait for Grason to walk up and finish him off. He rolled on one hip, stomach down, facing away from Grason. He surveyed the landscape back toward the pressure ridge. Ten yards to a snow-covered shard of worn ice, a nice little shield four feet high. No time to look, he thought, just move, five yards straight, five yards oblique.

He coiled one leg underneath his stomach. He studied the footing, sheets of slippery ice, mounds of crusted drifts. If he floundered, if he fell . . .

His chest ached. His heart pounded, an adrenaline high, but this one did not feel so good. He drew two deep breaths and then he exploded like a whitetail deer rising out of its bed.

He thought nothing of Grason. His every concentration was on the task assigned to him, pumping legs, pumping arms, eyes wide, watching the snow, anticipating when he might slip, when the crust might suddenly collapse. Grason was fast, that snap shot had taken less than a second to raise the rifle and fire at a target three hundred yards away. He felt the tightness in his back, the knowledge the bullet would tear into him before the shot was heard, a tiny 180-grain projectile, penetrating frail human flesh, mushrooming, ripping out systems that had taken billions of years to evolve.

His nerve failed. He abandoned the chosen path and swerved to his right, crossing a patch of ice he'd thought to circle around. His footing gave way, skidding, arms waving for balance. A hissing somewhere nearby, a bee buzzing through arctic air. A thunderclap. He touched snow and regained his balance. Five endless yards, fifteen feet, more than enough time for Grason to line up and shoot. Two steps, three, he dove, tumbling, rolling even as another shot zipped past.

As much as he desired, he did not hug the shelter of the ice. He peered over the top mound of snow. Grason, rifle held cross-arms, was trotting in his direction. As long as Grason was moving, he could not shoot. Keeping his head up and watching, Reed began to back toward the pressure ridge, keeping the patch of snow and ice between him and Grason. Once Grason stopped and raised the rifle. Reed ducked and continued to back. He counted sixty seconds then quickly rose. Grason had resumed his trot and was little more than a hundred and fifty yards away.

Reed had backed to the pressure ridge, but now he had to get up over the top, as exposed as a mountain climber hanging from a rope. No chance, he knew. He'd outsmarted himself.

A distant shout carried, Pewter standing in clear sight on top of the opposite ridge. His partner, Reed thought. Tears welled. Grason turned, looking back. In that same instant Reed moved, vaulting upward, touching the top of one sheared block, sliding on another, clawing with hands and feet at ice and snow. One second, two seconds, three seconds. Surely Grason had seen him move. He lurched to one side and then the other, rapid side-movement even as he slowly dragged to the top of a fifteen-foot-high ridge.

A hand reached up and tugged at his coat. A thunderclap with all the force of a jet breaking the sound barrier echoed across the ice. He dove across the top, tumbling and sliding down the opposite side like an otter going down a slide.

ESKIMO MONEY

But this was not for fun. He had no control. He braced and slammed off the side of an ice wall, raising a knot on his head. He grunted and without hesitation rose to his feet and set out at a trot. In combat there was a time for patience and there was a time to move. And when you moved you moved fast and hard.

The idea now was escape, to put distance between himself and Grason. Even as he moved his eyes took in the ice field, the black water of a nearby lead blocking any escape to the next pressure ridge. The sickness burned in his stomach. He'd known men who'd fought tooth and nail, bleeding, in terrible agony, giving no quarter for hour after hour, the most supreme effort possible and then, with the complete lack of compassion of real nature, the men ended up dead, another lifeless piece of meat.

Reed turned to survey the opposite direction. The ridge extended on, somewhere, lost in a fog. A quarter-mile or so down this same ridge Kurth and Wynona were concealed. He moaned as he turned. The burning seared like someone had placed a hot iron in the flesh high up beside his ribs. And then he saw the dark droplets of blood. The tug at his coat had been a bullet. Grason would be pleased.

He turned and began to run. No need to worry about sweating and then freezing now, he thought. He'd die from a bullet first.

Reed covered a hundred yards, staying tight against the ridge of ice, an undulating wall with fresh shards of ice so steep there were few places to cross. However, there were numerous bays, indentations, tiny tunnels, a thousand places to hide, albeit for the occasional indentation of his tracks and the tiny drops of blood coagulating in the snow. One thing here, Grason would have to pick one side or the other on this ridge. The top was far too jagged for movement.

Inside a circular bay, hidden from Grason's view, an old pool of water had refrozen into a pond of ice. He moved halfway down the pool and turned back. There were a couple drops of blood. He pressed his arm against his ribcage, hoping to stem the flow. He moved back along his tracks, leaped over a little mound of snow and ice and began to work upward to cross over the pressure ridge. With only one hand for pulling, the going was difficult. He could use his other arm in an emergency, Reed thought, but to do so now would only increase the flow of blood, leave a track, weaken him for the fight ahead.

He clawed up, scraping snow, leaving a mark, and then another. Grason might be fooled, but not for very long. He topped the jagged ridge and cautiously peeked over a mound. Nothing. His spirit ebbed. Was Grason lying in wait, ready to ambush his unwary prey? He had the advantage, the rifle, surely he'd stay with the track.

A cold wind scraped the side of Reed's face, a reminder of his exertion, the dampness of his clothes, the buildup of heat within his body core, and now this stillness, his exposed position, all invitations to a crash. He was dying of thirst and thought to compact some snow, more ice that would take away his heat and add to his demise. But he had to stay hydrated, pumped with enough moisture to ward off hypothermia and to keep the systems going. It was all so hard to decide.

He looked down through a small cave that ran straight down into the ridge. Light filtered into the side and the ice changed from clear to azure blue. One ridge leading down the side of the cave was cut as sharp as if someone had used a knife. At the bottom a turquoise pool of water had formed and tiny shrimp darted about. Pewter would enjoy this, he knew. He could tell her about eating the raw shrimp while on the hunt with Vitus.

He shivered and a flood of regrets filled his thoughts. If only they would have had time, a proper setting other than on a case.

Movement flickered in the corner of his eye. Reed moved only his eyes, a click left to see Grason walking down along the ridge, following his track. Fifty yards away and moving right along. Grason looked up, sweeping the ridgetop. Reed did not move. Grason passed behind a shard of ice. Reed ducked and worked down the opposite side of the ridge. More exertion needed now, something to take away the chill.

He trotted along the ridge, headed back in the direction he'd first come. He glanced toward the opposite ridge, Pewter should be on watch while Vitus tried to break inside the airplane. But he could see nothing. He continued on his way until he reached the path he'd first scaled. He saw the first spots of his own blood, and the indentation where Grason had knelt and then touched the blood, probably rubbing it between his thumb and forefinger, a badge of his shooting prowess.

There was the fact also, wounding an animal and doggedly staying on the trail, making it move, keep the blood flowing, using resources, worrying on the creature until you finally see the creature lying, either dead in its bed, or too weak to get up and run.

Reed perched on the center of the ridge, in a concealed spot so he could look down both sides. The wind lanced his skin. His arms and legs trembled. A spasm of shivering racked him head to foot. Ten minutes before he'd been as lucid as a fresh-melt pond, and now he felt lost in a fog.

The plan had been to wait and see which side Grason came down, then go on the opposite and begin to move, circles upon circles, until what? But he didn't have time, and he didn't have strength. Right now he needed to

ESKIMO MONEY

find a cave, someplace where he could hide.

He slid down the ridge, turned down in the direction where Kurth and Wynona were hiding and began to move. He should trot, a part of him thought, but his legs were heavy, his shoulders weary. A couple times he turned and glanced back. If Grason stayed with the trail, he might soon cross over the ridge. If he'd crossed over to begin with.

Reed spun quickly, crouched, fully expecting to see Grason leveling the rifle at his chest. Was that fog or was that clouds? Flakes of snow drifted at a forty-five-degree angle through the air. How far had he moved, fifty yards? A hundred? The passage of time seemed hard to grasp. Grason might cross over any second. He should cross over himself.

Or maybe Grason was smart enough to wait on the opposite side, knowing sooner or later he'd cross again. Or maybe Grason would just climb up on top and watch the best he could down either side.

Reed turned and began a rapid shuffle along the ridge. He had to figure this out, get inside Grason's mind, think as he would think. But then Grason would do the same, get inside him, think as he would think. But of course right now he was so tired he could not think. He giggled. That would throw Grason for a loop.

His foot hit a ridge of ice and slid out and he tumbled to his side. "Uhhh!" The hot slice of a knife through flesh cut his wounded side. He lay there, eyes trying to focus. A wad of cotton coated his mouth and he shoveled a handful of snow inside. It was gone in an instant and he shoveled in more. That he shivered violently he did not notice. He closed his eyes. A moment's rest. That was all he asked, just a moment or two.

Something stung his face. He tried to see through a swirl of blinding snow. Damn, a full-scale blizzard was beginning to brew. Something to cover his tracks, leave Grason behind.

Reed struggled to his feet. A piece of his mind acknowledged his foolishness, lying down and letting himself freeze to death. He knew better than that. Why the hell didn't he think?

He peered back down the ridge. Visibility had dropped markedly. But the ridge jutted out here, running him right out into the open. And he did not have the strength to crawl up through the spires. Could Grason see? Was he there?

"The hell with it," Reed muttered. "Whatever you do, Grason, make it clean, one shot. Remember your hunter ethics."

He smiled and began his relentless shuffle through the snow. The bad news was that the wind blew directly into his face. The good news was it would blow into Grason's face as well. But the bad news was the wind chill was taking away his warmth. The good news . . . Reed pawed at snow and ice crystals fusing his eyelashes into one. The good news . . . He didn't have much warmth to take away. Yeah, the good news was if he froze it wouldn't take long. Not long at all.

He shuffled on. The only chance now was to move, just move.

CHAPTER NINETEEN

"Reed?" the uncertain voice called out of the snow. Reed stopped. Only the muscles for straight-ahead movement seemed to have any blood. He slowly turned, feeling the strain tearing at his flesh.

Kurth peered out of a small enclave in the ice. He looked one direction and then the other. "Where is everyone? I heard the shots. I saw Grason chasing after you. Where is he?"

Reed negotiated the turn and shuffled forward a few steps. He stopped once and made a slow, creaking turn to peer back in the direction he had come. Swirling snow blocked his view and coated his eyelashes. "Gra . . . Grashun." He rubbed his frozen lips, trying for circulation. "I don't know." He shrugged and slipped inside the enclave and immediately felt the absence of the wind.

He looked at Wynona, a small dark figure huddled within herself. The side of her face was grotesquely swollen and the broken blood vessels in her eye glared out like a hot and bright red beacon. But she had no fire, no will, even he could see that.

He would become that, a part of Reed thought. He shuffled around in a tight circle. Keep moving. Keep moving. If only he weren't so tired.

"Do you think they got into the airplane?" Kurth asked.

Reed paused and looked up. Kurth's face was pale, pinched, the lines distinct, the boyish exuberance erased. "I donno. Go see. Tell others, come back. Get out of storm." Reed slurred out his little speech.

Kurth looked at his wife. "You'll stay with Wynona?"

Reed nodded.

"What about Grason?"

"I donno. Watch," Reed said simply. He shuffled around in a small circle, using his right arm to try to rub circulation into his face and pound warmth into his body. He kept his left arm sealed tight against the side of his rib cage, not willing to disturb the burning slice of the wound.

Kurth knelt to his wife. Her eyes flickered, staring at him but seemingly without comprehension. "I'll be back, honey. I'm going to get the others. Reed will stay here to protect you."

Wynona smiled. Her head rolled from side to side with mirth she could not contain. Kurth rose. He turned to Reed. "We have to do something. Her mind's gone. She's freezing to death."

"My mind's perfectly fine. Get the hell out," Wynona barked in a high, thin voice. "Just go, do it."

Kurth looked to Reed for help, but Reed was shuffling a tiny war-dance circle. "Jesus, is your mind gone too," Kurth muttered. He stepped outside the enclave.

"Watch for Grason," Reed said in his head. It was only after Kurth had disappeared from sight that he realized the words had not passed his lips.

Move or die. Move or die. The refrain burned. He shuffled in a tiny circle. One, two, three, four. One, two, three, four. Each time he faced the entrance he expected Grason to appear. "Hi, Reed. I've been looking for you."

"Terry. Let's sit down and talk. Remember that grizzly bear you drove past me with the Super Cub? You gave me one bullet and didn't tell me. I admit now I didn't want to kill a bear. But a charging grizzly and one bullet, that's a blast."

"Who the hell are you talking to?"

Reed turned. Wynona was looking up at him. "What?"

"I said, who the hell are you talking to?"

"I wasn't talking."

Wynona shrugged. She looked out the entrance. The snow was thicker, huge flakes angling down against the push of the wind. "How the hell could this happen? Who could believe we'd end up like this?"

"You never know," Reed muttered. "Good effort gives you the best odds. But there are no guaranties. I thought I knew Grason, thought he was just like me." He began to shuffle in a tiny circle. "Maybe it's what I wanted to see."

"Do you have to keep doing that?" Wynona snapped.

Reed slowly paused. "Blocking your view?"

"No, I'm sitting here trying to freeze, like you wanted me to freeze and you're irritating me."

Reed stared, considering her words, mulling them over in his mind. He suddenly brightened, like a drunk who has stumbled upon a lucid thought. "Well, maybe getting mad at me will get you warm. Think of that." He merrily began to shuffle. Move or die. "Move or die."

And then they heard the distant crack, a hollow thump carrying through the gloom of the snowfall. Reed slowly looked at Wynona.

"Grason just shot Kurth," Wynona muttered with just a hint of triumph. "I knew it. You sent him out there to die. Why didn't you go?"

Reed shook his head in the negative. "Ice. I think it was ice." He paused, considering. "Ice. I think it was ice." He began to shuffle in his tiny circle. "Move or die. Move or die."

In truth, he thought, he actually felt quite fresh. Wynona should move. But she really wasn't any business of his. He'd told Pewter. It wasn't lack of consideration, it was reality. The guys knew it in Vietnam. You didn't kill the platoon to rescue one guy who was going to die anyhow. Tough decision. It had to be made. "Move or die. Move or die." He'd say it aloud, he thought. Perhaps Wynona would understand.

Darkness blotted the opening of the enclave. Three forms entered, filling up the space. Reed continued to shuffle in his circle. They could do whatever they wanted. He was not going to quit. It was not part of his being. If you weren't the biggest, the strongest, the fastest, the smartest, you had only intestinal fortitude, the will to go on, the long-distance runner, the ultra marathoner, just keep going, sooner or later the others would fall by the way. Even the bigger, the stronger, those like Grason, rifle in hand. At least Grason had to give him that, he hadn't succumbed without a fight.

Hands gripped his arms. Reed looked up, blinking, trying to focus, a man, short, pug features, a nose almost recessed in order to fight against the cold. Vitus. His old hunting partner. He'd once hunted walrus with Vitus, years ago, back when he'd been a special agent.

"Reed. Look at me." Someone gripped his cheeks. An angel, smooth tan skin, high cheekbones, black shiny hair, deep, dark eyes. There'd been an attraction there, physical at first. But there could have been more, a love of the outdoors, a shared camaraderie, a shared warmth, someone opening his coat, his shirt, taking off his clothes.

"You're damp. Look, Vitus, he's shot."

"Pewter," Reed said. He grinned. She was taking off her clothes. Reed leered. "No. This isn't right." He motioned at Vitus. "People." They pulled something over his head, and then around his shoulders. Pewter moved in close, pressing her chest and stomach tight against his, arms wrapped down around his ribcage even as someone pressed in against his back.

He was not alone, Reed thought. He could relax, give himself to others, let the body succumb, take over.

"No, damn you. Stand up. We have a lot to do. Vitus couldn't break into the airplane. Grason came back. He's inside the airplane, waiting out the storm."

Reed struggled to stand, to comprehend. Pewter pressed into him, her cheek against his, her body as molded as she could make it just as someone else pressed against him from behind. Reed closed his eyes. If only he could sleep. A few minutes. Couldn't they give him that.

"Stand, you damn sonofabitch!"

Reed looked. Why was Pewter screaming at him? He shook his head. Grason was right. A man tried to do right and it all came back in his face.

"Here, we'll march," Pewter said. "Left foot, right foot. You were in the army, march. March dammit!"

Screaming again, at him. Reed dutifully shuffled his feet. He'd tried to be considerate. He'd tried to be strong. It just didn't seem to work. They marched and they marched, and they marched, a neverending process that became a goal in itself, anything to stop Pewter from screaming in his face.

Gradually lucidity emerged. The first clear thought was that his fingers tingled. And then they burned, excruciating pain like someone was holding his hands in boiling water. He glanced at Pewter, her face an inch away and saw the exhaustion in her eyes. He bussed her cheek. "Thanks. Now if you'll turn me around, I'll kiss Vitus thanks as well."

Pewter smiled. "Just keep moving. Get completely warm. We couldn't break into the airplane, although Vitus smashed the rudder even more."

They turned, the three of them shuffling together. "Kurth," Reed said. "There was a shot. I thought you were dead."

"No. When I started across, I saw Grason ahead of me. I just stayed back."

"Good. Good." They shuffled around and around. Eventually Reed buttoned his shirt and his coat over Pewter's dry thermax underwear and the three of them edged in and crowded in next to Kurth and Wynona on a slanted block of ice.

"How's Wynona?" Reed asked through thickened lips.

"Still here, asshole, no thanks to you," Wynona said.

"First I have to walk and then I have to walk and now we sit. I'm afraid I don't see the point."

"We're out of the wind," Pewter said to Reed. "But sitting on the ice sucks away warmth also. I'm sitting on my gloves."

"Yeah, good idea," Reed said and repositioned himself. He could feel Pewter watching and tried to steady his movements as he lay his gloves down and repositioned himself. "Grason's in the airplane, probably wrapped up in a sleeping bag."

"But not zipped up," Vitus said. "With this wind he has to worry about the airplane getting blown on its back."

184   ESKIMO MONEY

"If the airplane sinks we're dead," Kurth said.

"We're dead anyhow," Wynona snapped. "Before my toes were stinging. Now I can't feel my feet."

"Better walk," Pewter said. "At least get up and jump up and down in place. Ten minutes."

Wynona protested. Kurth joined in and they finally dragged her to her feet and made her move.

Pewter joined Reed back on the ice, moving in close, almost affectionate, Reed thought. He trembled violently. Vitus pushed in from the other side. He sensed Vitus and Pewter looking past him at each other. "I'm all right, dammit," he snarled. "Just a few minutes rest, a little time out of the wind."

Distant rumbling carried. The ice suddenly jolted beneath their feet. Showers of snow rained off the walls. Wynona cursed. "Damn. What are we going to do, sit here and wait until we're crushed or freeze to death? Maybe a bear will come, or Grason. Who knows. Or maybe we'll hear the airplane when he flies over."

"If you like, you can go out and stand watch," Reed snarled. "I give you twenty minutes, thirty tops. We can sit on your boots. I can use your coat. Every layer helps."

Wynona's dark eyes flashed. "You are a sonofabitch."

"Honey, please," Kurth said. His eyes were red. A white splotch of frostbite had formed on the tip of his nose. He stared at Reed as if trying to judge the man. "I could go stand watch."

"No," Reed muttered. "The wind's too strong. Grason's inside the airplane. He's not working on it now. If the wind tips it over there's nothing we can do. Our fight now is with the cold and the wind. We have to work on that."

In time Wynona and Kurth rejoined them on the slanted slab of ice. They sat quietly, listening to the sounds of the ice, the creakings, the moanings from inside the pressure ridge. The wind whistled five feet over their heads and blew snow dust down on their shoulders and blew a dust covering across the lumpy and open ice to their front.

In time visibility closed to less than a hundred yards. The distinction between the horizon and the sky became blurred, near whiteout conditions that confined their world even more. Once, through the low sheets of blowing snow, Reed thought he saw a polar bear, a huge, pigeon-toed creature slowly crossing the ice plain. It looked their direction, the consummate hunter covered by white, hollow hair and four inches of fat. But then snow blew and it was gone. His imagination, Reed wondered? It had only been there a second, maybe two. He glanced at Vitus, but the half-Yupik did not move.

He looked to see if Pewter noticed, but only saw pity and wondered why. What was between them? What counted? What mattered? Why now did she have to see him weak?

Here they sat, like five little birdies perched on a limb and huddled against the storm. Grason could look inside their little enclave and pick them off one by one.

Or, more likely, Reed thought, they would huddle here while the warmth of their bodies slowly ebbed into the chilly air and the surrounding ice. Ever so slowly the flow of blood to their extremities would cease. Veins would close and freeze. Fingers, toes, arms, and legs would become useless, without feeling. Blood flow would concentrate within the body core, keeping vital organs alive even as cold invaded the body from every direction. Eventually blood flow to the brain would become minimal. The mind would grow numb, unable to focus, unable to reason. Perhaps there would be hysteria, brief seconds of lucidity as the knowledge of painless death drew near. Perhaps they would struggle. But more likely their capabilities would be gone. They'd go to sleep, five people huddled inside a pressure ridge in the midst of the Arctic pack ice. A touching little scene, Reed thought with a smile, if they were ever found.

They should walk. They should move, Reed thought. But it was so comfortable where they were, Pewter at his side. He smiled. His head bobbed on his chest. At the moment he needed to sleep. Just a few minutes sleep. Then he'd be all right.

ESKIMO MONEY

CHAPTER TWENTY

The winds had abated. They'd spent hours huddled together. Sometimes they moved, Kurth with Wynona and Pewter or Vitus helping, Reed with Vitus and Pewter assisting him on either side. The ice rumbled beneath them, a subtle motion reminding them of instability. Once the ice cracked loudly, a shot that jerked their heads and made hearts race. The new, erratic fractures exposed a dark sea that was warmer than the air. The water steamed, a water sky, a direction for boats during ancient times, a jagged escape route or a dead-end alley where moving ice would crush those unaware. Gradually an ice fog covered all the floes.

After hours of relative silence, Vitus began to talk. "My people have earned their living on the ice like this for twenty thousand years. A man can become lost in the fog, sometimes for weeks. At one time we distracted polar bears with dogs and men stepped in and killed them with a lance. Very often a hunter would die. Other times a hunter would go onto the ice and cover himself and sit by a seal hole, sometimes for half a day."

"The patience of the hunter," Reed said. He held his elbows at his side, his arms crossed over his stomach trying to retain core body heat as much as he could. He'd slept, he'd walked, he'd shivered. Now, with the wind abated, he'd gained a measure of warmth, a measure of renewed strength. "Like the polar bear. One bear was observed waiting by a seal hole for fourteen hours."

"I've seen a polar bear snorkel through the water with just his nose in the air," Vitus said. "A sea bear. They jump out of the water and try to catch the seal on the edge of the ice. That's what the polar bear does with his life, like the Eskimo, he hunts."

Reed shifted his weight. Neither Pewter nor Vitus appeared cold. Once he'd noticed Pewter shivering, but the walks seemed to help her regain her warmth. Although her face was drawn, the firm lines seemed to sag with the weight of exhaustion. She'd used herself, saving everyone else, a hero for the cause, if he could ever write a report. Reed looked down at his boots. He'd misjudged himself, worked up a sweat then stayed in the wind too long. He'd been losing it. If it wasn't for Pewter and Vitus he'd probably be gone.

"When a polar bear stalks a seal on the ice, when the seal looks up, the polar bear keeps moving, slow and steady, belly to the ice," Vitus continued. His head was down, he talked almost as if to himself, remembering the past. "In the old days men would cover themselves with sealskin and crawl out to where a seal lay in the open. When they got close they would use a stick and rake the ice as if they had flippers. In time the seal would ignore them, as if they were another seal. People had great respect for the animals. The death of a polar bear was met with reverence and offerings; the death of a whale with great ceremony and sharing. Blanket tosses and prayer. We were a community then."

Kurth jumped to his feet. He flapped his arms wildly, trying to gain warmth. "Jesus, Vitus, do we have to listen to this? Those are the old days. They're past. Your people are dead and are just waiting for the funeral. We have to think about surviving. What are we going to do, just sit here and freeze?"

"The last time I looked, Grason had turned the airplane around. He was working on the tail," Vitus said in the same mild tone he'd used telling his stories. He directed his words at Reed.

"Was he watching close? Did he appear alert?" Reed asked.

"Not much," Vitus said. "It was not as foggy as this, but it was hard to see. He might have had the rudder in place. But I don't know if it would turn."

Reed stood up. He shuffled his feet, trying to gain warmth. He looked at the others one by one. Wynona was grotesque, Kurth frightened and tense, Pewter had aged, her teeth clenched, her dark eyebrows twisted with worry. She'd withdrawn, because of the exhaustion or fear he could not tell. Perhaps she'd given too much, just as had he. Only Vitus appeared unchanged, perhaps a little sad, a little melancholy, but fully capable, fully willing.

"It's not the best chance," Reed said, "but it might be our only chance. Vitus' stories gave me an idea. I think we have to go for something. And now, before it's too late. Pewter." She looked him in the eyes. "Get undressed."

For several seconds no one spoke. Reed showed the hint of a smile. "Get undressed. I need that white nightgown you wore underneath your underwear. Vitus and I are going to pretend we're a white mound of snow and ice. If Grason's not watching and with this fog, we've got a damn good chance to get close."

"He's got a gun. If he spots you in the open you're dead," Pewter said. "Besides, you're wounded."

"We're dead anyhow," Reed said. "If we get close enough we can jump him before he gets his gun free. You and Kurth can be down the ridge. If you have to you can distract him before he sees us. When we get hold of him, you come running out to help. Kurth, you help us. Pewter, you go for the airplane. There's a rifle inside, maybe another pistol." As Reed talked, he became more forceful, giving orders, feeling the warmth flooding back into his veins. There was a chance here, something they could do.

They talked, discussing the options, the possibilities. Abruptly Pewter turned her back. She slipped off her coat, her sweater, the gray Thermax top of Reed's long underwear that she'd taken to replace her own. And then she pulled her nightgown out of her pants and over her head. Goose bumps rose on the smooth expanse of her naked and muscled back. Reed handed her the underwear top and she quickly redressed.

Reed ripped the nightgown down the front so he had one flat sheet. They could crawl on hands and knees behind it and keep it draped in front of them. The gown was not snow white, but then the ice and snow was in various shades of gray and blue and white. The blend would be close enough. And their outline would be erased. The two problems lay unmentioned, how they would withstand the cold, and what they would do with Grason even if they got close enough to jump him. Two, even three half-freezing men did not seem like enough.

They rose to depart. "What about Wynona?" Kurth asked. "She's so cold."

"This is her only chance at warmth," Reed said. "She can come or she can stay. There isn't any wind. But when we jump Grason you can't hesitate. You come and you come fast. I don't know if four of us can take Grason or not, but it's our only chance."

"He ain't that tough," Kurth argued. "Four of us on one? If you get hold of him and I get there, we'll have him, no problem."

Reed frowned. "Just be there, as hard and as fast as you can. Either that or it'll be you and Grason one-on-one."

"I'll be there," Kurth promised. He was eager, seeing the same chance as did everyone else. "You can bet on it."

"Good," Reed said.

They started out across the ice, heading for the pressure ridge closest to the airplane. With the exception of Wynona and Kurth who moved together at the rear, they moved in a spread single file, dark forms shrouded in fog and moving across a carpet of white. The wind-chill had abated, but the fog was damp, penetrating. The purposeful movement served to bring warmth.

They reached the base of the pressure ridge. Vitus climbed up and peered over the top. Grason still had the airplane turned and was hard at work.

"Okay," Reed said when Vitus returned. His breath billowed into the fog. "Pewter, you and Kurth and Wynona move down that way about fifty yards. That'll give us a better angle if you have to distract Grason. Vitus and I are going to go down the line here, cross over the ridge and come down right along the edge of the lead. We should be able to walk to within thirty or forty yards before we have to get down and crawl. There's no reason for Grason to be watching along the lead, unless of course he's worried about bears. But I don't think he's too worried about that because he left the rifle inside the airplane."

"All right," Pewter said.

"Kick him in the balls," Kurth said. "We'll come just as fast as we can." He turned with Wynona and started down along the ice. Vitus turned and started in the opposite direction.

Reed stood face to face with Pewter. He swallowed. When he spoke his voice came out a croak. "Well, this is it."

Pewter took both of his gloved hands in her gloved hands. She struggled to speak. "In my wildest nightmares I never imagined any of this, Grason, the ice, you."

"Me, a nightmare."

Pewter smiled. "And you can still joke? No. I just . . . I've never killed anything. It's been on my mind, trying to get set, just like you said. You say you need Kurth's strength. You want me to go for the airplane, for a pistol, a rifle. And then what?"

"You do what you have to do, and do it fast," Reed said. He tightened his grip on her hand. "Don't think, just do it."

Pewter stepped back. Tears brimmed in her eyes. "You're so damn tough. Born and raised in the jungle. It's easy for you. Everything's changed. How can I go back? Even if we survive this, things will never be the same." She backed away, one step and then another, her face slowly obscured by the fog. When she was but a black outline against the gloom, she raised a hand, the sad and tentative gesture of someone resigned to their fate. Reed waved back. He turned and walked a few steps. When he stopped to look back she was gone.

Reed trailed Vitus down the ice then wallowed up through the snow and crossed the pressure ridge. The airplane lay out of sight, but they could hear metal pounding on metal, the sound amplified by the fog. They crossed the ice and walked down near the black water of the lead. They'd stay fifteen or twenty feet away, Vitus suggested. The ice could be washed out from underneath, a cornice that could break beneath their weight. But to stay close would mean the lapping water would cover the sound of their approach.

Slowly but steadily they advanced in the direction of the airplane. Pounding carried, and was followed by a muttered curse. The vague outlines of the airplane emerged from the mist. Reed motioned Vitus to his side and they unfurled the nightgown and each held one edge up in front of their nose and let the gown hang down toward their knees, something so that if Grason glanced their way it would blot out most of their dark shapes.

Soon Grason's dark figure emerged more clearly. For the most part he faced in their direction — unfortunate, for he simply had to raise his eyes to see them. When he turned away, Reed tugged Vitus's elbow and the two of them sank to the snow on hands and knees. Reed grunted in agony as the movement tore open the wound under his arm. A wet, sticky sensation trickled down his arm. As best as they could they arranged the nightgown so it covered their backs and hung down in front of their faces. Reed had one little slit where he could peek out with one eye. Seventy or eighty feet, Reed thought. They slowly began their crawl.

He felt the wet packed snow beneath his hands and knees. A dampness ran down his burning side — blood. He gritted his teeth against the pain. Small ripples of water lapped at the nearby edge of the ice. The fog lay heavy and damp, cutting through their clothes, a conduit sucking away their warmth.

Reed whispered, "I can't tell when he's looking this way or not. We'll have to do it like your polar bear, slow and steady and hope we blend."

Vitus nodded. In the gloom under the nightgown, his dark eyes twinkled. If anything, Reed thought, Vitus was more excited and determined than scared. He felt the man's closeness, their shoulders rubbing, their hips touching as they crawled. He understood, Vitus he could trust.

Their cold, weakened, unnourished condition was quickly revealed. Reed's legs from the knees and thighs became soaked, as did the thin gloves on his hands. His knees ached, his arms ached, his sopping fingers slowly became numb. Resolve and strength oozed away on the cold. What the hell had he been thinking? Grason would see them ten feet away. One man would be shot. The other might hit Grason, but it would be like flinging themselves against a steel pylon. One blow or one shot and they'd be crushed. Kurth and Pewter would come one at a time. They'd die one at a time. Wynona would freeze.

Reed's arms trembled, unable to hold his weight. The spectre of failure pushed down.

But the reality was pain. And just when the agony became most excruciating, he realized he could see Grason clearly, the curled hair, the solid jaw, the towering figure twenty feet away. His arms all but collapsed. But the slightest miscue now and they would be dead.

He thought of Grason sitting in his huge log mansion, classical music booming, stuffed animal heads on the walls, wolf rugs, bear rugs, moose in the yard, a river down the bank. He'd worked and he'd built like a beaver building a dam. And then chance, a sudden break in the dam, outside intruders took it all away. But to kill five people?

People had faced worse and picked themselves up and continued on. But Grason had surrendered, unable to face his weakness. Reed huffed with surprise, the marathoner still huffing along. Just like the time Guy dislocated his shoulder when a Widow-Maker, a green poplar bent under the weight of another green poplar, snapped and knocked him out. Guy had walked from the woods, drove himself to the doctor's office, had the shoulder jerked into place, refused admission to the hospital, and the next day went back out to cut pulp. Never quit, never give in to emotion, never hug your kids. A sob clucked deep in Reed's throat.

Vitus gave him an elbow and a strange look.

"Sorry," Reed barely mouthed the word. They crawled on, the cutting ice slicing at his knees. He licked at his cracked lips and managed a smile. All this snow and ice and his throat was as parched as if they crawled upon the Sahara Desert.

Vitus elbowed Reed and they stopped. The nightgown had slipped forward, hanging down in front and barely covering half their backs. Reed glanced through his tiny peephole. He could see Grason's feet, unmoved, pointing in their direction. Had Grason picked them up, pulled his pistol and was even now pointing it at them?

He dared not raise his head. His knees screamed. His arms quivered. A violent shivering swept his body from head to foot. Surely Grason saw the movement. Throw the gown up and make a rush. Maybe they could knock him into the water, give the others a chance. Reed tensed, ready to explode. Vitus touched his hand, a simple pat, to wait, to be patient.

Grason's legs turned away. They each reached back with one hand and pulled the nightgown down so it covered their rear ends. They slowly began to crawl, drawing closer and and closer. Reed recalled the stories, you never saw the polar bear that stalked you until the final charge. Nevertheless, it seemed ridiculous Grason could not know they were there.

Someone hissed. Vitus's hand closed on his, a warning.

Reed glanced through his peephole. Ten feet. Life or death. Reed brought his legs up underneath him. Vitus did the same. Grason turned. Reed and Vitus rose, the nightgown dropping behind them. As one they rushed ahead like a polar bear making the final charge. They jolted Grason from either side as they each took an arm and drove him face first into the snow. Grason roared like a dinosaur. He whirled, kicking and flailing and easily ripping his arms free. He dug into his coat pocket and extracted a pistol. He half rose, Vitus hanging on the arm with the pistol, Reed on the other. The pistol discharged, a thunderous roar burning just past Reed's face.

Reed struggled. He'd hit Grason in the head, but the blow had no impact. He fought to hold an arm, but his numb fingers could not retain a grip on such a thrashing, powerful force. He glimpsed Kurth running, falling, Pewter coming from behind. Vitus had one hand on the pistol, trying to force it into the air. And then Vitus bit into Grason's hand and the pistol flew.

Reed ducked in behind Grason, trying for a Full Nelson. But the man's shoulders were too broad, his clothes too bulky. It was like wrestling a grizzly, the differences in strength were so immense the effort was a joke. The first sense of despair sucked at his resolve.

Grason slipped backward, and fell on top of Reed. The air exploded from Reed's chest. He saw Grason swing, heard the smack into Vitus's face.

As Grason clawed upward, Reed gasped for air and tried to follow. He glanced toward the snow and ice, searching for the pistol. Vitus had fallen off to one side. Kurth was there but had stopped. Grason swung. Reed ducked, trying to stay close, inside the range of a haymaker. Kurth picked up the grapple hook and anchor for the airplane and, with jagged edge raised, advanced on Grason from behind.

Grason turned, swinging wildly, tumbling Kurth sideways toward the back of the airplane and the black water of the open lead. Kurth yelped as he slithered into the brine. The airplane rocked and drifted out from the ice.

Reed backed, searching frantically in the snow for the pistol. But then Grason was on him, straddling, hands around his throat. Reed pawed ineffectually, but his arms were too short to reach Grason's face. He tried with his leg but he could not bring it up to Grason's head. A veil of blackness began to erase the light.

And then something crashed down on top of Grason's head. A shower of ice stung Reed's face. The grip loosened. He kicked and clawed and managed to slither free. He whirled to his feet. Pewter stood nearby, crouched and backing after slamming a block of ice on top of Grason's head. Vitus lay motionless on his back. Kurth screamed and clawed at the eighteen-inch-high ice ledge. The airplane, the anchor pulled from the ice, drifted a good twelve or fifteen feet from the edge of the ice. And was getting further away.

Grason slowly rose to his feet. He looked at Pewter and then Reed. His movements were casual, his voice amused. "Nice effort. Out there on the ice as well." He shook his head in admiration. "I knew you were pretty good. I guess you were right about that. It's the morality thing, the betrayal. I keep forgetting, even the Commies had good soldiers. Sometimes better. They knew deprivation." Grason looked down at the snow, searching for the pistol.

"Stay out of his reach," Reed instructed Pewter. His voice was little more than a croak.

Grason smiled. "Got a frog in your throat? What are you going to do now, the two of you, come and grab me?"

Reed circled, moving around Grason toward the edge of the ice. "It's over, Grason. Can't you see?"

"Help! Jesus, someone help," Kurth whined. He jumped and struggled and somehow managed to crawl out onto the ice. He coiled into a tiny, violently shivering ball. "Help, please." No one paid him any heed.

"Ten minutes and he'll be out of it. Half an hour and he'll be dead," Grason said. "Airplane's gone. How long do you think we'll survive?"

Reed passed near Pewter. "Stay out of his reach. If he gets that pistol, run back into the fog."

Pewter nodded, puzzled that Reed was still coiled, still in the fight even though Grason had handled him with ease.

Abruptly Reed turned, two racing steps and then he leaped out toward the drifting airplane. He went down, sinking into the obscene cold, an icy mask collapsing his blood, blasting his system with all the force and surprise of a booby trap. The edge of panic blackened his brain and he clawed for the surface. He sputtered and gasped as blood rushed to his inner core. A band of steel springs constricted his chest and he was certain the shock had triggered a massive coronary. He could not breathe. His boots and sopping clothes dragged him down. He could barely keep his chin above the freezing water. He kicked and paddled as hard as he could. It was just a few feet and then he reached the pontoon. But how the hell would he get aboard?

After several futile grabs, Reed gripped the edge of the float, pushed himself as far under the black, icy water as he could and then kicked and pulled upward and launched himself until one hand gripped a cross-brace. He grunted, kicking, thrashing, pulling his legs up.

Somehow he made it to the top of the float. He wanted to lie down, to die, to surrender to the shocking, all-encompassing cold. But he had a mission, an assignment. He could not quit. He struggled to his feet and climbed the metal step and fumbled for the door handle. Everything seemed uncoordinated, in slow motion. His fingers had no feeling. He crawled

194   ESKIMO MONEY

inside the airplane and immediately saw the rifle lying on the seat. He fumbled with the safety and turned back to shore.

Kurth still lay on the ice tucked into a fetal ball. Pewter stood off to one side, a smaller and darker figure behind her in the fog. Vitus had climbed to his feet, or else Grason had hauled him. For Grason hugged Vitus from behind and held a knife to his throat.

"You can kill me. But if you raise that rifle, I slit Vitus's throat," Grason yelled. The casual tone of a minute before had left him. His voice was a rage, his eyes were wild.

A spasm of shivering swept Reed from head to foot. He had not much left for strength. The theory was you do not sacrifice the many for the few. But to sacrifice the few for the many, the Yupik for the white . . . He could not move. His teeth chattered. His body was racked by spasms. His arms were as limp as wet rags. He looked into Vitus's eyes. The man was dimly conscious, somehow aware. He stared calmly, waiting on his death.

"Agghhh," Reed clenched his teeth and screamed to the enclosed fog. If he killed Grason, he killed Vitus, the blood would be his forever. So Pewter could live. So he could live. The law of the wild.

And then he saw the movement, the rush, Pewter running headlong and then launching herself at the back of Grason's knees. Reed seized the rifle, clicking the safety off as he brought it around. He had a second, a window. As he brought the rifle to his shoulder he saw Grason stagger, not even knocked off his feet. But Vitus pulled to one side even as Pewter pawed at Grason's legs. The knife flashed, a stainless steel blade gleaming in the fog. Within the same heartbeat, both eyes open, Reed's concentration turned to look through the scope. It was fogged. A dark blob moved. Vitus? Grason? No time. His finger continued the squeeze.

The rifle exploded, slamming him back. With the automation of the long-experienced hunter, Reed worked the bolt and chambered another round.

Grason rose like a bear on its hind legs. He staggered back, one step, then two. He sat down and then slowly dropped on his back. He raised his head and looked in Reed's direction. And then his head dropped back in the snow.

For maybe a second Reed did not move. He floated in space, the great universe, the great emptiness, a hollow void displacing his guts. Everything was gone. Everything was changed, never to be restored.

But no time now, Reed thought. There was still the matter of life. He had to get back and help. He lay the rifle aside and stepped down on the pontoon. He shivered violently, teeth rattling, his limbs quivering uncontrollably. He found the rope and the grappling hook hanging straight down into the water.

He pulled the line aboard, coiling it at his feet. With each second his fingers grew more numb. Would the line reach? Already it was turning stiff.

"Pewter," he called. He gave the hook a throw. It landed at her feet and Pewter quickly grabbed it before it slipped into the water. She towed the airplane toward shore.

But then Grason raised his head and looked at Reed. He shook his head from side to side as if in shame. And then he lay back in the snow. As the airplane bumped into the ice, Reed could see the huge pool of dark red forming at Grason's side. His work. His hand. If the truth be known, a part of him lay dying on that ice.

Reed's throat was as raw as if it had been eaten by acid. They were a sorry lot, in desperate straits, but somehow they had survived. Even Grason, shot through the side of his rib cage, gurgled for life. But it would not be for long.

Fortunately, as they had before, Pewter and Vitus took command. They anchored the airplane sideways. Reed and Kurth were quickly stripped, shoved up inside the airplane and zipped into down-filled sleeping bags.

As they climbed inside, Grason, still gurgling for air, raised his head. Pewter looked at Reed, questioning. Reed, shivering out of control, simply shook his head. "No. No."

Grason blinked. He struggled to speak. "It took five of you. You tell them what it took to bring Terry Grason down. You tell them. They won't forget."

Vitus moved in beside Pewter and helped push Wynona up into the airplane. "Please, Miss. Very quickly. The Arctic does not wait." He slammed the door and moved into the pilot's seat.

Reed huddled in the seat beside Pewter. His lips were purple, his fingers numb, his body vibrating as if under constant electric current. He huddled inside himself, sleeping bag zipped up to cover everything but his face.

Vitus turned on the motor. The battery had good power. The Pratt and Whitney engine roared. It didn't take long and they were soon flooded with heat. Vitus hand-tripped the ELT, Emergency Location Transmitter and then tried the emergency radio band. Perhaps they could contact a passing ship, a freighter carrying oil drilling supplies for the North Slope.

Reed tried to look out the windows to where Grason lay. But the windows were fogged, just as the scope had been fogged. Grason was dark, indistinct, a man alone, bleeding and freezing to death on the ice. Reed closed his eyes in shame, he had not the strength, nor the means to render aid. If it was cruel, it was nature. Still he could not escape Grason's eyes, the pain, the twisted look of a man betrayed. He moved over toward Pewter. She put her arm around his shoulder, holding him close, giving to him her warmth. The only thing, Reed wondered, was it real? The cost of too many years living two lives. Other than nature, he no longer knew what was real.

EPILOGUE

As it turned out the oil industry came to their rescue. Vitus managed to gain radio contact with a freighter carrying drilling supplies to the North Slope. In addition they hand-tripped the airplane's ELT-Emergency Location Transmitter and a rough location fix was picked up by the Rescue Coordination Center at Elmendorf Air Force Base near Anchorage. By the time the fog lifted, a Huey helicopter, under charter from Energy Resources Associates, was dispatched to home-in on their location, transmitted by the emergency beacon through a satellite relay. Only Kurth gave a yell when the helicopter hovered into view. With Grason's stiffened body lying inside a bodybag at their feet, the flight back to Kotzebue was somber.

Reed could not remove his eyes from Grason, a lifeless form, the result of his hand, his squeeze of the trigger. A man as big as all of Alaska, his spirit erased, a towering and powerful presence that would never again dominate a Fairbanks bar. He'd heard stories from hunters Grason had guided; the man was a legend. Just walking into camp made men need to pee. And yet he'd been a father, a husband, carved a home out of the wild, the last frontier. To Grason it became a joke. And now he lay unomved, his life gone into a dark splotch of blood oozed onto the ice. There'd been anger there, pain, a man's life washed away by change, and then betrayal, his betrayal, Reed thought. Did he have a choice?

They reached Kotzebue. Fortunately Doug and other Fish and Wildlife agents were available to handle logistics. A regularly scheduled commercial jet flight was due to leave for Nome and then Anchorage, and Kurth and Wynona, accompanied by a Fish and Wildlife agent, were sent on that. They later learned that, as suspected, Wynona's jaw had been broken. Her toes were black and severely frostbitten, but luckily none had to be amputated.

The next day Reed, Doug and Pewter returned to Anchorage. They had to meet with a U.S. Attorney, review evidence, issue charges, write reports. The entire process was going to take time. Plus there was Grason's death, and the investigation by state authorities. The mounds of paperwork and the hours of interviews quickly took their toll. Whenever they could, Reed and Pewter broke away, jogging or biking down the paved trails along Knik Arm, hiking in the Chugach Mountains, or just sitting quietly and watching a movie. The warmth, safety and comfort of a motel room were a welcome change from the freezing pack ice.

Red looked at Pewter's bright, clean features and saw the age in her eyes. There was a distance between them, a wariness, like a husband and wife moving in together after a trial separation. But there was also a closeness, an ability to look at each other with a certain understanding, like men in combat, members of a special fraternity, people who'd been there, faced shared dangers, tread common ground. No matter what else transpired between them, they at least had that.

After two weeks, Pewter flew back to California where she intended to pick up duties as an ordinary field agent. Another week later and Reed returned to Washington D.C.

The simple fact of entering his dark and dingy basement apartment almost drove Reed to tears. He was so seldom in town his contacts were non-existent, his social life almost nil. He stood there all alone and looked around. Was this any way for a man to live?

He set up a routine with Trish, going running for her cross-country workouts, hiking on the Appalachian Trail, watching her volleyball games with Pam, his ex-wife, and the three of them going out for a bite afterwards.

Stacy was another matter. He'd promised himself he'd forgive. But how can a person stand and watch someone they love die?

Reed sat on a tattered chair. There was no escape from the sordid, unclean smell of soiled clothes and unwashed dishes and spectre of human flesh going to rot. Stacy sat on a black vinyl sofa, her clothes uncharacteristically rumpled, although she still wore a half-dozen bracelets on each wrist and large blue earrings. Strung out or just tired, he could not tell. Her eyes and nostrils were inflamed. No judgments, Reed had promised, just try to reconnect.

"Look, what happened in Alaska happened. I think we should put it behind us. Go on, try to at least be civil with one another."

Stacy regarded him suspiciously. She'd been upset over Grason's death. "Such a nice man," she'd said. How had he felt about killing a man like that?

"Not good," Reed said. "But like I described, there was no choice."

And now he'd returned, deliberately picking a time when Derrick, her current unemployed boyfriend, had sauntered out of the tiny, white-painted apartment.

"Why?" Stacy asked of Reed's offer to be civil. "I ruined the vacation. I cost all that money. Those are just words. You're just saying that to put the guilt on me."

Reed smiled. Any direction he chose, Stacy could counter. The expert at confrontation and self-destruction. "If I got furious, as I initially was furious, you'd get angry back. We'd shout at each other and then I'd leave. We're of the same flesh and blood, family if you will. We have to stand by each other."

"Now you say that. What happened before? You forced me into those clinics. You forced me to go live in the woods with Guy."

Reed spoke quietly, in total control. "No. You agreed to live with Guy in lieu of juvenile detention. It was your option, your decision. We just don't understand the grip this stuff has on you."

Stacy looked away. "I've tried. But it's there. The night drags. You never know what a trip's going to be like, where you'll go, where you'll end up. It's exciting. Like you and your cases, same thing."

"I have a name," Reed said. He laid a piece of paper on the pressed-wood coffee table. "It's a woman you can visit whenever you feel the need."

"I can't afford a shrink and neither can you."

"She's not a shrink. She's been where you've been. Don't worry about any bills." Reed stood. He handed Stacy the slip of paper. She stared until Reed finally lay it on the table. He started to depart.

Stacy spoke in her sarcastic tone. "That's good. It's like being rich. If you can't be there for me, you'll hire someone who can."

"The thing is, Stacy, you have to understand there's still hope, especially for someone with a mind as sharp as yours." They stared. Her struggle was his struggle. Maybe she saw that now. He turned, but not before he saw the hint of a smile, the gleam of a tear.

* * *

The next day, his first day in the office, Reed informed Peter, "As soon as we get these trials wrapped up, I've got to get out of here. No more Washington, Peter. I have to be out."

Behind his rimless glasses, Peter's clear blue eyes flickered with concern. As usual he worried about his agents, in the field and in their personal lives. "I thought you'd be happy to get back, visit Stacy and Trish."

"That's the only reason I come back. But they are older, into their own lives. It's almost a strain for Stacy to find time to even let me visit. Trish and I do things, but that takes her away from her friends. I can tell she'd rather be with them."

Peter patted Reed on the shoulders. "Home life and this job are a tough mix, even for the field agents. You know how we appreciate what you've done. You get these court cases put together and out of the way and we'll expand that preliminary work you've been doing on the bear gall bladder trade. I don't want just the poachers this time around. I want to target the market and get an international ban on the trading in bear parts."

"Yeah," Reed said with some enthusiasm. He knew the background. Trading black bear gall bladders and bear paws through the Oriental market was big business. Dried bear gall bladder powder, used for medicinal purposes, was more expensive than cocaine, fetching as much as eight hundred dollars an ounce in Hong Kong. Federal and state conservation officers in California, Washington, West Virginia, New England and in the Great Smoky Mountains National Park had uncovered rings, each of which had supplied several hundred bear galls to Oriental animal-parts traffickers. He'd already been on fall hunts with suspected poachers, part of the long-term process of establishing his cover. "Incidentally, Pewter has some time in the Orient."

"If you need her and if she's willing, strictly volunteer, go ahead. But let's get this walrus thing put to bed first. Breismeister and his wife are fighting it. The way Fortuno talks, they have a high-powered, obnoxious defense attorney. Expend your time and energy there for now. Take Trish up to Alaska like you planned. We need favorable publicity out of this. The President line-itemed the biologists' money for walrus research and monitoring. If we can't get a handle on what's out there, we can't manage the herd. Maybe a little positive publicity will help the cause. What law enforcement does could give biologists the money to do their job."

✳ ✳ ✳

"There's one reason for the delays," Dan Fortuno said to Reed and Pewter. They'd flown to Anchorage for the third time to visit with the U.S. attorney handling the ivory trading cases. The were in the Federal Office Building in Fortuno's office. "Vance McElroy," Fortuno continued. He was short with thick black hair combed straight back and dark eyes exactly like those of Pewter. In fact when they talked, it was Pewter at whom he mostly stared. "McElroy's the biggest sonofabitch of a defense lawyer I've ever seen. His primary tactics are to delay. He files every discovery motion he can think of, and he always waits until the eleventh hour. Well this time I think we have him. You've been up here twice, I've had Inokenti flown in from Gambell twice. The expenses keep mounting. But this time the judge said this was it. If I get everybody here, we have the trial. No matter what."

"How's Vitus doing?" Reed asked.

"Not well. We filed minimal charges as you requested. But he got divorced. Sold his airplane to settle that and moved back to Gambell. That's where most of them go eventually, back home."

"Nothing more on Tanaka?" Pewter asked.

"Nope. That's dead." Fortuno paced as he talked, a man continually in motion. " We haven't been able to resolve that. We have the one tusk with one transmitter, but we couldn't prove Tanaka knew it came from Kurth. Tanaka pleaded guilty to one charge of illegal exportation and one charge of trafficking with a non-native, that being Breismeister. He paid two thousand on each count. And he's still in business, although maybe a little wiser."

"And nothing on the Keelachuck brothers?" Reed stated.

"Nope. They cover themselves too well. We tried for a wasteful hunting charge as you suggested, but they brought in several witnesses who swore they went back out and brought in all the walrus meat. So we took that plea to one charge of wasteful hunting, two-thousand-dollar fine and that was it. The small-timers that came into the shop got fines and jail time. The others," Fortuno shrugged, an indication that that was the way the world went.

Two days later the government agreed to a plea. Charges against Wynona were dropped. Kurth was fined twenty thousand dollars and sentenced to six months in jail.

As he left the court room Kurth offered to shake Reed's hand. He spoke enthusiastically. "No hard feelings. I know you were doing your job."

"No hard feelings," Reed said. Wynona silently glared.

"I'm going straight now," Kurth continued. "You won't have to watch me anymore. I've got my rigs still going up north. Sooner or later they'll have to open the Arctic National Wildlife Refuge for oil. They'll run the pipeline from there to Prudhoe. They'll need trucks. I'll get a couple more."

"Well, I'm happy for you," Reed said sourly. "What I want to know, Kurth, is Vitus claims that over the years he'd probably sold you fifty tons of ivory. A hundred thousand pounds. That's ten to twelve thousand walrus. Where's all the money?"

Kurth grinned and shrugged. "Well, Wynona has her house, that's free and clear. But you know, over the years, it just goes. There are so many things to buy."

"Yeah," Reed muttered. He slowly trudged down the hallway. For all they risked, too often the disposition of cases made it all seem insignificant. What he needed just now was an escape.

* * *

Samuel Inokenti's arms ached. St. Lawrence island lay as a long black scar obscured by a wall of fog and mist. He sat in the front seat of the two-man kayak, balancing with his hips, working the paddle, knowing his father watched to see that he did not quit. A hard chop rolled beneath their rounded bottom. They balanced precariously over the black, icy water. Vitus deftly made a side-pull with his paddle and they slid gracefully into the trough and were buried from all sight of land.

They were headed for shore, their two-hour daily workout almost complete. But then they would spend two hours working on the umiaq, the skin boat Vitus had resolved to build. Hot, steel rods of pain worked across Samuel's shoulders. He did not wish to disappoint, but his father made it so hard.

At first Samuel had been pleased when his father moved to the island. His brother and sister remained in Eagle River with his mother. Samuel and his father moved into a small, one-room house, little more than an old fish camp. Now he could remain in Gambell the entire year, Samuel had thought. He would not have to attend a gussuk school. There would be no more feelings of being different. Now he could hunt and fish and drive his four-wheeler all year long.

But Vitus said no. First they must work, become strong, two hours paddling, two hours on their boat, and one hour carving ivory. He'd rather carve with Grandfather Jake, Samuel thought. Everyone could see his father had no carving skill. Everyone but Vitus.

When they returned to land they paused for lunch, maktak from a fresh-killed bowhead whale and strong tea for Vitus and a soda for Samuel. Then they worked on the umiaq, patiently sewing skin from the uguruk, the bearded seal, over the heavy thwarts. As he had for the previous three days, Samuel spotted Grandfather Jake watching them work. Since the day of his father's arrest, the two did not speak. Even now, weeks later, when Vitus entered a room, Jake got up and left. It was not good, Grandmother Lulu said. Everyone felt bad.

"You're not working good today, Samuel," Vitus said. He pretended not to notice his step-father watching. "A lazy man in summer is a hungry man in winter. We must work hard in order to be ready for the fall hunt."

"Time is almost up," Samuel said.

"A true hunter knows no time," Vitus replied. He paused, watching Jake slowly cross the rocky field. It was a rare Gambell day with a light breeze and bright sunshine.

A boy on a four-wheeler circled between two houses and stopped and stared. Thomas Keelachuck, Samuel thought. Thomas knew it was time. They'd planned fishing down the shore.

Jake walked up and slowly circled the boat, inspecting their work. His face was scarred and wrinkled as dark as burnt leather. He nodded as if in approval then picked up a long curved needle made from the wing of a sea gull and slowly began to sew.

"I need two more uguruk," Vitus said.

"I had good luck. I have one," Jake replied.

"Father," Samuel implored.

Vitus waved a hand of dismissal. Work time had expired. Samuel quickly ran toward Thomas. Why, he wondered, did his father have tears? Nothing made sense anymore. Now his father talked of killing walrus with a lance. He looked at Thomas's rounded face. What would Thomas say when he learned that Samuel and Vitus Inokenti were to hunt aiviq with spears? The Keelachuck brothers were the best hunters on the island. With their big, fast motors and powerful rifles they killed many more walrus than anyone else. Many elders depended upon the Keelachucks for food.

Samuel jumped on the back of Thomas' four-wheeler and they drove back to his house. He started his four-wheeler, and with a spray of gravel, followed Thomas down the beach. As he passed his grandfather and father, he waved. The two waved, stared briefly as if in disapproval then returned to their side-by-side work on the sealskin boat.

The wind blew in Samuel's face, throwing his long black hair in a wave behind him. He was thankful for the wind, a reason for tears he could not explain streaming down his brown cheeks.

* * *

Pewter led the way up the steep trail. She wore tan shorts, hiking boots, knee-high socks, a long-sleeve shirt, and a blue fanny-pack with a water bottle and windbreaker inside. Reed followed close behind, grabbing limbs and clumps of grass to assist in the ascent. He tried not to stare at her smooth, trim legs and her taut, rounded buttocks. A dirty old man, he thought. But it was behind them now, the last case closed. They were free, their last day before separating and flying back to the Lower 48.

What could he say?

They pulled themselves up the last steep rise and walked side by side across spongy tundra. They crossed the packed finger of snow leading off the icefield. They climbed the rocky glacial alluvial, more snow and then crossed to a rocky promontory overlooking a small pool of glacial melt. To one side the Harding Icefield extended into the evening. In front of them the blue scales of Exit Glacier stacked itself in a line of turquoise crevasses dropping 3,500 feet down the mountain. At the bottom of the glacier, green swirls of dark finger-painted forest rose up the sides of nearby mountains. Tendrils of fluffy gray clouds pushed into the valley.

Reed paused on a piece of the mountain that, a thousand generations ago, had been scraped smooth by tons of glacier ice. Small lines revealed where tiny pebbles had ground rivulets in the rock. He located a small boulder next to a larger one and sat down so he could rest his back. He looked up at Pewter and then the scenery and before he looked again she came to him and settled on his lap, her arm around his neck, her shoulder on his cheek. He felt her warmth, her flesh on his flesh, the giving of herself, the saving of his life.

A reddish hue colored the sky. Hints of pink, like the flashing stripe on a rainbow trout, coated the clouds in the valley. The blue of the glacial ice paled at the top and darkened at the bottom. The greens in the valley deepened, almost a friendly black. In silent appreciation their heads turned, one direction and then another, absorbed by the surrounding amphitheater, the ultimate art, each scene altered every second, living, moving, evolving.

Was it his imagination or could he feel Pewter's heart throbbing next to his, the warmth flowing between them as connected and necessary as sun rays succoring the earth? There was no need to speak. He could not speak. There'd never be a world as perfect as this.

But then the moment was ruined, at a nagging thought he could not erase; how long could perfection last?